SPE(**DERS**

THE [barcode: C70243563%] ATION
(regis~~tered UK charity number~~ 264873)

was established in 1972 to provide funds for
rese~~arch, diagnosis and treatment of eye disea~~ses.

Eye

reat

and
ogy,

up,

tern

oyal

You

tion

E

ou

w

or

Tel: (0116) 236 4325

website: www.foundation.ulverscroft.com

A PELICAN AT BLANDINGS

Unwelcome guests are descending on Blandings Castle — particularly the overbearing Duke of Dunstable, who settles in the Garden Suite with no intention of leaving, and Lady Constance, Lord Emsworth's sister and a lady of firm disposition. Skulduggery is also afoot involving the sale of a modern nude painting (mistaken by Lord Emsworth for a pig). It's enough to take the noble earl on the short journey to the end of his wits. Luckily, Clarence's brother Galahad Threepwood, cheery survivor of the raffish Pelican Club, is on hand to set things right, restore sundered lovers, and solve all the mysteries.

Books by P. G. Wodehouse
Published in Ulverscroft Collections:

JEEVES & WOOSTER:
CARRY ON, JEEVES
THE INIMITABLE JEEVES
VERY GOOD, JEEVES
THANK YOU, JEEVES
RIGHT HO, JEEVES
THE CODE OF THE WOOSTERS
JOY IN THE MORNING
THE MATING SEASON
JEEVES IN THE OFFING
JEEVES AND THE FEUDAL SPIRIT

BLANDINGS:
SOMETHING FRESH
SUMMER LIGHTNING
FULL MOON
HEAVY WEATHER
PIGS HAVE WINGS
GALAHAD AT BLANDINGS

P. G. WODEHOUSE

A PELICAN AT BLANDINGS

Complete and Unabridged

ULVERSCROFT
Leicester

First published in Great Britain in 1969 by
Barrie & Jenkins
London

This Ulverscroft Edition
published 2019
by arrangement with
Rogers, Coleridge & White Literary Agency
London

A catalogue record for this book is available
from the British Library.

ISBN 978–1–4448–4130–5

Published by
F. A. Thorpe (Publishing)
Anstey, Leicestershire

Set by Words & Graphics Ltd.
Anstey, Leicestershire
Printed and bound in Great Britain by
T. J. International Ltd., Padstow, Cornwall

This book is printed on acid-free paper

1

The summer day was drawing to a close and dusk had fallen on Blandings Castle, shrouding from view the ancient battlements, dulling the silver surface of the lake and causing Lord Emsworth's supreme Berkshire sow Empress of Blandings to leave the open air portion of her sty and withdraw into the covered shed where she did her sleeping. A dedicated believer in the maxim of early to bed and early to rise, she always turned in at about this time. Only by getting its regular eight hours can a pig keep up to the mark and preserve that schoolgirl complexion.

Deprived of her society, which he had been enjoying since shortly after lunch, Clarence, ninth Earl of Emsworth, the seigneur of this favoured realm, pottered dreamily back to the house, pottered dreamily to the great library which was one of its features, and had just pottered dreamily to his favourite chair, when Beach, his butler, entered bearing a laden tray. He gave it the vague stare which had so often incurred the censure — 'Oh, for goodness sake, Clarence, don't stand there looking like a goldfish' — of his sisters Constance, Dora, Charlotte, Julia and Hermione.

'Eh?' he said. 'What?' he added.

'Your dinner, m'lord.'

1

Lord Emsworth's face cleared. He was telling himself that he might have known that there would be some simple explanation for that tray. Trust Beach to have everything under control.

'Of course, yes. Dinner. Quite. Always have it at this time, don't I? And recently been having it here, though I can't remember for what reason. Why am I having dinner in the library, Beach?'

'I gathered that your lordship preferred not to share the meal in the dining-room with Mr. Chesney.'

'Mr. who?'

'Mr. Howard Chesney, m'lord, Mr. Frederick's friend from America.'

The puzzled frown that had begun to gather on Lord Emsworth's forehead vanished like breath off a razor blade. Once more Beach with that lucid brain of his had dispelled the fog of mystery which had threatened to defy solution.

'Ah yes, Mr. Howard Chesney. Mr. Howard Chesney, to be sure, Mr. Frederick's friend from America. Are they feeding him, do you know?'

'Yes, m'lord.'

'I wouldn't want him to starve.'

'No, m'lord.'

'Is he having his dinner?'

'Mr. Chesney went to London by the afternoon train, m'lord, planning, I understand, to return tomorrow.'

'I see. So he'll probably dine there. At a restaurant or somewhere.'

'Presumably, m'lord.'

'The last time I dined in London was with Mr. Galahad at a place in one of those streets off

2

Leicester Square. He said he had a sentimental fondness for it because it was one he had so often been thrown out of in his younger days. It was called something or other, but I forget what. That stuff smells good, Beach. What is it?'

'Leg of lamb, m'lord, with boiled potatoes.'

Lord Emsworth received the information with a gratified nod. Good plain English fare. How different, he was thinking, from the bad old era when his sister Constance had been the Führer of Blandings Castle. Under her regime dinner would have meant dressing and sitting down, probably with a lot of frightful guests, to a series of ghastly dishes with French names, and fuss beyond belief if one happened to swallow one's front shirt stud and substituted for it a brass paper-fastener.

'And,' Beach added, for he was a man who liked to be scrupulously accurate, 'spinach.'

'Capital, capital. And to follow?'

'Roly-poly pudding, m'lord.'

'Excellent. With plenty of jam, I hope?'

'Yes, m'lord. I instructed Mrs. Willoughby — '

'Who is Mrs. Willoughby?'

'The Cook, m'lord.'

'I thought her name was Perkins.'

'No, m'lord, Willoughby. I instructed her to be careful that there was no stint.'

'Thank you, Beach. Are you fond of roly-poly pudding?'

'Yes, m'lord.'

'With plenty of jam?'

'Yes, m'lord.'

'It's quite essential, I always feel. Unless there

3

is lots of jam, roly-poly pudding is not worth eating. All right. Bring it when I ring, will you?'

'Very good, m'lord.'

Left alone, Lord Emsworth attacked his good plain English fare with gusto, musing as he did on the stupendous improvement in conditions at the castle since his sister Constance had married that American fellow James Schoonmaker and gone to live in New York. Providence, moreover, never niggardly when attending to the welfare of a deserving man, had seen to it that there was no danger of any of his other sisters taking her place. At their last meeting he had so deeply offended Hermione that they were no longer on speaking terms, and as for Dora, Charlotte and Julia, they never left London except to go to fashionable resorts on the Riviera and in Spain. The peril of a visit from any of them was so remote that it could be dismissed, and it is scarcely to be wondered at that by the time Beach brought in the roly-poly pudding he was in so euphoric a frame of mind that he would probably not have noticed it if there had been a shortage in the accompanying jam. His brother Galahad had once said that it had been a mistake to have sisters and that they ought to have set their faces against it at the outset, but almost as good as no sisters were sisters who kept their distance.

There was just one small crumpled rose leaf. His younger son Frederick, now employed in a firm in Long Island City, N.Y., which manufactured dog biscuits, had most unnecessarily sent this chap Chesney to him with a letter of

4

introduction and he had had to ask him to stay, but he had neutralized the man's menace by cleverly having all his meals in the library and in between meals keeping out of his way. A host can always solve the problem of the unwanted guest if he has a certain animal cunning and no social conscience.

He finished the roly-poly pudding to the last speck of jam and took his coffee to the arm-chair in which he always reclined when in the library. It was within easy reach of the shelf of pig books which were his main source of mental refreshment. Selecting one of these, he became immersed, and it was not for some considerable time that his attention was diverted from its magic pages. What diverted it was the sound, plainly audible through the open window, of a car drawing up at the front door. It alarmed him, and when shortly afterwards Beach appeared, he addressed him in a voice that shook with pardonable anxiety. Callers at the castle had been infrequent since Connie's departure, but he knew that they still lurked in near-by lairs and it was possible that in spite of his efforts he had not entirely stamped out the neighbourly spirit he so deplored.

'Was that a car, Beach?'

'Yes, m'lord.'

'If it's someone for me, say I'm in bed.'

'It is her ladyship, m'lord.'

'Eh? What? What ladyship?'

'Lady Constance, m'lord.'

For one awful moment Lord Emsworth thought he had said 'Lady Constance'. In the moment which succeeded it he realized that he had, and he quivered with natural resentment. In the long years during which Beach had been to him more a crony than a butler he had never detected in him a disposition to try to be funny, but it now seemed plain that the man was in the grip of the spirit of whimsy, and he burned with justifiable indignation. Too bad of the fellow to come bursting in like this and saying things like that, presumably as some sort of crude practical joke. Might have given one heart failure.

Then the mist before his eyes cleared and he saw the look in the eyes that met his. It was a look in which sadness, understanding and pity were blended; the look of one who knew how grave was the announcement he had made; of one who fully appreciated how his employer must be feeling and who, had their social relations permitted of it, would have patted him on the head and urged him to bear up like a man, for these things are sent to try us and make us more spiritual.

It convinced Lord Emsworth. He no longer felt that he had been cast in the role of straight man supporting a butler who was playing for laughs. Hideous though the truth was, it could not be evaded.

'Where is she?'

'In the amber drawing-room, m'lord. Her ladyship is accompanied by a Miss Polk — from her voice, I gather, of American origin.'

The pig book had long since fallen from Lord Emsworth's nerveless hand, as had the pince-nez from his nose. He reeled the latter in at the end of their cord.

'I suppose I had better go down,' he said in a low, toneless voice, and with faltering steps made for the door. Beach, who sometimes read historical novels, though he preferred Rex Stout and Agatha Christie, was reminded of an apprehensive aristocrat in the days of the French Revolution on his way to the tumbril.

II

Precisely as stated Lady Constance was in the amber drawing-room, sipping sherry and looking as formidable and handsome as ever. All Lord Emsworth's sisters were constructed on the lines of the severer type of Greek goddess, except Hermione, who looked like a cook, and Connie in particular was remarkable for aristocratic hauteur and forcefulness of eye. One felt immediately on seeing her that there stood the daughter of a hundred earls, just as when confronted with Lord Emsworth one had the impression that one had encountered the son of a hundred tramp cyclists. He was wearing at the moment patched flannel trousers, a ragged shirt, a shooting coat with holes in the elbows and bedroom slippers. These, of course, in addition to the apprehensive look always worn by him when entering this formidable woman's presence. From childhood onward she had always dominated him, as she would have dominated Napoleon, Attila the Hun and an all-in wrestling champion.

'Oh, there you are, Clarence,' she said, and her

eye told him more plainly than words could have done that he had failed to satisfy her fastidious taste in the matter of dress. 'I want you to meet my friend Vanessa Polk, who was so kind to me on the boat. This is my brother Clarence, Vanessa,' said Lady Constance with that touch of the apologetic which always came into her voice when she introduced him to visitors. Don't go blaming me, it seemed to say, it's not my fault.

Looking at Vanessa Polk one could readily imagine her being kind to people, whether on or off ocean liners, for her warmth and geniality were obvious at a glance. Where Lady Constance had winced at the sight of Lord Emsworth like a Greek goddess finding a caterpillar in her salad, she smiled upon him as if their meeting were something to which she had been looking forward for years. It was a wide, charming smile, and it brought about a marked improvement in his morale. He felt, as so many people did when smiled upon by Vanessa Polk, that he had found a friend.

'How do you do?' he said with a cordiality of which a short while before he would not have been capable. Then, remembering a good one, he added, 'Welcome to Blandings Castle. Tomorrow,' he said, 'I must show you my pig.' It was not an invitation he often extended to female visitors, for experience had taught him that the Empress was wasted on their shallow minds, but here, he saw, was one worthy of the privilege. 'Are you fond of pigs?'

Miss Polk said she had not met many socially, but had got along fine with those which had come her way, never an angry word. Was this, she asked, kind of a special sort of pig, and Lord Emsworth answered eagerly in the affirmative.

'Empress of Blandings,' he said proudly, 'has won the silver medal three years in succession in the Fat Pigs event at the Shropshire Agricultural Show.'

'You're kidding!'

'I can show you the medals. It was an unparalleled feat.'

'To what did she owe her success?'

'Careful feeding.'

'I thought as much.'

'Some pig owners are guided by other authorities and for all I know,' said Lord Emsworth generously, 'get quite good results, but I have always pinned my faith on Wolff-Lehman. According to the Wolff-Lehman feeding standards a pig must consume daily nourishment amounting to fifty-seven thousand calories, proteins four pounds five ounces, carbohydrates twenty-five pounds.'

'Exclusive, of course, of the last thing at night raid on the ice box?'

'These calories to consist of barley meal, maize meal, linseed meal and separated butter-milk. I occasionally add on my own initiative a banana or a potato . . . '

One of those short, sharp, steely coughs proceeded from Lady Constance. It stopped Lord Emsworth like a bullet. He was not a very perceptive man, but he understood that he was expected to change the subject. Regretfully but with the docility of a well-trained brother he did so.

'Bless my soul, Connie,' he said with as much heartiness as he could manage on the spur of the moment, 'this is certainly a surprise. Your being here, I mean. Quite a surprise, quite a surprise.'

This time the sound emitted by his sister was not, like the previous one, bronchial, but resembled more that made by drawing a wet thumb across a hot stove lid.

'I don't know why it should be,' she said tartly. 'You got my letter saying I was sailing.'

Lord Emsworth had not gulped since coming into the room, but he did so now, and with good reason. He had an odd sensation of having been slapped in the face with a wet fish. He was guiltily conscious that the communication she referred to had been lying unopened for some two weeks in a drawer of the desk in his study. Now that he was alone without a secretary to pester him and make him observe the ordinary decencies of life he seldom opened letters if they were not from the Shropshire, Herefordshire and South Wales Pig Breeders Association.

'Oh, ah, yes, of course, certainly, your letter saying that you were sailing, yes, quite.'

'To refresh your memory, I said in it that I was coming to spend the summer at Blandings — '

The faint hope Lord Emsworth had had that she might be just passing through on her way to join Dora or Charlotte or Julia at one of those Continental resorts of theirs choked and died.

' — and that James will be here soon. He has been delayed in New York by an important business deal.'

The words 'Who is James?' started to frame

themselves on Lord Emsworth's lips, but fortunately before he could utter them she had gone on to another subject.

'Whose hat is that?'

Lord Emsworth could not follow her. She seemed to be asking him whose hat that was, and he found the question cryptic.

'Hat?' he said, puzzled. 'Hat? When you say hat, do you mean hat? What hat?'

'I noticed a hat in the hall, much too good to be yours. Is someone staying here?'

'Oh, ah, yes,' said Lord Emsworth, enlightened. 'A fellow . . . I can't think of his name . . . Gooch, was it? Cooper? Finsbury? Bateman? Merryweather? . . . No, it's gone. Frederick sent him with a letter of introduction. Been here some days. He has several hats.'

'Oh, I see. I thought for a moment it might be Alaric. The Duke of Dunstable, an old friend of mine,' Lady Constance explained to Miss Polk. 'I do not see as much of him as I should like, as he lives in Wiltshire, but he comes here as often as he can manage. A little more sherry, Vanessa? No? Then I will show you your room. It is up near the portrait gallery, which you must see as soon as you are settled. Be careful of the stairs. The polished oak is rather slippery.'

III

Lord Emsworth returned to the library. He should have been feeling in uplifted mood, for he had certainly been lucky in the matter of that letter. Connie might quite easily have probed and questioned until the awful truth was revealed, and at the thought of what the harvest would then have been his blood froze. For far less serious offences he had often been talked at for days. Her comments on that paper-fastener in his shirt front had run to several thousand words, and even then she had seemed to feel that only the fringe of the subject had been touched on.

But what she had said about thinking that the Duke of Dunstable might be staying at the castle had shaken him. It seemed to him ominous. The hour that had produced her, he felt, might take it into its head to round the thing off by producing the Duke as well. Morbid? Perhaps so, but it was a possibility that could not be overlooked. He knew that she had an inexplicable affection for the fellow, and there was no telling to what lengths this might lead her.

Many people are fond of Dukes and place no obstacle in the way if the latter wish to fraternize with them, but few of those acquainted with Alaric, Duke of Dunstable, sought his society, Lord Emsworth least of all. He was an opinionated, arbitrary, autocratic man with an unpleasantly loud voice, bulging eyes and a walrus moustache which he was always blowing at and causing to leap like a rocketting pheasant, and he had never failed to affect Lord Emsworth unfavourably. Galahad, with his gift for the telling phrase, generally referred to the Duke as 'that stinker', and there was no question in Lord Emsworth's mind that he had hit on the right label. So as he sat in the library with his pig book he was feeling uneasy. For the first time in his experience its perfect prose failed to grip him.

It is possible that solitude and a further go at the pig book might eventually have soothed him, but at this moment the solitude was invaded and the book sent fluttering to the floor. Lady Constance was standing in the doorway, and one look at her told him that trouble was about to raise its ugly head.

'Well, really, Clarence!'

He wilted beneath her glare. Galahad, similarly situated, would have met it with a defiant 'Well, really, *what?*', but he lacked that great man's fortitude.

'Those trousers! That coat! Those slippers! I can't imagine what Vanessa Polk must have thought of you. I suppose she was wondering what a tramp was doing in the drawing-room, and I had to say 'This is my brother Clarence.' I have never felt so embarrassed.'

Sometimes in these crises Lord Emsworth had found that it was possible to divert her thoughts from the item uppermost on the agenda paper by turning the conversation to other topics. He endeavoured to do so now.

'Polk,' he said. 'That's a very peculiar name, isn't it? I remember noticing when I was over in America for your wedding how odd some of the names were that people had. Neptune was one of them. So was Stottlemeyer. And a colleague of Frederick's in that dog biscuit concern of his was a Bream Rockmetteller. Curious, it struck me as.'

'Clarence!'

'Not that we don't have some remarkable names over here. I was reading my Debrett the other day, and I came on a chap called Lord Orrery and Cork. I wondered how you would address him if you met. One's natural impulse would be to say 'How do you do, Lord Orrery?', but if you did, wouldn't he draw himself up rather stiffly and say '*And* Cork'? You'd have to apologize.'

'Clarence!'

'That fellow Neptune, by the way, was the head of a company that manufactures potato chips, those little curly things you eat at cocktail parties. I met him at a cocktail party Frederick took me to, and we got into conversation and he happened to mention that his firm had made the very potato chips we were eating. I said it was a small world, and he agreed. 'Sure,' he said. 'It's a very small world, no argument about that,' and we had some more potato chips. He said the great thing about being in the potato chip business was that nobody could eat just one potato chip, which of course was very good for the sales. What he meant was that once you've started you haven't the strength of mind to stop; you've got to go on, first one potato chip, then another potato chip, then — '

'Clarence,' said Lady Constance, 'stop babbling!'

He did as directed, and there was silence while she paused to select for utterance one of the three devastating remarks which had come into her mind simultaneously. It was as she stood

14

wavering between them that the telephone rang.

Had he been alone, Lord Emsworth would have let it ring till it became exhausted, for his views on answering telephones were identical with those he held on reading letters not from the Shropshire, Herefordshire and South Wales Pig Breeders Association, but Lady Constance, like all women, was incapable of this dignified attitude. She hurried to the instrument, and he was at liberty to devote himself to thoughts of names and potato chips. But even as he started to do so he was jerked from his meditation by the utterance of a single word.

It was the word 'Alaric!' and it froze him from bald head to the soles of the bedroom slippers on which Lady Constance a moment before the bell rang had been about to comment. He feared the worst.

It happened. Five minutes later Lady Constance came away from the telephone.

'That was Alaric,' she said. 'He has had a fire at his place, and he is coming here till everything is all right again. He says he wants the garden suite, so I had better be going and seeing that it is just as he likes it. He is coming by the early train tomorrow with his niece.'

She left the room, and Lord Emsworth sank back in his chair looking like the good old man in some melodrama of Victorian days whose mortgage the villain has just foreclosed. He felt none of the gentle glow which he was accustomed to feel when one of his sisters removed herself from his presence. The thought of a Blandings Castle infested not only by

Connie but also by the Duke of Dunstable and his niece . . . probably, if she was anything like her uncle, one of those brassy-voiced domineering girls who always terrified him so much . . . left him as filletted as the Dover sole he had enjoyed at breakfast.

He sat there for several minutes motionless. But though his limbs were inert, his brain was working with the speed which so often accompanies the imminence of peril. He saw that he was faced with a situation impossible for him to handle alone. He needed an ally who would give him moral support, and it was not long before he realized that there was only one man who could fill this position. He went to the telephone and called a London number, and after what seemed to him an eternity a cheery voice spoke at the other end of the wire.

'Hullo?'

'Oh, Galahad,' Lord Emsworth bleated. 'This is Clarence, Galahad. A most terrible thing has happened, Galahad. Connie's back.'

2

At about the moment when Lady Constance was mounting the stairs that led to the library of Blandings Castle, all eagerness to confront her brother Clarence and let him know what she thought of his outer crust, a dapper little gentleman with a black-rimmed monocle in his left eye paid off the cab which had brought him from Piccadilly, trotted in at the front door of Berkeley Mansions, London W.I. and ascended to the fourth floor where he had his abode. He was feeling in excellent fettle after a pleasant dinner with some of his many friends, and as he started upward he hummed a melody from the music halls of another day.

Thirty years ago it would have been most unusual for Galahad Threepwood to return home at so early an hour as this, for in his bohemian youth it had been his almost nightly custom to attend gatherings at the Pelican Club which seldom broke up till the milkman had begun his rounds — a practice to which he always maintained that he owed the superb health he enjoyed in middle age.

'It really is an extraordinary thing,' a niece of his had once said, discussing him with a friend, 'that anyone who has had as good a time as Gally has had can be so frightfully fit. Everywhere you look you see men who have led model lives pegging out in their thousands, while good old Gally, who was the mainstay of Haig and Haig for centuries and as far as I can make out never went to bed till he was fifty, is still breezing along as rosy and full of beans as ever.'

But a man tends to slow up a little as the years go by, and he was not averse nowadays to an occasional quiet home evening. He was looking forward to one tonight. The Pelican Club had been dead for ages and with its going had taken much of his enthusiasm for the more energetic forms of night life.

Opening the door of his apartment and passing through the little hall into the sitting-room, he was surprised to see pacing the floor a human form. This naturally startled him, but it did not give him the instant feeling of impending doom which it would have done in his younger days, when a human form on his premises would almost certainly have been a creditor or a process server. A moment later he had recognized his visitor.

'Why, hullo, Johnny, my boy. I thought for a second you were a ghost someone had hired to haunt the place. How did you get in?'

'The hall porter let me in with his pass key.'

Gally could not repress a slight frown. Of course it did not really matter now that he was respectable and solvent, but it was the principle of the thing. Hall porters, he felt, ought not to let people in; it undermined the whole fabric of civilized society. Like one wincing at the twinge of an old wound, he recalled the occasion many years ago when a landlady had admitted to his little nest a bookmaker trading under the name of Honest Jerry Judson, to whom a shortage of funds had compelled him to owe ten pounds since the last Newmarket Spring Meeting.

'I told him I was your godson.'

'I see. Still . . . Nevertheless . . . Oh, well, never mind. Always delighted to see you.'

Gally had quite a number of godsons, offspring of old Pelican Club cronies. They were practically all of them orphans, for few of the Pelicans had had the stamina which had enabled him to take the life of that institution in his stride and thrive on it. John Halliday, the young man who had dropped in on him this evening, was the son of the late J.D. ('Stiffy') Halliday, one of the many for whom the club's pace had proved too rapid. He had signed his last I.O.U. in his early forties, and it was a matter of surprise to his circle of intimates that he had managed to continue functioning till then.

Scrutinizing John through his monocle, Gally, as always when they met, was impressed by the thought of how little resemblance there was between poor old Stiffy and this son of his. The former — splendid chap, but let's face it not everybody's cup of tea — had presented, as so many Pelicans did, the appearance of a man with a severe hangover who had slept in his clothes and had not had time to shave: the latter was neat, trim, fit and athletic looking. There was about him something suggestive of a rising young barrister who in his leisure hours goes in a good deal for golf and squash racquets, and that, oddly enough, was what he was. His golf handicap was six, his skill at squash racquets

19

formidable, and he had been a member of the Bar for some five years, and while far from being one of the silk-robed giants whose briefs are marked in four figures, was doing quite nicely.

During these brief exchanges he had continued to pace the room. Passing the open window, he paused and looked out, drawing an emotional breath.

'What a night!' he said. 'What a night!'

To Gally it appeared an ordinary London summer night. He conceded that it was not raining, but was not prepared to go further than that.

'Seems pretty run-of-the-mill to me.'

'The moon!'

'There isn't a moon. You must have been misled by the lights from the pub on the corner.'

'Well, anyway, it's a wonderful night, and to hell with anyone who says it isn't.'

For the first time Gally became aware of something unusual in his godson's manner, a sort of fizzing and bubbling like that of a coffee percolator about to come to the height of its fever. In the old Pelican days he would automatically have attributed a similar exuberance in a fellow member to his having had one, if not more, over the eight, but he knew John to be as abstemious as befits a rising young barrister and told himself that it would be necessary to probe more deeply for an explanation.

'What's the matter with you?' he said. 'You seem very happy about something. Did you back a winner today?'

'I certainly did.'

'What odds?'

'A thousand to one.'

'What on earth are you talking about?'

'A thousand to one against was what I was estimating my chances at. Gally, I came here to tell you. I'm engaged.'

'What!'

'Yes, you can start pricing wedding presents. A marriage has been arranged, and will shortly take place.'

An elderly bachelor with a record like Gally's might have been expected to receive such an announcement from a godson whose best interests he had at heart with pursed lips and a shake of the head, for nothing saddens a benevolent senior more than the discovery that a junior of whom he is fond is contemplating a step which can only lead to disaster and misery. Gally, however, though his sisters Constance, Dora, Charlotte, Julia and Hermione would have contested such a description of him hotly, was a man of sentiment. In the long ago he too had loved, the object of his affections a girl called Dolly Henderson who sang songs in pink tights at the old Oxford and Tivoli music halls. It had been the refrain of one of them that he had hummed tonight as he went up to his apartment.

Well, nothing had come of it, of course. A Victorian father with enough driving force for two fathers had shipped him off to South Africa, and Dolly had married a fellow named Cotterleigh in the Irish Guards and he had never seen her again, but the memory of her still lingered, and this made him a sympathetic

21

listener to tales of young love. Instead, therefore, of urging his godson not to make an ass of himself or enquiring anxiously if he couldn't possibly get out of it, he displayed the utmost interest and said:

'Good for you, Johnny. Tell me more. When did this happen?'

'Tonight. Just before I came here.'

'You really clicked, did you?'

'I know it's hard to believe, but I did.'

'Who is she?'

'Her name's Linda Gilpin.'

Gally frowned thoughtfully.

'Gilpin. I know a young chap called Ricky Gilpin. The Duke of Dunstable's nephew. Any relation?'

'His sister.'

'So she's Dunstable's niece?'

'Yes.'

'Have you ever met Dunstable?'

'No. I suppose I shall soon. What's he like?'

'He's a stinker.'

'Really?'

'And always has been. I've known him for thirty years. He once tried to get elected to the Pelican, but he hadn't a hope. The top hat we used at committee meetings burst at the seams with black balls, several handfuls of them contributed by your father. We were very firm about letting stinkers into the Pelican.'

'Why is he a stinker?'

'Don't ask me. I'm not a psychiatrist.'

'I mean what's wrong with him? What does he do?'

'He doesn't do anything in particular. He just is. Too fond of money, for one thing. When I first knew him, he was a Guardee with an allowance big enough to choke a horse, and he hung on to it with both hands. Then he married a girl who had the stuff in sackfuls, the daughter of one of those chaps up North who make cups and basins and things, and she died and left him a fortune. Then he came into the title and all the land and cash that went with it, and now he's a millionaire twice over. But though so rich, he is constantly on the alert to become richer. He never misses a trick. If the opportunity presents itself of running a mile in tight shoes to chisel someone out of twopence, he springs to the task. I can't understand what these fellows see in money to make them sweat themselves to get it.'

'Money's always useful.'

'But not worth going to a lot of fuss and bother to get more of if you've already got your little bit. Dunstable makes me sick. I'm beginning to feel dubious about this step you're taking, Johnny. I wonder if you're being wise.'

John reminded him of the fact, which he seemed to have overlooked, that it was not the Duke of Dunstable whom he was planning to marry, but merely a relative of his, and Gally admitted that he had a point there. It was not pleasant, though, to think that John would have to go through life calling the Duke Uncle Alaric, and John said that love would enable him to face even that prospect with fortitude.

'Not that I expect to see enough of him to have to call him anything.'

'You'll see him at the wedding.'

'I'll be in a sort of trance at the wedding and won't notice him.'

'Something in that,' Gally agreed. 'Bridegrooms are seldom in a frame of mind to take a calm look at their surroundings as the situation starts to develop. How well I remember your father when the parson was putting him through it. White as a sheet and quivering in every limb. I was his best man, and I'm convinced that if I hadn't kept near enough to him to grab him by the coat tails, he'd have run like a rabbit.'

'I shan't do that. I shall quiver all right, but I'll stay put.'

'I hope so, for nothing so surely introduces a sour note into the wedding ceremony as the abrupt disappearance of the groom in a cloud of dust. Tell me about this girl of yours.'

'Don't tempt me. I should go on for hours.'

'Nice, is she?'

'That describes her exactly.'

'Big? Small?'

'Just the right size.'

'Slim? Slender?'

'Yes.'

'Eyes?'

'Blue.'

'Hair?'

'Brown. Sort of auburn. Chestnut.'

'Make up your mind.'

'All right, chestnut, then, damn you.'

'No need to let your angry passions rise. Naturally I'm interested. I've known you since you were so high.'

'I suppose you dandled me on your knee when I was a baby?'

'I wouldn't have done it on a bet. You were a revolting baby. More like a poached egg than anything. Well, from what you tell me she seems to be all right. A godfather's blessing is yours, if you care to have it. Where are you going for the honeymoon?'

'We were thinking of Jamaica.'

'Expensive place.'

'So I hear.'

'Which brings me to a point I should like to discuss. How about your finances? I know you're doing pretty well at the Bar, but will it run to marriage?'

'I'm all right as far as money's concerned. I've got a nest egg. Do you know the Bender gallery?'

'Shooting gallery?'

'Picture gallery.'

'Never heard of it.'

'It's in Bond Street. Not one of the big ones, but doing all right, and I'm a kind of sleeping partner. Joe Bender does all the running of it. He's a man I knew at Oxford, and he took over the gallery from his father. He needed more capital and I had just been left quite a bit by an aunt of mine, so I put it in.'

'All you'd got?'

'Most of it.'

'A rash move.'

'Not rash at all. Joe's a very live wire, all tortoiseshell-rimmed spectacles and zip. We'll make our fortunes.'

'Says who?'

'I read it in the crystal ball. Joe's just pulled off a big deal. Ever heard of Robichaux?'

'No.'

'French painter. One of the Barbizon group.'

'What about him?'

'He's suddenly started getting hot. That's always happening with these old French artists, Joe tells me. They jog along all their lives hardly able to give their stuff away, and then they die and suddenly the sky's the limit. There was a time when you could buy a Renoir for a few francs, and now look at him. If you want a Renoir today, you have to sell the family jewels. It's getting to be the same with this bloke Robichaux. A year or two ago nobody would touch him, but now a regular boom has started, and what I was going to say was that Joe sold a Robichaux the other day for a sum that made me gasp. I wouldn't have thought it possible.'

'Anything's possible with the world as full of mugs as it is. Who was this cloth-headed purchaser?'

'I was saving that up for the big surprise at the end. None other than my future uncle-by-marriage.'

Gally snorted incredulously.

'Dunstable?'

'Yes, Uncle Alaric.'

'I don't believe it.'

'Why not?'

'Dunstable never bought a picture in his life. A comic seaside postcard would be more his form.'

'Perhaps he mistook it for a comic seaside postcard. Anyway, he bought it. You can ask Joe.'

'Amazing. Was he tight?'

'Not having been there when the deal went through, I couldn't tell you. I'll enquire if you like.'

'Don't bother. We'll just take it as read that he must have been. There's a boom, you say, in this Robichaux chap's work?'

'Price going up all the time, I believe.'

Gally shook his head.

'It still doesn't explain Dunstable's departure from the form book. With any ordinary man one would assume that he bought the thing on spec, hoping to sell at a profit, but not your Uncle Alaric. He wouldn't risk a bob on the deadest of certs. No, we fall back on our original theory, that he must have been stewed to the gills. Now who would that be?' said Gally, as the telephone rang. He went out into the hall, where the instrument was, and John was at liberty to devote his thoughts to the girl he loved.

His had been a long and cautious courtship, culminating with unforeseen suddenness in an abruptly blurted out proposal in the cab in which he was taking her home from a cocktail party, and his elation at the happy outcome of that proposal had been marred by the fact that there had been no time for anything in the nature of extended conversation. He was looking forward to going into the matter in what is called depth at their next meeting.

He was just thinking how infinitely superior Linda Gilpin was to any of the poor female fishes of whom in the last few years he had mistakenly supposed himself to be enamoured, and was thanking his guardian angel for his excellent staffwork in not allowing him to become really involved with any of them, when Gally returned.

He seemed amused.

'Odd coincidence,' he said, 'that we should have been talking about Dunstable. That was my brother Clarence, and he was talking about him, too. It seems that hell has broken loose at Blandings. My sister Connie has blown in from America with a female friend, which alone would have been enough to shake Clarence to his foundations, and on top of that Dunstable is arriving with his niece on the early train tomorrow. No wonder he's feeling like the Lady of Shalott when the curse had come upon her. Connie and friend would be bad enough. Add Dunstable and niece and he feels — rightly — that the mixture is too rich. Niece,' said Gally. 'Would that be your donah, or has he several?'

His words had stunned John. He knew that the Duke had only one relative of that description. He said he could not understand it.

'What puzzles you?'

'Linda didn't say anything about going to Blandings.'

'When would this be?'

'In the taxi, when I asked her to marry me.'

'She probably didn't know about it then. Dunstable must have sprung it on her when she got home.'

'We were to have had lunch tomorrow.'

'You weren't going to see her earlier than that? A whole morning wasted?'

'I have to be in court all the morning. Some

damned motor accident case.'

'Oh? Well, I'm sorry, but I'm afraid that lunch is off. And so am I. A brother's call for help is not a thing to be ignored,' said Gally. 'I leave for Blandings Castle in the morning.'

3

To get from London to Market Blandings, which is where one alights for Blandings Castle, the traveller starts from Paddington, and at 11.12 on the following morning Gally, smoking a cigarette on the platform outside his compartment and waiting for the 11.18 to begin its journey, looked about him with the approval he always felt for this particular terminus.

He liked its refined calm, so different from the hustle and bustle of such stations as Liverpool Street and Waterloo. Here all was cloistral peace. The trains as they got up steam puffed in a quiet undertone. The porters went about their duties with the reserve of junior Cabinet ministers. Guards, when compelled to whistle, whistled softly. And even the occasional cocker spaniel, on its way back to its Worcestershire or Shropshire home, postponed its barking to a more suitable time, knowing instinctively that a raised voice in these surroundings would be the worst of form.

But all too soon it was borne in upon him that snakes could sometimes penetrate into this gentlemanly Garden of Eden. One of them was coming along the platform at this moment, a large, stout, walrus-moustached man with a brown paper parcel under his arm. He was brushing aside like flies the little groups of cultured men accustomed to mingling with basset hounds and the women in tailored suits who looked like horses, and at the sight of him Gally dived hastily into his compartment and tried to lurk behind his morning journal.

It was a wasted effort. Not so easily as this was it possible to evade Alaric, Duke of Dunstable.

'Thought it was you, Threepwood,' said the Duke, seating himself. 'Must be two years since we met.'

'Two wonderful years.'

'Eh?'

'I was saying how wonderful it was seeing you again.'

'Ah.'

'Clarence tells me you've had a fire at your place.'

'Yes. Wires fused.'

'So you're coming to Blandings.'

'Never could stand London.'

'Bad fire, was it?'

'Made the place smell. I cleared out.'

'And Connie came to the rescue of the homeless waif.'

'Eh?'

'She invited you to Blandings.'

The Duke snorted a little. It was as though his pride had been touched.

'Good God, she didn't invite me. I rang up last night and said I was coming.'

'I see.'

'I was surprised to find she was over here. I was expecting Emsworth to answer the telephone. What made her leave America, do you know?'

'I've no idea.'

'Some sudden whim, I suppose. In a week or so she'll get another and go dashing back. Women are all potty. Never know their own minds from one day to another. What's taking you to Blandings?'

'Clarence was anxious for my company.'

'Why?'

'Who can say? Some sudden whim, do you think?'

'Could be. Is he still mooning over that pig of his?'

'He courts its society a good deal, I believe.'

'Much too fat, that pig.'

'Clarence doesn't think so.'

'No, because he's as potty as Connie. Pottier. Fact of the matter is, the whole world's potty these days. Look at Connie, going off to live in America with a man with a head like a Spanish onion. Look at those two nephews of mine, both married to girls I wouldn't have let them so much as whistle at if I'd been able to stop them. And look at my niece. Came back to the hotel last night giggling and humming, and wouldn't tell me what it was all about. Definitely potty.'

Gally could of course have shed light on the mystery of the humming niece, but he felt that if she herself had been so reticent, it was not for him to speak. He allowed the slur of mental instability to continue to rest upon her.

'Where is this unbalanced niece? Clarence said she would be coming with you. Not ill, I hope?'

'No, she's all right except for all that humming and giggling. She's got to appear in court today; she's a witness in some case that comes on this morning. She'll be coming later. Do you know

32

anything about pictures?' asked the Duke, wearying of the subject of nieces and changing it with his customary abruptness.

'Not much. I heard you had bought one.'

'Who told you that?'

'A usually reliable source.'

'Well, it's quite true. It's what they call a reclining nude. You know the sort of thing. Girl with no clothes on, lying on a mossy bank. By some French fellow. I bought it at one of those art galleries.'

'I suppose they told you it was a monument to man's attainment of the unattainable and the work of a Master with his brush dipped in immortality?'

'Eh?'

'Let it go. I was only thinking that that's the way art galleries generally talk when a mug walks into the shop.'

The Duke's moustache shot up. His manner showed resentment.

'Think I'm a mug, do you? Well, you're wrong. I knew what I was doing, all right. Shall I tell you why I bought that reclining nude? Do you know a chap called Trout? Wilbur J. Trout?'

'Not had that pleasure. What about him?'

'He's an American. What the Yanks call a playboy. He's in London, and I ran into him at the club. He has a guest card. We got into conversation, and he told me he loved his wife. Blotto, of course.'

'What makes you say that?'

'Well, would a chap tell a chap he loved his wife, if he wasn't?'

'He might if the other chap had your charm.'

'True. Yes, something in that.'

'Yours is a very winning manner. Invites confidences.'

'I suppose it does. Yes, I see what you mean. Well, anyway, as I was saying, he told me he loved his wife. She was his third wife. Or did he say fourth? Never mind, it's immaterial. The point is that she recently divorced him, but he still loves her. He said he was carrying the torch for her, which struck me as a peculiar expression, but that's what he said. He was crying into his cocktail as he spoke, and that seemed odd, too, because he was a big, beefy chap who you'd have thought would have been above that sort of thing. He told me he used to be a great footballer, played for Harvard or Yale or one of those places. Ginger-coloured hair, broken nose which I suppose he got at football unless one of his wives gave it him, inherited millions from his father, who was a big business man out in California.'

Gally stirred uneasily in his seat. He had always been a better raconteur than listener, and it seemed to him that his companion was a long time coming to the point, assuming that there was a point to which he was coming.

'All this,' he said, 'would be of the greatest help if I were planning to write a biography of Wilbur Trout or doing The Trout Story for the films, but how does it link up with reclining nudes and you as an art collector?'

'I'm coming to that.'

'Good. Come as quick as you can.'

34

'Where was I?'

'He told you he loved his wife.'

'That's right. And then he said something that held me spell-bound.'

'Like me. I can hardly wait for the plot to unfold. I'll bet it turns out that it was the butler who did it.'

'What do you mean, the butler? What butler? I never mentioned any butler.'

'Don't give it another thought. What did he say that interested you so much?'

'He said he saw this picture in the window of this picture gallery, and blowed if it wasn't the living image of his third wife, the one he was carrying the torch for. And when he told me he was going to buy it because he had to have it just to remind him of her, no matter what it cost, I naturally said to myself 'What ho!'.'

'Why did you say that to yourself?'

'Because I saw that this was where I could make a bit. Ten minutes later I was round at the gallery buying the thing, confident that I would be able to sell it to him for double the price I'd paid, which, let me tell you, was stiff. It's a crime what these galleries charge you. Still, I'll get it all back and more.'

'You look on it as an investment?'

'Exactly. The profit should be substantial. So don't let me hear any more of that talk of mugs walking into shops. Care to see the ruddy object? I've got it in this parcel. On second thoughts, no,' said the Duke, changing his mind. 'Too much trouble untying the string and doing it up again, and I'm feeling drowsy. Couldn't get a wink of sleep last night, pondering over that niece of mine. Giggling she was and all starry-eyed. I didn't like the look of her.'

II

Train journeys never bored Gally unless they involved extended conversations with an uncongenial companion, and he found the time pass very pleasantly with his thoughts. Nevertheless he was glad when he was able to wake the Duke, who had fallen into another coma after lunch, and inform him that in five minutes they would be arriving at Market Blandings.

The first person he saw on the platform was his brother Clarence, the second his sister Constance. Her welcoming smile as the Duke alighted vanished from her face as if wiped off with a squeegee when she observed what was coming out of the train behind him. Her attitude towards Gally had always been austere. No matter how great his popularity in the circles in which he moved, to her, as to her sisters, he was a blot on the escutcheon of a proud family and something one preferred to hush up and try to forget. For years she had been haunted by the fear that he was going to write his Reminiscences, and though this threat had blown over, she still had a tendency to shudder when she saw him. She disliked his presence, his conversation and his monocle. She sometimes thought that she could almost have endured him if he had not worn an eyeglass.

A certain chill, accordingly, marked this little gathering on the platform of Market Blandings station, and it was a relief to Lord Emsworth, who was in momentary fear lest his responsibility for Gally's arrival might be revealed, when the Duke went off with her to see about his luggage, which on these visits was always considerable.

'It was very good of you to come so promptly, Galahad,' he said. 'I was afraid you might have other engagements.'

'My dear Clarence! As if any engagement, however other, could keep me from answering a cry for succour like yours. You were very wise to send for me. It must have shaken even a strong man like you when Connie suddenly popped up out of a trap like the Demon King in a pantomime.'

'It did indeed.'

'And the shock of hearing that Dunstable was coming must have been almost worse. Still we ought, standing shoulder to shoulder, to be able to cope with Dunstable. It only needs a firm hand. What about this friend of Connie's?'

'Oh, she is charming. I like her very much.'

'Well, that's something.'

'Very sound on pigs. Nothing she actually said, but I could see that she had the right attitude when I was telling her about the Empress's feeding schedule.'

'What's her name?'

'I've forgotten.'

'Well, no doubt I shall find out in God's good time. You said something about some fellow young Freddie had sent to you with a letter of introduction. What's *his* name?'

'I can't remember.'

'No need for you to join the Foreign Legion, where men go to forget, Clarence. You can do it comfortably without stirring a step from Blandings Castle. What's he like? Nice chap?'

'No, I wouldn't say that. He kept trying to sell me oil stock. Just the American business drive, I suppose, but it was embarrassing having to keep refusing, so I told Beach I would have all my meals in the library, and of course avoiding him in between meals was a simple task.'

'Child's play to one who has spent years avoiding Connie.'

'Beach tells me he left for London yesterday.'

'But he may be coming back.'

'I fear so.'

'In fact, I shouldn't be surprised if this were not he whom I see approaching us. No, not there; the other direction; slightly more to your left.'

'Yes, that is Mr . . . Mr . . . Mr . . .'

'Call him X,' said Gally.

Howard Chesney was a slender young man of medium height, distinctly ornamental in appearance, his flannel suit well cut, his hat just as good as the one Lady Constance had admired on the previous evening. The only criticism a purist could have made of him was that his eyes were a little too wary and a little too close together.

Knowing at what a disadvantage Lord Emsworth would be if called upon to introduce him to a man whose name he had forgotten, Gally took it on himself to start the conversation.

'Good afternoon,' he said. 'I am Lord

Emsworth's brother. Threepwood is the name. I hear you are a friend of my nephew Freddie. How was he when you left him?'

'Oh, fine.'

'Selling lots of dog biscuits?'

'Oh, sure.'

'Splendid. That's the spirit one likes to see. My brother tells me that you and he have been whooping it up together these last days.'

It was not quite how Howard Chesney would have described his association with Lord Emsworth, but he allowed the phrase to pass and spoke appreciatively of Blandings Castle and the many attractions it had to offer. He also had a good word to say about the beauties of the Shropshire countryside. He had walked to the station yesterday, he said, and was preparing now to walk back.

'That,' said Gally approvingly, 'will be satisfactory to all parties concerned, for with Clarence and me and my sister Constance and the Duke . . . that is my sister over there and the substantial object with her is the Duke of Dunstable . . . it would be something of a squash if we all climbed into the car. The Duke takes up quite a bit of room, and Clarence has a way of spreading his legs about like an octopus's tentacles. You'll be happier singing gypsy songs along the high road. How right you were, Clarence,' said Gally as Howard moved away, 'not to invest in oil stock sponsored by our young friend. I don't hold it against him that his eyes are so close together . . . some of my best friends are men with eyes close together . . . but if ever I saw a con man, and in the course of a longish life I've seen dozens, he's one. Where on earth do you think Freddie dug him up?'

III

Up at the castle Beach was in his pantry sipping his evening glass of port, and seeing him one would have said that there sat a butler with his soul at rest and not a disturbing thought on his mind.

One would have been in error. His soul was not at rest. It would perhaps be too much to put it that vultures were gnawing at his ample bosom, but he was certainly far from carefree. Sensitive to atmosphere, he found that which now prevailed at Blandings trying to his nervous system. It seemed to him that with the return of Lady Constance a shadow had fallen on the home he loved. He had not failed to note his lordship's reaction to his announcement of her arrival, and he foresaw hard times ahead. If only, he was thinking, Mr. Galahad could have been here to lend aid and comfort to his stricken employer: and even as he framed the thought the door opened and Gally came in.

To say that he leaped from his seat would be an overstatement. Men of Beach's build do not leap from seats. He did, however, rise slowly like a hippopotamus emerging from a river bank, his emotions somewhat similar to those of a beleaguered garrison when the United States Marines arrive.

'Mr. Galahad!'

'Why not? Someone has to be. Beach, you see before you a bison making for the water hole with its blackened tongue hanging out.'

'I shall be taking the tea into the drawing-room shortly, Mr. Galahad.'

'Tea is no good to me. I want port. And in any case I wouldn't go to the drawing-room. It will be full of Society's lowest dregs. As a matter of fact, one of my motives in coming to your pantry was to discuss those dregs with you and get your opinion of them.'

Beach was pursing his lips a little as he produced a second glass and prepared to play the host. His guest, he perceived, was about to be frank about the castle's personnel, and he knew that he ought to disapprove. But though his lips were pursed, there was a gleam in his eyes. As a butler he deplored Mr. Galahad's habit of gossiping with the domestic staff, but as a man he simply loved it.

'What, to start with, do you make of this chap Chesney?' said Gally.

It was a subject on which Beach held strong views. His reply was austere.

'He is not what I have been accustomed to, Mr. Galahad.'

'And you've seen some pretty weird specimens in your time.'

'I have indeed, sir.'

'Remember the fellow who wanted to eat jam with his fish?'

'Very vividly, sir.'

'And the one who put water in his claret?'

41

'Please, Mr. Galahad. I have been trying to forget him.'

'I have yet to observe Chesney at the dinner table, but I imagine he stops short of those awful extremes. Still, I know what you mean when you say he's not what you've been accustomed to. He's obviously a crook.'

'Indeed, Mr. Galahad?'

'No question about it. I can tell them a mile off.'

'It seems strange that he should be a friend of Mr. Frederick.'

'I don't suppose he is. Probably just a casual acquaintance he picked up in a bar. Freddie wouldn't see anything wrong with him, and he would give a letter of introduction to anyone who asked him.'

'But what — '

' — makes me think he's a crook? He tried to sell Clarence oil stock. And though you may say that that's only what John D. Rockefeller used to do when he met people, I find the fact damning. Be very careful how you have dealings with Chesney, Beach.'

'I will indeed, sir.'

'We now come to His Grace the Duke of Dunstable, and this is where we really shudder. You will agree with me, I think, that his presence at it would lower the tone of a silver ring bookies' social and outing picnic?'

Though his words were music to Beach's ears, for the Duke was no favourite of his, routine called for a mild protest.

'It is scarcely for me, Mr. Galahad, to express

derogatory opinions of the guests whom her ladyship sees fit to invite to — '

'All right, I get your point. But however much you may wear the mask, you know in your heart that he's utterly devoid of all the finer instincts which raise Man above the level of the beasts that perish. He's a twister to end all twisters.'

'Sir?'

'Well, look at the way he's doing down the unfortunate Trout.'

'I am afraid I do not understand you, Mr. Galahad.'

'Only because you weren't there when he was telling me that story on the train. It appears that there is a harmless innocent American of the name of Wilbur Trout whose only fault is that he marries rather too often, which is the sort of thing that might happen to anyone. King Solomon, if you remember, had the same tendency. Well, Trout saw a picture in the window of an art gallery which was the image of his latest wife. She divorced him recently, but in spite of that he still loves her. He was planning to buy the picture, to remind him of her, and was ass enough to tell Dunstable so, with the result, of course, that Dunstable nipped in ahead of him and bought it, so as to be able to sell it to him at an exorbitant price. He knows Trout wants the thing so badly that he will cough up anything he's asked, even unto half his kingdom. What do you think of that for chiselling and skulduggery, Beach?'

'Tut, tut.'

'You may well say Tut, tut. I wouldn't blame

43

you if you'd said Gorblimey. So there you have His Grace of Dunstable in a nutshell, and it's not a pleasant thought that he will be with us for days and days, probably for weeks and weeks. One wonders how Clarence will bear up, especially as her ladyship will make him dress for dinner every night. She will, won't she?'

'I fear so, Mr. Galahad.'

'And he hates it even more than having to wear a top hat at the school treat. Ah well, we must just hope that his frail form will not crack beneath the strain. And now, Beach, with many thanks for your hospitality, I must be leaving you. The train journey, as always, has left me feeling like a cinder track and an immediate plunge into the waters of the bath tub is of the essence. We shall meet at Philippi, if not sooner.'

4

Two days elapsed before Linda Gilpin arrived. She came in her car late at night and went straight to bed, tired from the long journey, and after breakfast next morning Gally, naturally anxious to have a confidential talk with her, took her to see the yew alley which was one of the features of the place and often got flattering notices in books with titles like 'British Gardens' and 'Olde Worlde England'. The brief glimpse he had had of her had impressed him favourably. She was, as John had said, slim, blue-eyed, just the right height, topped off with chestnut-coloured hair, and so unlike her uncle the Duke of Dunstable that it did him good to look at her. A girl, in short, whom any godfather would be glad to think his godson would at an early date be going off on honeymoons to Jamaica with. He could hardly wait to make her better acquaintance.

The Duke and Lady Constance were up in the portrait gallery. On the previous day the former's reclining nude had been hung there, and Lady Constance was scrutinizing it without pleasure. She was a woman who, while not knowing much about Art, knew what she liked, and the kind of paintings she liked were those whose subjects were more liberally draped. A girl with nothing on except a quite inadequate wisp of some filmy material, she told the Duke, was out of place in the company of her ancestors, and the Duke in rebuttal replied that her ancestors were such a collection of ugly thugs that it was a charity to give the viewer something to divert his attention from them. With a flight of imagery of which few would have thought him capable he compared the Blandings Castle portrait gallery to the Chamber of Horrors at Madame Tussaud's.

The critique ruffled Lady Constance, though anyone less prejudiced would have felt compelled to admit that some of the Earls of Emsworth, notably the third, fifth and seventh, had been rash to allow their portraits to be painted, but she checked the sharp response she would have liked to make. The Duke, when responded to sharply, was apt to take offence, and she had that to say to him which called for amiability on his part, or something as close to amiability as could be expected of him.

She was about to take up once again the matter of his marrying. For many years he had been a widower, and her own happy union with James Schoonmaker had made her feel more strongly than ever that this was a state of affairs that should be adjusted. She was a firm believer in a wife's influence for good over her husband, and she held the view that the Duke needed all the influence for good that he could get. Someone who would improve his manners and habits and general outlook on life was, in her opinion, what he ought to be supplied with as soon as possible.

She had often spoken to him on the subject before, but only in a vague, general way. Now that Vanessa Polk had come into her life and was actually here at Blandings with him, it seemed to her that the time had come to be more specific; to get, though she would never have used such an expression, down to brass tacks and talk turkey. She edged gently into her theme.

'How charming American women are,' she said. 'So pretty, so chic, so well dressed.'

The Duke saw that she was under a misapprehension. Only to be expected of a female, of course. In the sex to which she belonged one took muddleheadedness for granted.

'She isn't American. Chap who did the thing was French, so she must have been French, too. Stands to reason a fellow painting in France would have a French model. Probably her name was Gaby or Brigitte or Mimi or something. And if you think she's well dressed, you're potty. She hasn't got a ruddy stitch on.'

Lady Constance bit her lip and had to pause for a moment before speaking. The uncharitable thought floated into her mind that there were times when Alaric was just like her brother Clarence.

'I was not alluding to the woman in that picture,' she said coldly. 'I was thinking of — '

'Does she remind you of anyone?' the Duke proceeded. It was only inadvertently that he ever allowed anyone to finish a sentence. 'I ask because a fellow I know, an American fellow called Trout, says she's the image of his third wife, while Emsworth insists that she has a distinct look of that pig of his.'

'I was thinking — '

'Something about the expression in her eyes, he said, and the way she's lying. He said he had seen his pig lying like that a hundred times. It does it after a heavy meal.'

'What I was going to say — '

'And oddly enough I notice quite a resemblance to our vicar's wife down in Wiltshire. Only the face, of course, for I never saw her lying in the nude on a mossy bank. I doubt if the vicar would let her.'

'If you would just listen, Alaric — '

'By the way, meant to have told you before, I've invited Trout here. I thought it was the decent thing to do. His wife divorced him, and he's carrying the torch for her, so naturally the more he sees of a picture that reminds him of her, the better he'll like it. He's arriving this afternoon.'

Had Lady Constance been conversing with Lord Emsworth and had he let fall the statement that he had invited an American fellow called Trout to Blandings Castle without her permission, something reminiscent of the San Francisco earthquake must inevitably have resulted. But true to her policy of keeping the Duke in the best mood of which he was capable she allowed only the merest suggestion of annoyance to creep into her words.

'I wish you would not invite people to my house, Alaric.'

The Duke, a clear-headed man, saw the objection to this immediately, and once again the inability of females to reason anything out impressed itself upon him. It was something, he believed, to do with the bone structure of their heads.

'How the devil are they to get here, if they aren't invited?'

Lady Constance might have retorted that men who invited themselves were not unknown to her, but she merely heaved a weary sigh.

'Who is this Trout?'

'Aren't you listening? I told you. A Yank. I met him at the club. We got talking, and he told me about his wife. Not a bad chap. Potty, of course.'

'Why do you call him that?'

'Marrying all those women. As far as I can make out, he does it every hour on the hour. Do you remember that song 'They call me Otto of roses' in one of those Gaiety shows? 'If you don't like what you've go-to, pick another from the grotto, that's the motto of Otto of roses'. That's Trout.'

'He sounds charming.'

'He's all right. Tight all the time, I imagine. At least he was when I met him. He was crying into a cocktail, and he told me about his wife. This was his third wife, or it may have been his fourth. He marries at the drop of a hat. Odd hobby to have, but everyone to his taste and I suppose he enjoys it.'

He had given Lady Constance the cue she needed. Pigeonholing for the moment the rather disquieting thought that in her capacity of chatelaine of Blandings Castle she was about to entertain for an indeterminate visit a mentally unbalanced alcoholic, she said:

'Don't you think it's time you married again, Alaric?'

An exasperated snort echoed through the portrait gallery like a fog horn.

'That's what you say every blasted time I see you. Nag, nag, nag. Who do you want me to marry now?'

'Vanessa Polk.'

'That American female you've brought along? Who is she? One of your New York friends?'

'No, I met her on the boat. I had an attack of neuralgia, and she was very good to me. I was obliged to spend two days in bed, and she came and sat with me and looked after me.'

'Probably working up to a touch.'

'Don't be ridiculous.'

'Has she tried to borrow money?'

'Of course she has not. She's much richer than I am. At least, her father is.'

'How do you know that?'

'She told me. She is J. B. Polk's daughter. You must have heard of J. B. Polk.'

'I seem to know the name.'

'Of course you do. He's a financial emperor. Controls all sorts of businesses ... banks, railroads, mines, everything.'

'*Does* he?' said the Duke.

'Nobody could call James a pauper, but he feels like one when he compares himself with J. B. Polk. And he has a very high blood pressure.'

'James has?'

'Polk has. He might die of apoplexy at any moment, and Vanessa would become one of the wealthiest women in America.'

'Would she?' said the Duke thoughtfully. '*Would* she?'

The gleam which had come into his prominent eyes did not escape Lady Constance's notice, nor did it surprise her. She had expected her words to create a powerful reaction. Revolted though she would have been had someone informed her that her views on anything could coincide with those of her brother Galahad, on the subject of the Duke's affection for money they were identical. This partiality of his for coin of the realm had been drawn to her attention twenty years ago, when he had informed her that their engagement was at an end because her father refused to meet his terms in the matter of dowry, and she could never be sufficiently grateful to her late parent for his parsimony. She was fond of Alaric in a sisterly way, but her intelligence told her that for one of her impatient temperament marriage with him would have been a disaster. Vanessa was different. Her cheerful equable nature would enable her to cope even with an Alaric.

'She would be ideal for you,' she said.

'Seems nice,' the Duke agreed.

'And of course it would be a wonderful match for her.'

'Of course.'

'She went to the library after breakfast. Why don't you go there and talk to her?'

'I will.'

'She will be delighted to see you.'

'I suppose so. I'll go at once. And I don't want you coming along, Connie, so buzz off.'

Gally had had to change his plans. He had not been able to fulfil his intention of showing Linda Gilpin the beauties of the yew alley, for after the briefest of conversations on the way there they had parted, she to return to the house, he to go to the Empress's sty, where he knew Lord Emsworth was to be found. As the result of his talk with the moon of his godson's delight he was feeling perplexed and bewildered, and he had a faint hope that Clarence might have something constructive to suggest. Such a miracle was not of course likely, for Clarence in the course of a longish life had never suggested anything constructive to anybody on any subject whatsoever, but it often happens that talking something over with someone has the effect of clarifying one's thoughts, even if that someone merely gapes at one like a goldfish.

He found Lord Emsworth, as usual, draped like a wet sock over the rail of the Empress's G.H.Q. with a large potato in his hand, and came immediately to the point.

'Clarence,' he said, 'I'm worried.'

'I am sorry to hear that, Galahad,' said Lord Emsworth, courteously transferring to him the attention monopolized till then by the silver medallist, who was busying herself among the proteins and carbohydrates with a gusto which would have drawn a smile of approval from Wolff-Lehman. 'Is it Connie?' he asked, seizing on what he thought the obvious explanation for anyone's mental disturbance at Blandings Castle.

'No, not Connie. It's about a godson of mine.'

'I did not know you had a godson.'

'I have several. People ask you to officiate, and you can't very well refuse. Not that I have any complaints to make about my little lot. I'm very fond of them all, particularly this one. I hope I am not interrupting you in an early lunch, Clarence.'

'I beg your pardon?'

'That potato you're brandishing.'

'Oh, that is for the Empress. I was about to give it to her.'

'Do it now. Then you will be able to concentrate on my story.'

'Quite. Yes, go on, Galahad. You were saying you were thinking of adopting a godson.'

'I wasn't saying anything of the sort. You don't adopt godsons, they just adhere to you like some sort of growth. This one is the son of an old friend of mine, and he's in trouble.'

Lord Emsworth was concerned.

'Money? I should be glad to do anything in my power.'

'That's extremely kind of you, Clarence, but he's all right as far as money is concerned. He's doing well at the bar and has an interest in one of those Bond Street picture galleries. It's his love life that has come a stinker. You remember that night you phoned me about Connie breaking out again. He was with me at the time, and he had just been telling me he had become engaged to be married.'

'Indeed?'

'To the Gilpin girl.'

53

'Who is the Gilpin girl?'

'You've met her. She's staying here. Came last night, smallish, with blue eyes and chestnut hair.'

'Ah yes, I do seem to have some sort of recollection. Isn't she something to do with Alaric?'

'His niece.'

'And she is going to marry your godson?'

'According to him it was all set. He babbled about how much he loved her and distinctly gave me to understand that she loved him with equal intensity.'

'They loved each other?' said Lord Emsworth, having worked it out.

'Exactly. It seemed as if it was all over except buying the licence and rounding up the parson.'

'When is the wedding to be? And will it mean . . . ' said Lord Emsworth in sudden panic, 'that I shall have to wear a top hat?'

'The way it looks, you need have no anxiety.'

'You don't think Connie will insist?'

'She won't be given the opportunity.'

'She makes me wear one for the school treat.'

'What I'm trying to tell you is that there probably won't be a wedding.'

'You said there would.'

'And the girl says there won't.'

'She ought to know. Well, that's a relief. It isn't the top hat I really object to, it's the clothes that go with it. The stiff collar — '

'If you will just let me get on with it, Clarence.'

'Certainly, my dear fellow, certainly.'

'Then I will proceed. Not so many minutes

ago I took her — or started to take her — to see the yew valley. It being the first time I had been able to get her alone, my opening move was naturally to touch on the engagement.'

'To your godson?'

'To my godson. 'I hear I have to wish you happiness,' I said. To which she replied with a simple 'Why?'. A little surprised by her slowness at the uptake, I explained that I was referring to her betrothal.'

'To your godson?'

'To my godson. And she gave me a quick, cold, haughty look, as if I had offended her with a four-letter word. 'Are you under the impression,' she said, 'that it is my intention to marry that ruddy Gawd-help-us? If so, here is something for your files. I wouldn't marry him to please a dying grandmother. If I saw him perishing of thirst, I wouldn't give him the dew off a Brussels sprout. And if I heard that he had been run over by a motor omnibus and had broken his spine in three places, I would go about Blandings Castle trilling like a nightingale.' Those may not have been her exact words, but that was the gist, and her attitude left me disturbed. I may be hypersensitive, but I got the definite feeling that the wedding was off. I can't imagine what Johnny has done to get her thinking along those lines. It'll probably turn out to be something quite trivial. A thing I've noticed as I've gone through life is that girls never need much of a reason for breaking engagements. It's their first move when anything goes wrong. I remember a fellow named Ponderby at the old

Pelican — Legs Ponderby we used to call him — short for Hollow Legs — because of his remarkable capacity for absorbing buttered rums — who got engaged to a girl who did a snake act on the suburban Halls and always took her supporting artists around with her in a wickerwork basket. And one night, when they were having a bite of supper at the Bodega, a long green member of the troupe got loose and crawled up Legs's leg, and wanting to sell his life dearly he hit it on the nose with a bread stick. He explained to the girl that seeing snakes always affected him profoundly, but she broke the engagement just the same and went off and married a comedy juggler. And then there was poor Binks Holloway — '

The Binks Holloway anecdote was one of Gally's best. He had told it perhaps a hundred times in the course of his career to rapturous audiences, but he was not to tell it now. Lord Emsworth had uttered a strangled yelp and with a shaking finger was pointing at something in the sty. What it was, Gally was unable to see. Everything looked perfectly normal to him, no suggestion that the Empress had fallen in a fit or was being snatched up to heaven in a fiery chariot. Always a pig chary of exhibiting the stronger emotions, she seemed even more placid than usual.

'What on earth's the matter, Clarence?' he asked with petulance. That sudden yelp had made him bite his tongue.

For a moment Lord Emsworth struggled for speech. Then he achieved utterance, though in a shaking voice.

'The potato!'

'What about it?'

'She has not eaten it. Such a thing has never happened before. She is passionately fond of potatoes. She must be sickening for something.'

'Shall I send for the vet?'

Gally's query had been satirical in intent. He resented this agitation about a pig which was obviously at the peak of its form, and his tongue was still paining him.

'Or notify the police? Or call out the military?'

All that penetrated to Lord Emsworth's consciousness was the operative word.

'Yes, will you telephone the vet, Galahad. I would do it myself, but I ought to stay with her. His name is Banks. Beach will know the number. Please go and see Beach without delay.'

III

It had been well said of Galahad Threepwood from the old Pelican days onward that blows beneath which lesser men reeled and collapsed left him as cool and unconcerned as a halibut on a fishmonger's slab, and indeed there were very few socks on the spiritual jawbone that he could not take with a stiff and nonchalant upper lip. Nevertheless, it was with heart bowed down that he made for Beach's pantry to perform his errand of mercy. It seemed abundantly clear to him from her remarks on the way to the yew alley that what had sundered Linda Gilpin and the godson for whom he had always felt a

57

paternal fondness had not been one of those passing lovers' tiffs which can be put right with a few kisses and a bottle of scent, but the real big time stuff. For some reason which had still to be explained John had fallen back so badly in the betting in the matrimonial stakes that he might as well have been actually scratched.

It was not a pleasant state of things for a loving godfather to have to contemplate, and he was pondering deeply as he reached the house. He was an optimist and throughout his checkered career had always clung stoutly to the view that no matter how darkly the clouds might lower the sun would eventually come smiling through, but this time it looked as though the sun had other intentions.

Musing thus, he was passing across the hall, when his meditations were interrupted by a voice calling his name. Lady Constance was standing in the doorway of the amber drawing-room, looking, he thought, extraordinarily like the Statue of Liberty.

'Please come here, Galahad.'

Conversations with Connie, tending as they so often did to become acrimonious, were never among the pleasures Gally went out of his way to seek, and at the moment, with so much on his mind, he was feeling particularly allergic to a tete-a-tete. He replied promptly.

'Can't now. I'm busy. Fully occupied.'

'I don't care how fully occupied you are. I want to talk to you.'

'Oh, all right, but talk quick. The Empress has refused to eat a potato, Clarence is distracted, and I've got to call the vet. It's a major crisis, and all good men have been notified that now is the time for them to come to the aid of the party.'

He followed her into the drawing-room, sank into a chair and gave his monocle a polish, an action which drew from her a sharp 'Oh, for goodness sake don't *do* that!'

'Do what?'

'Fiddle with that revolting eyeglass.'

It was evident to Gally that his sister was in one of her moods, which were roughly equivalent to those which Cleopatra and Boadicea used to have when things went wrong, and he braced himself to play the man. One of the rules he lived by was 'When Connie starts throwing her weight about, sit on her head immediately'. It was a policy he had repeatedly urged on Lord Emsworth, but never with success.

'I don't know why you call it revolting,' he said with dignity. 'For years it has been admired by some of the most discriminating jellied eel sellers in London. What's on your mind, Connie? You didn't lug me in here merely to heap vulgar abuse on me.'

'I lugged you in here, as you put it, because I want to speak to you about Vanessa Polk.'

'That's better. I am always happy to be spoken to about the Polk popsy. Charming creature.'

'She is, and you have a habit of monopolizing charming creatures who visit the castle and never letting anyone else come near them.'

'One tries to be civil.'

'Well, this time don't. There are others who

would like to have an occasional word with Vanessa.'

It was only a kindly reluctance to inflame passions beyond control that kept Gally from polishing his eyeglass again. The significance of her words had not escaped him. Excluding Howard Chesney, there could be only one person she had in mind, and it was unlikely that she would be concerning herself about Howard Chesney.

'Do you mean Dunstable?'

Lady Constance started irritably, like the Statue of Liberty stung by a mosquito which had wandered over from the Jersey marshes. She spoke with the petulance that always came into her manner sooner or later when she conversed with her brother Galahad.

'Why do you persist in calling him that? You've known him for years. Why not Alaric?'

'Never mind what I call him. If you knew some of the things I'd like to call him you would be astounded at my moderation. Are you telling me that that human walrus has fallen in love at first sight with Vanessa Polk?'

'Alaric is not a human walrus.'

'You criticize my use of the word human?'

Lady Constance swallowed twice, and was thus enabled to overcome a momentary urge to hit her brother over the head with a glass vase containing gladioli. It is one of the tragedies of advancing age that the simple reactions of child-hood have to be curbed. In their mutual nursery far less provocation than she was receiving now would have led her to an attack with tooth and claw. With an effort she forced herself to preserve the decencies of debate.

'I am not going to waste the morning bickering with you, Galahad,' she said. 'Naturally I am not saying anything so foolish as that Alaric has fallen in love at first sight, but he is very interested in Vanessa and I'm not surprised. She is very attractive.'

'But he isn't,' said Gally.

Lady Constance gave him a stony glance. Wasted on him, for being too humane to polish his eyeglass he was assisting thought by lying back in his chair with his eyes closed. Her voice was icy as she said:

'Alaric is extremely attractive.'

'If you like walruses.'

'And I want you to understand that you are not to interfere with — '

'His wooing?'

'If that is the word you care to use.'

'Very well. But may I say in parting that if you're trying to get Dunstable off this season, you haven't a hope. He's much too set in his ways and much too fond of his comforts to marry anyone. Don't fool yourself. He may put on an act and make you think he's going to jump off the dock, but he'll always remember how snug he is as a widower and draw back in time.'

And so saying Gally trotted off to Beach's pantry to fulfil his mission.

Beach was polishing silver when he arrived. Abandoning this duty for the moment, he called the veterinary surgeon at his office in Market Blandings and bade him hasten to the Empress's

61

sty; and he had scarcely replaced the receiver when the telephone rang again.

'For you, Mr. Galahad. A Mr. Halliday.'

'Ah, I was expecting him to call. Hullo, Johnny.'

The conversation that ensued was brief, too brief for Beach, whose curiosity had been aroused. He gathered that this Mr. Halliday was speaking from the Emsworth Arms and wished to see Mr. Galahad at the earliest possible moment, but beyond that all was mystery.

At length Gally hung up, and with a curt 'Got to go to Market Blandings' hurried out.

Odd, thought Beach, most peculiar. Sinister, too, if you came to think of it, like those telephone calls in the novels of suspense which were his favourite reading.

He hoped Mr. Galahad had not got mixed up with a gang of some kind.

IV

The hollowness of John's voice over the telephone had deepened Gally's conviction that this rift between him and the Gilpin popsy must be the real West End stuff, and when he reached his destination and saw him, he realized how well-founded his apprehensions had been.

What with the excellence of its beer and the charm of the shady garden running down to the river in which its patrons drink it, haggard faces are rarely seen at the Emsworth Arms, and the haggardness of John's was all the more

62

noticeable. In these idyllic surroundings it could not but attract attention, and Gally was reminded of his old friend Fruity Biffen on the occasion when he had gone into the ring at Hurst Park wearing a long Assyrian beard in order to avoid recognition by the half dozen bookmakers there to whom he owed money, and the beard, insufficiently smeared with fish glue, had come off. The same wan, drawn look.

Until they were seated at one of the garden tables with tankards of Emsworth Arms beer before them no word was spoken. But it was never in Gally to refrain from speech for long, and after he had fortified himself with a draft of the elixir he leaned forward and gave his companion's shoulder a fatherly pat.

'Tell me all about it, my boy,' he said in the hushed voice of one addressing a stretcher case on his stretcher. 'I should mention that it was only an hour or so ago that Miss Gilpin and I were in conference, so I understand the situation more or less. That is to say, while short on details, I'm pretty clear on the general all-over picture. Your engagement, I gather from her, is off, and as it's only a day or so since you plighted your troth it struck me as quick work. I was mystified.'

'What did she say about me?'

'Better, far better not to enquire. Suffice it that her obiter dicta differed substantially from the sort of thing Juliet used to say about Romeo. What on earth happened?'

A beetle, descending from the tree in the shade of which they were sitting, fell on the

63

table. John gave it a cold look.

'It wasn't my fault,' he said. 'I was simply doing my duty. Women don't understand these things.'

'What things?'

'She ought to have realized that I couldn't let Clutterbuck down.'

'Clutterbuck?'

'G. G. Clutterbuck.'

Gally had intended to be all gentleness and sympathy at this interview, but he could not repress an irritated snort. If he had to listen to a story instead of telling one, he liked it to be clear and straightforward.

'Who the hell is G. G. Clutterbuck?'

'A chartered accountant for whom I was appearing in the action of Clutterbuck versus Frisby. And Frisby is the retired meat salesman whose car collided with Clutterbuck's in the Fulham Road, shaking Clutterbuck up and possibly causing internal injuries. The defence, of course, pleaded that Clutterbuck had run into Frisby, and everything turned on the evidence of a Miss Linda Gilpin, who happened to be passing at the time and was an eye witness of the collision. It was my duty to examine her and make it plain to the jury that she was cockeyed and her testimony as full of holes as a Swiss cheese.'

It is probable that Gally would have made at this point some ejaculation expressive of interest and concern, but he chanced at the moment to be drinking beer. It was not till he had finished choking and had been slapped on the back by a passing waiter that he was in a condition to offer any comment, and even then he was unable to, for John had resumed his narrative.

'You can imagine my feelings. The court reeled about me. I thought for a moment I wouldn't be able to carry on.'

The drama of the situation was not lost on Gally. His eyeglass flew from its base.

'But you did carry on?'

'I did, and in about a minute and a half I had her tied in knots. She hadn't a leg to stand on.'

'You led her on to damaging admissions?'

'Yes.'

'All that 'Would it be fair to say' and 'Is it not a fact' sort of thing?'

'Yes.'

'Did you wag a finger in her face?'

'Of course I didn't.'

'I thought that was always done. But you gave her the works?'

'Yes.'

'And she resented it?'

'Yes.'

'Did you win your case?'

'Yes.'

'That must have pleased Clutterbuck.'

'Yes.'

'Did you see her afterwards?'

'No. She wrote me a note saying the engagement was off.'

Gally replaced his monocle. The look in the eye to which he fitted it and in the other eye which went through life in the nude was not an encouraging one. Nor was his 'H'm' a 'H'm'

65

calculated to engender optimism.

'You're in a spot, Johnny.'

'Yes.'

'You will have to do some heavy pleading if those wedding bells are to ring out in the little village church or wherever you were planning to have them ring out. And the problem that confronts us is How is that pleading to be done?'

'I don't follow you. She's at the castle.'

'Exactly, and you aren't.'

'But you'll invite me there.'

Gally shook his head. It pained him to be compelled to act as a black frost in his young friend's garden of dreams, but facts had to be faced.

'Impossible. Nothing would please me more, Johnny, than to slip you into the old homestead, but you don't realize what my position there is. Connie can't exclude me from the premises, I being a chartered member of the family, but she views me with concern and her conversation on the rare occasions when she speaks to me generally consists of eulogies of the various trains back to the metropolis. Any attempt on my part to ring in a friend would rouse the tigress that sleeps within her. You would be lucky if you lasted five minutes. She would have you by the scruff of the neck and the seat of the trousers and be giving you the bum's rush before you had finished brushing your feet on the mat. I know just how you are feeling, and I couldn't be sorrier not to be able to oblige you, but there it is. You'll have to go back to London and leave me to look after your affairs. And if I may say so,' said Gally modestly, 'they could scarcely be in better hands. I will do the pleading with L. Gilpin, and I confidently expect to play on her as on a stringed instrument.'

The words brought to his mind a very funny story about a member of the Pelican Club who had once tried to learn to play the banjo, but something whispered to him that this was not the moment to tell it. He gave John's shoulder another fatherly pat and set off on the long trek back to the castle.

John, his face more than ever like that of Fruity Biffen, put in an order for another beer.

5

In order to avoid the glare of the sun and the society of the Duke of Dunstable, who had suddenly become extremely adhesive, Vanessa Polk had slipped away after lunch to one of the shady nooks with which the grounds of Blandings Castle were so liberally provided, and was sitting there on a rustic bench. Lord Emsworth's father had been a man much given to strewing rustic benches hither and thither. He had also, not that it matters, collected birds' eggs and bound volumes of the proceedings of the Shropshire Archaeological Society.

As she sat there, she was thinking of Wilbur Trout. The news that he was expected on the afternoon train had given her a nostalgic thrill. He had probably forgotten it, his having been a life into which feminine entanglements had entered so largely, but they had once for a short time been engaged to be married, and though it was she who had broken the engagement, she had always retained a maternal fondness for him. Whenever she read of another of his marriages she could not help feeling that she had been wrong to desert her post and stop looking after him. Lacking her gentle supervision, he had lost all restraint, springing from blonde to blonde with an assiduity which seemed to suggest that he intended to go on marrying them till the supply gave out.

Wilbur Trout was a young man of great amiability whose initial mistake in life had been to have a father who enjoyed making money and counted that day lost which had gone by without increasing his bank balance. Had he been the son of someone humble in the lower income tax brackets, he would have gone through the years as a blameless and contented filing clerk or something on that order, his only form of dissipation an occasional visit to Palisades Park or Coney Island. Inheriting some fifty million dollars in blue chip securities unsettled him, and he had become New York's most prominent playboy, fawned on by head waiters, a fount of material to gossip columnists and a great giver of parties whose guests included both the rich and the poor. It was at one of these that Vanessa had met him, and she now sat in the shady nook thinking of old times.

In favour of this shady nook there was much to be said. It was cool. It was pleasantly scented. The streamlet that trickled through it on its way to the lake gave out a musical tinkle. And above all Alaric, Duke of Dunstable, was not there. But against these advantages had to be set the fact that it was a sort of country club for all the winged insects in Shropshire. Wearying of their society after a while, Vanessa rose and made her way back to the house, and as she approached it Lord Emsworth came down the front steps.

She greeted him cordially.

'Playing hooky, Lord Emsworth?'

'I beg your pardon?'

'Or has the Empress given you the afternoon

off? Aren't you usually on duty at this time of day?'

Lord Emsworth, who had been looking gloomy, brightened a little. He was fond of Vanessa. He found her sympathetic, and a sympathetic ear into which to pour his troubles was just what he had been wanting. He explained the reason for his despondency.

'Connie told me to meet this man Trout at the station. He is arriving on a train that gets in soon. I forget when, but Voules will know. And I ought to be with the Empress every minute. She needs me at her side.'

'Why didn't you tell Lady Constance that you had a previous engagement?'

The blankness behind Lord Emsworth's pince-nez showed that this revolutionary idea had not occurred to him. When Connie told you to do things, you did not say that you had a previous engagement. Galahad, of course, would be capable of such an act of reckless courage, but Galahad, in addition to being a man of steel and iron, veteran of a hundred battles with bookmakers, process servers and racecourse touts, wore an eyeglass and had only to twiddle it to daunt the stoutest sister. It was not a feat to be expected of a man in pince-nez. With a shiver at the mere thought of such a thing, he said:

'Oh, I couldn't do that.'

'Why not?'

'She would be furious.'

Wheels grated on gravel, and the car came round the corner, chauffeur Voules at the helm.

'Oh dear,' sighed Lord Emsworth, seeing it.

'Look,' said Vanessa. 'Why don't I go and meet Trout?'

The start Lord Emsworth gave at this suggestion was so violent that it detached his pince-nez from the parent nose. Hauling them in on their string, he gazed at her reverentially. On his visit to New York to attend the wedding of Connie and James Schoonmaker he had become a great admirer of the American girl, but he had never supposed that even an American girl could be as noble as this.

'Would you? Would you really?'

'Sure. A privilege and pleasure.'

'There would be no need to tell Connie.'

'None whatever.'

'Well, it is extremely kind of you. I don't know how to thank you.'

'Don't give it a thought.'

'You see, it's the Empress. I mean — '

'I know what you mean. Your place is at her side.'

'Exactly. I ought not to leave her for a moment. They keep assuring me that there is no reason for concern, Banks said so in so many words, but the fact remains that she refused to eat a potato which I had offered her.'

'Bad.'

'No, that is what is so sinister about it. It was a perfectly good potato, but she merely sniffed at it and — '

'Turned on her heel?'

'Precisely. She sniffed at it and walked away. Naturally I am anxious.'

'Anyone would be.'

'If only I could consult Wolff-Lehman.'

'Why can't you?'

'He's dead.'

'I see what you mean. That does rather rule him out as an adviser. Though you might get him on the ouija board.'

'So if you will really go to the station — '

'I'm on my way. Market Blandings, here I come.'

'I'm afraid it is asking a great deal of you. You will find it boring having to talk to Mr. Trout as you drive back. It is always a strain finding anything to say to a stranger.'

'That's all right. Willie Trout's not a stranger. I knew him on the other side.'

'Where?'

'In America.'

'Oh, ah, yes, of course, yes. The other side of the Atlantic, you mean.'

'We'll have all sorts of things to talk about. Not a dull moment.'

'Capital,' said Lord Emsworth. 'Capital, capital, capital.'

The train was just coming in as the car reached the station, and as Wilbur Trout stepped from it Vanessa started picking up the threads with a genial 'Hi!', and he responded with the same cordial monosyllable. There was no embarrassment on his side at this unexpected meeting with a woman he had loved and lost. If meeting women he had loved and lost could have embarrassed Wilbur Trout, he would have had to spend most of his time turning pink and twiddling his fingers. Vanessa was an old friend whom he was delighted to see. If he was a little vague as to who she was, he distinctly recalled having met her before. And when she told him, after he had called her Pauline, that her name was Vanessa, he had her placed. It helped, of course, that she was the only one on his long list to whom he had been engaged and not married.

She explained the circumstances which had led to her being at Blandings Castle, and they spoke for awhile of the old days, of parties he had given at Great Neck and Westhampton Beach, of guys and dolls who had been her fellow guests at those parties, and of the night when he had dived into the Plaza fountain in correct evening dress. But the frivolous memories did not detain him long. His mind was on deeper things.

'Say, is there anywhere around here where you can get a drink?' he asked, and she replied that beverages of all kinds were to be obtained at the Emsworth Arms not a stone's throw distant. There were other hostelries in Market Blandings . . . one does not forget the Goose and Gander, the Jolly Cricketers, the Wheatsheaf, the Waggoner's Rest, the Blue Cow and the Stitch In Time . . . but these catered for the proletariat rather than for millionaire visitors from New York. This she explained to Wilbur, and soon, having brightened Voules's afternoon by telling him to go and refresh himself at the bar, they were seated at one of the tables in the Emsworth Arms' charming garden with gin and tonics within easy reach and Vanessa was clothing in speech a thought which had been in her mind from the first moment of their meeting.

'Willie,' she said, 'you look like the Wreck of the Hesperus.'

He took no offence at an old friend's candour. He had indeed arrived at the same conclusion himself when peering into the mirror that morning. He merely heaved a sombre sigh.

'I've had a lot of trouble.'

'What's gone wrong this time?'

'It's a long story.'

'Then before you start on it tell me how in the name of everything mysterious you come to be headed for Blandings Castle.'

'That's part of the story.'

'All right, then, carry on. You have the floor.'

Wilbur drank deeply of his gin and tonic to assist the marshalling of his thoughts. After a moment's brooding he appeared to have got them in order.

'It started with my divorce.'

'Which one? Luella?'

'No, not Luella.'

'Marlene?'

'No, not Marlene. Genevieve.'

'Oh, Genevieve? Yes, I read about that.'

'It was a terrible shock when she walked out on me.'

The thought crossed Vanessa's mind that after his ample experience of that sort of thing the exodus of another wife should have seemed pure routine, but she did not say so. She was a tactful girl, and it was plain to her that for some inscrutable reason the loss of the third Mrs. Trout, who had chewed gum and talked baby-talk, had affected him deeply.

'I loved her, Pauline I mean Vanessa. I worshipped her. And she ditched me for a guy who plays the trumpet in a band. And not a name band, either.'

'Tough,' said Vanessa, but purely out of politeness. The character in the drama calling for sympathy was, she considered, the guy who played the trumpet. Unsuccessful in his profession, chained to a band that was not a name band, and now linked to Mrs. Genevieve Trout. One would have had to be hard-hearted indeed not to feel a pang of pity for a man with a record like that.

Wilbur attracted the attention of a waiter and ordered two more gin and tonics. Even if his heart is broken, the prudent man does not neglect the practical side of life.

'Where was I?' he said, passing a weary hand over his forehead.

'You had got as far as the trumpeter, and you were saying how much you loved Genevieve.'

'That's right.'

'Still?'

'Do you mean Do I love her still? I certainly do. I think of her all the time. I lie awake nights. I seem to hear her voice. She used to say the cutest things.'

'I can imagine.'

'She used to call roses woses.'

'So she did.'

'And rabbits wabbits.'

'Yes, I remember.'

'So you can understand how I felt when I saw that picture.'

'What picture would that be?'

'It was in the window of one of those art galleries on Bond Street, and it was the image of Genevieve.'

'You mean a portrait?'

'No, not a portrait, a picture of a girl by some French guy. And I said to myself I'd got to have it to remind me of her.'

'So you bought it, and they threw in an invitation to Blandings Castle? Sort of like trading stamps?'

'Don't joke about it.'

'I'm not joking. Something must have happened, to bring you here, and I'm waiting to be told what.'

'That was the Duke.'

'What Duke?'

'Dunstable he calls himself. He invited me.'

Vanessa flung her arms out in a despairing gesture. Wilbur had always been a story-teller who got his stories muddled up, but with his present conte he was excelling himself.

'I don't get it,' she said. 'I just don't get it. Maybe you'll make it clearer as you proceed, so go on from when you bought the picture. In words of one syllable, if you can manage it.'

Wilbur fortified himself with gin and tonic. From now on every word he uttered was going to be a knife in his bosom.

'I didn't buy it. That's the whole point. It was past one o'clock, and like a sap I thought I might as well have lunch first, so I went to a club where I've a guest card and was having a drink at the bar before going into the dining-room, when this duke came along and sat down next to me and started telling me what was wrong with the Government. We hit it off pretty well and I had some more drinks, and before I knew what was happening I was telling him about Genevieve and this picture in the art gallery.'

'And while you were having your lunch he popped around the corner and bought the picture, and now he's got you here to sell it to you at a large profit.'

Amazement held Wilbur speechless for a long moment. He stared blankly at the clairvoyant girl.

'How did you guess?' he gasped.

'It wasn't difficult, knowing the Duke. It must be the picture that's in the castle portrait gallery now. And I'll bet he didn't buy it from any love of art. He's in this for what he can get.'

With another of his sombre sighs Wilbur endorsed this theory.

'And he's invited me here so that I can keep on seeing the thing. He knows I won't be able to stop myself buying it, no matter what he asks. And that,' said Wilbur moodily, 'will be about double what he paid for it. I'm in a spot.'

'Then say 'Out, damned spot.''

A long train journey and several gin and tonics had left Wilbur's brain on the sluggish side. There was, he presumed, some significance in her words, but what it was eluded him. Pure baloney, he would have said if asked to criticize them.

'How do you mean?'

'You say you're in a spot. Why are you in a

77

spot? Ask me, you're sitting pretty. You're here, the picture's here, and all you've got to do is swipe it.'

Wilbur's eyes widened. He uttered a low bronchial sound like the croak of a bull frog. It is never easy for a man of slow mind to assimilate a novel idea.

'Swipe it?' he said. 'Do you mean *swipe* it?'

'Sure. Why not? He as good as swiped it from you. You can find out from the art gallery what he paid for it and reimburse him, if that's the word.'

A gleam came into Wilbur's eyes, but it was only momentary. He was able to recognize the suggestion as a good one, but he knew that he was not the man to carry it out.

'I couldn't,' he said with something of the emphasis which Lord Emsworth had employed while saying the same thing a little earlier in the afternoon, and Vanessa reacted as she had done on that occasion.

'Then I will,' she said, and Wilbur, like Lord Emsworth, stared for a moment unbelievingly. In the days of their brief engagement he had come to know Vanessa as a girl of unconventional trend of thought, but she had never given him a surprise of this magnitude.

'You really think you could do it?'

'Of course I can do it. It only wants thinking over. As a matter of fact, I've got a glimmering of an idea already. I'm only hesitating because it means bringing Chesney into it.'

'Who's Chesney?'

'Man who's staying at the castle. I'm pretty

sure he's a crook, but I'll have to be certain before I start anything. You don't want to take chances with a thing of this kind.'

'You bet not.'

'I'll be able to tell when I've studied him a bit longer. I hope he'll turn out to be what I think he is, for if there's one thing that sticks out of this situation like a sore thumb, it is that His Grace the Duke must not be allowed to pull quick ones on the young and innocent and get away with it. And now,' said Vanessa, 'let's dig that chauffeur out of the bar and be getting along to the castle.'

6

Night had fallen when John got back to London. He found Paddington still its refined and unruffled self, and his forlorn aspect struck as discordant a note there as it had done at the Emsworth Arms. Paddington porters like to see smiling faces about them. They may feel pity for young men with drawn brows and haggard eyes, but they prefer not to have to associate with them, and this applies equally to guards, engine drivers and the staff of the refreshment room. The whole personnel of the station felt a sense of relief when he had removed himself in a taxi and was on his way to Halsey Court in the W.1. postal division, his London address.

His interview with Gally had deepened the despondency with which he had set out on his journey to Shropshire. He had been so certain that he would have received an invitation to Blandings Castle, that essential preliminary to a reconciliation with the girl whose gentle heart he had bruised with all those 'Would it be fair to say's' and 'I suggest's' when battling under the banner of G. G. Clutterbuck. Once at the castle he would have been in a position to start pleading, and by pleading he meant really pleading — omitting no word or act that would lead to a peaceful settlement. Let him once get Linda to the negotiating table, he had told himself, let her once hear the tremolo in his voice and see the melting look in his eyes, and all would have been well.

Gally's refusal to co-operate had come as a stunning blow, dislocating his whole plan of campaign. Nor had Gally's parting words done anything to raise his spirits. He had spoken of playing on Linda as on a stringed instrument with the confidence of a man who had been playing on girls as on stringed instruments since early boyhood, but there was little solace to be drawn from that. A third party can never accomplish anything solid on these occasions. Delicate negotiations between two sundered hearts cannot be conducted through an agent; one needs the personal touch.

Halsey Court, when he reached it, set the seal on his depression. It was a gloomy cul-de-sac full of prowling cats and fluttering newspapers, almost its only merit being that living there was cheap. Halsey Chambers, where he had had a flat for the last two years, was a ramshackle building occupied for the most part by young men trying to get along — journalists like Jerry Shoesmith, at one time editor of that seedy weekly paper *Society Spice*, and writers of novels of suspense like Jeff Miller, the Rugger international. John had inherited the latter's apartment when Jeff had married and gone to live in New York, and with it Ma Balsam, the stout motherly soul who had looked after him. She emerged from the kitchen as he opened the front door, and he greeted her with a 'Hullo, Ma' which he hoped did not sound too much like a death rattle.

81

'Good evening, sir,' she said. 'So you're back. Did you have a nice time in the country?'

John tightened his lips and held his breath and was thus enabled to prevent the escape of the hollow laugh which had tried to get out in response to this query. He had no wish to reveal to this good woman that she was conversing with a tortured soul, for let her find that this was the case and he would be overwhelmed by a tidal wave of sympathy with which at the moment he was incapable of coping. Ma Balsam when in sympathetic vein could be stupefying.

'Very nice,' he said, having counted ten.

'Where was it you went?'

'Shropshire.'

'That's a long way.'

'Yes.'

'A good thing the weather kept up.'

'Yes.'

'So nasty if it comes on to rain when you're having a pleasure trip in the country.'

'Yes.'

'Well,' said Ma Balsam, seeming to feel that what might be called the pourparlers could now be considered completed, 'it's a pity you weren't here, because that friend of yours, that Mr. Ferguson, was trying to get you on the telephone all day.'

'I don't know any Ferguson.'

'Might have been Bostock. He's been to dinner here often. Artistic-looking. High voice. Tortoiseshell-rimmed specs.'

'You don't mean Joe Bender?'

'That's the name. He's an artist or something.'

'He runs a picture gallery in Bond Street.'

'Well, he can't have been running it much today, because he was on the buzzer all the time, asking for you. Very impatient he was. Kept saying 'For G's sake isn't he back yet?', and I had to speak to him for using the expression 'Oh, aitch!' when I told him you wasn't. Last time he phoned, which wasn't more than twenty minutes ago, he told me to get him the minute you showed up. Like me to do it now?'

John weighed the question. His impulse was to answer it in the negative. He was fond of Joe Bender and in normal circumstances always enjoyed his company, but a man reeling from a blow of the kind he had so recently received shrinks from the society of even the closest of friends. Harrowing though his thoughts were, tonight he wanted to be alone with them.

Then his natural goodness of heart prevailed. Joe, he reflected, would not have been telephoning so urgently unless he were in some sort of trouble, and this being so he would have to do the decent thing and let him come and cry on his shoulder.

'Yes, do, Ma,' he said. 'I'm going to have a shower. If he comes before I'm dressed, tell him to wait.'

When John reappeared, a good deal restored by his bath, Joe Bender had arrived and was in conversation with Ma Balsam, though conversation is not perhaps the right word for what had been a monologue on her part, a series of grunts on his. Like a good hostess, she drew John into their little circle.

'I've been telling Mister Who-is-it he doesn't look well,' she said. 'Noticed it the minute he came in.'

Her eye had not deceived her. Joe Bender was looking terrible. A man, to use an old-fashioned phrase, of some twenty-eight summers, he gave the impression at the moment of having experienced at least that number of very hard winters. He was even more haggard than John, so much so that the latter, forgetting his own troubles, uttered a cry of concern.

'Good heavens, Joe! What's the matter?'

'Just what I was wondering,' said Ma Balsam. 'If you ask me, he's coming down with something. He's got the same pasty look Balsam had before he was stricken with whatever it was and passed beyond the veil. Lost the use of his legs to begin with,' she said as Joe Bender collapsed into a chair, 'and it wasn't long after that that he came out in spots. We ought to send for a doctor, Mister Who-is-it.'

'I don't want a doctor.'

'Then I'll go and heat you up a nice glass of hot milk,' said Ma Balsam. She belonged to the school of thought which holds that a nice glass of hot milk, while not baffling the death angel altogether, can at least postpone the inevitable.

As the kitchen door closed behind her, Joe Bender heaved a sigh of relief.

'I thought that woman would never go. Tell her I don't want any damned milk.'

'Have a whisky and soda.'

'Yes, I'll do that. In fact, I shall need several.'

John went to the kitchen and came back

84

successful, though not without argument, in having countermanded the Ma Balsam specific. 'He's liable to expire all over the floor,' she warned, 'but have it your own way.'

'Now then,' he said. 'What's all this about?'

It is possible that had this meeting taken place earlier, Joe Bender would have been in a frame of mind to break gently the news he had come to impart, for he was a man of sensibility who if compelled to give people shocks liked to do his best to soften them. But a whole long day of ever-growing agitation had sapped his morale. For an eternity, it seemed to him, he had kept pent in what Shakespeare would have called his stuffed bosom a secret calculated to stagger humanity or at least that portion of humanity with the interests of the Bender gallery at heart, and it came out with the abruptness of a cork leaving a champagne bottle.

'That picture, John! It's a fake!'

It is also possible that if John had been less preoccupied with his own tragedy, he would have grasped the import of these words more readily. As it was, he merely stared.

'Picture? What picture?'

Joe Bender, too, stared. The eyes behind their tortoiseshell-rimmed spectacles widened to their fullest capacity.

'What picture?' he echoed. He found it incredible that John of all people should find it necessary to ask such a question. There was only one picture in the world. 'The Robichaux. The one we sold to the Duke. Don't you understand, dammit? It's a fake. It's a forgery.'

He had no need to explain the situation further. John had grasped it now, and it was as if Ma Balsam, not that she was capable of such a thing, had crept up behind him and poured a brimming beaker of ice water down his back. He would not have thought such a thing possible, but he actually stopped thinking of Linda Gilpin. It was an appreciable time before he found speech, and when he did it was only to ask a fatuous question.

'Are you sure?'

'Of course I'm sure. The real one had been vetted by Mortimer Bayliss, who's about the best art critic in the world. He said it was genuine, and when he says a picture's genuine, that settles it.'

John was still far from understanding. He was clear as to there being in circulation not one reclining nude from the brush of the late Claude Robichaux, but two reclining nudes. Beyond that he found himself in a fog, and he fell insensibly into his professional manner when cross-examining a witness.

'Explain it from the beginning,' he said, only just refraining from a 'Then will you kindly tell the jury'. 'Where did the one you sold the Duke come from?'

'I bought it in Paris, from a couple of Rumanians who have a small place near the Madeleine. I might have known,' said Joe Bender bitterly. 'I ought to have asked myself 'Bender, if you were a forgery, where would you go?', and the answer would have been 'To a Rumanian art gallery'.'

'And this other one, the genuine one?'

'My father had it before I took over the business. That's what hurts so. It had been there all the time. I suppose Father had been holding on to it, waiting for a rise in the market.'

'Then why — ?'

'Because it had been sent to be cleaned. That's why I knew nothing about it. It came back this morning. What on earth are we going to do, John?'

'Explain to the Duke and give him the genuine one, I suppose.'

'And have him spread the story everywhere that you can't rely on anything you buy at the Bender Gallery because every second thing they sell you is bound to be a forgery. We should be ruined in a month, if not sooner. There's nothing so vulnerable as a picture gallery. It lives on its reputation. That's the last thing we must do. Fatal, absolutely fatal.'

'But we can't take his money under false pretences.'

'Of course not.'

'Then what?'

'We'll have to buy it back from him, probably for about double what he paid us.'

'That's not a pleasant thought.'

'I don't like it myself.'

'And how do we explain our sudden switch from seller to buyer?'

'I don't know.'

'He's bound to suspect a trap and put the price up even higher than you said. I've been hearing a lot about the Duke of Dunstable from my godfather, who has known him for years, and one of the things I heard was that he always likes to get all the money that's coming to him. We shan't have a penny left after he's done with us. What we ought to do is smuggle the forgery away and put the real picture in its place.'

'Yes?'

'Then everybody would be happy.'

'So they would. Smuggle the forgery away and put the real picture in its place. Mind if I ask you something?'

'Go ahead.'

'How?'

John agreed that this was a good question, and there was a silence of some duration. Joe Bender helped himself to another whisky.

'Yes,' he said, 'that's what we must do, smuggle the forgery away and put the real picture in its place. And we don't even know where it is.'

'The Duke's got it.'

'And where's the Duke?'

'At Blandings Castle.'

'I hope he's having a wonderful time.'

'He's bound to have the picture with him.'

'And nothing simpler than to grab it. All we need is an invitation to Blandings Castle.'

'My God!' cried John, so loudly that his voice penetrated to Ma Balsam in the kitchen, causing her to shake her head sadly. She felt that association with that Mister Who-is-it was corrupting her employer.

Joe Bender was endeavouring to dry his trousers, on to which the major portion of his

88

whisky had fallen. That clarion cry had startled him.

'Gally!' John shouted, and Ma Balsam shook her head again. The expletive was new to her, but it sounded worse than G or Aitch. 'Gally's at Blandings, too.'

'He is?' said Joe Bender. He had heard tales of Gally from John, and the first time a faint light of hope flickered behind his tortoiseshell-rimmed spectacles. 'You mean — ?'

'We can place the whole conduct of the thing in his hands with the utmost confidence. It's the sort of job that's right up his street. I'll go to Market Blandings first thing tomorrow and give him full particulars.'

II

It was not, however, till the following afternoon that John was at liberty to leave for Market Blandings. He had forgotten that he had been briefed to appear in court in the morning on behalf of Onapoulos and Onapoulos in their suit against the Lincolnshire and Eastern Counties Glass Bottling Company, and the sunlight was blotted still further from his life, when he did so appear, by the fact that he lost his case, was rebuked by the judge and harshly spoken to by both Onapouloses, who held the view that it was only the incompetence of their advocate that had prevented them winning by a wide margin. When he caught the 2.33 train at Paddington, everybody there winced at the sight of his haggard face. They thought he looked even worse than when they had seen him last.

The parting with Ma Balsam had done nothing to induce equanimity. When a motherly woman of strong inquisitive trend sees a young man, to whom she has attached herself as a guide, philosopher and friend, making preparations for a journey the day after he has returned from one, she is naturally curious. And when the Ma Balsams of this world are curious, they do not hesitate to ask questions. The following dialogue took place as John packed his suitcase.

'You off somewhere?'

'Yes.'

'You went off yesterday.'

'Yes.'

'Where you going this time?'

'Shropshire.'

'What, again?'

'Yes.'

'What takes you there?'

'I have to see a man.'

'In Shropshire?'

'Yes.'

'Whereabouts in Shropshire?'

'A place called Market Blandings.'

'Never heard of it.'

'Well, it's there.'

'Was that where you went yesterday?'

'Yes.'

'It'd have saved a lot of trouble if you'd stayed the night there. I suppose that didn't occur to you.'

'I had to be in court this morning.'

90

'Balsam used to go to court a lot when he was with us. There was a copper with a cast in one eye who kept pinching him for street betting. What's that thing in brown paper?'

'A picture.'

'You taking it to this man you're seeing?'

'Yes.'

'Cheaper to send it parcel post.'

'Yes.'

'Then why don't you?'

'Oh, aitch!' said John, and Ma Balsam realized that the bad influence of Mister Who-is-it had made even more progress than she had supposed.

The meeting with Gally got off to a bad start. When the last of the Pelicans arrived at the tryst on the following morning, he was in no welcoming mood. John's telephone call had come when he was out taking a stroll in the grounds, and its purport had been relayed to him by Beach. All he knew, accordingly, was that his godson, contrary to the most definite instructions, had returned to the Emsworth Arms, and he was naturally annoyed. No leader of men likes to hear that his orders have been ignored by a subordinate. His greeting of John was brusque.

'I thought I told you to go back to London and leave everything to me,' he said.

His manner was stern, but John remained unmoved.

'This isn't that.'

'What do you mean, this isn't that?'

'It has nothing to do with Linda.'

'Nothing to do with her?'

'No.'

'Then what's it all about? If,' said Gally, 'you've dragged me all the way to Market Blandings on a sweltering summer morning for some trifle . . . What are you giggling about?'

John corrected his choice of verbs.

'I was not giggling. I was laughing hollowly. Your use of the word 'trifle' amused me. It's anything but a trifle that brings me here. I'm sorry you've had a warm walk — '

'Warm? I feel like Shadrach, Meshach and Abednego in the burning fiery furnace.'

' — but I had to see you. The most ghastly thing has happened, and we need your help.'

'We?'

'Joe Bender and I.'

'Who's Joe Bender?'

'I told you that night I came to your place. Don't you remember? He runs the Bender gallery.'

'Ah yes. You put some money into it, you said.'

'I put practically all the money I had into it. And now I'm going to lose it, unless you come to the rescue.'

Gally stared, amazed that anyone should think him possessed of cash. Not that he did not appreciate the compliment.

'My good Johnny, what on earth can I do? Heaven knows I'd like to help you out of a tight place, but all I've got is a younger son's pittance, and I'm not allowed to dip into the capital. I could manage twenty quid, if that's any use. And even that would mean getting an overdraft at my bank.'

John expressed gratitude for the offer, but said that Gally was under a misapprehension.

'I don't want money.'

'Then why did you say so?'

'I didn't say so.'

'It sounded like it to me.'

'I'm sorry. No, what I want you to do is switch a couple of pictures.'

'To . . . what?'

'Yes, I know it sounds odd, but it's really quite simple.'

'Then perhaps you would explain.'

'I will.'

Gally, as has been mentioned, was always a better raconteur than a listener, but he gave on this occasion no cause for complaint in the latter role. Nobody could have been more silently attentive. He sat drinking in every word of John's story, never interrupting and not even saying at its conclusion that it reminded him of something that had happened to a friend of his in the Pelican Club. All he said was that he would be charmed to perform the absurdly simple task required of him. To take the forgery to John and return to the castle with the genuine painting and deposit it in the portrait gallery would, he assured him, be the ideal way of filling in the time. Time, he said, always hung a little heavy on one's hands in the country, and one was grateful for something to occupy one.

'You've brought the genuine goods with you?' he said, all executive bustle and efficiency. 'Capital, capital, as Clarence would say. Where is it?'

'Up in my room.'

'I can't take it now, of course.'

'Why not?'

'My dear boy, use your intelligence. What would I say if I met Connie and she asked me what I thought I was doing, sneaking about with a whacking great picture under my arm? I should be at a loss. I wouldn't know which way to look. No, stealth is essential.'

'Yes, you're right.'

'It's a thing that must be done at dead of night, the deader the better. We must arrange a rendezvous. Where can we meet? Not in the ruined chapel, because there isn't a ruined chapel, and other spots I could name wouldn't convey a thing to you, you being a stranger in these parts. I think I'll walk round in a circle for a bit and muse, if you have no objection.'

Permission granted, he walked in a circle for a bit and must have mused to good purpose, for on completing his eleventh lap he announced that he had it.

'The sty!'

'The what?'

'The bijou residence of my brother Clarence's prize pig, Empress of Blandings. The ideal locale, for however dark the night the old girl's distinctive aroma will lead you to it unerringly. It's near the kitchen garden. Go there and sniff, then follow your nose. There was a song popular before you were born, the refrain of which began with the words 'It ain't all lavender'. It might have been written expressly with the Empress in mind. Her best friends won't tell her, but she

94

suffers from B.O. How is your sense of smell? Keen? Then you can't miss. And we must make it tonight, for time is of the essence. Dunstable bought that picture with the intention of selling it to an American chap called Trout. Trout got here yesterday. As soon as they've concluded their deal he will presumably leave and bang will go our chance of making the switch. So meet me at the Empress's sty at midnight, and I will carry on from there.'

A belated spasm of remorse stirred John. For the first time it occurred to him that however lightly Gally might speak of his assignment as absurdly simple, he was asking a good deal of the most accommodating godfather.

'I hate landing you with a job like this, Gally.'

'My dear boy, I shall enjoy it.'

'Midnight's not too late for you?'

'The shank of the evening.'

'Suppose you're caught?'

'I won't be caught. I'm never caught. They call me The Shadow.'

'Well, I can't tell you how grateful I am. You've taken a load off my mind.'

'Though there must still be plenty on it.'

'There is.' John choked for a moment as if afflicted by a sudden catarrh. 'Have you . . . Have you . . . Have you by any chance had a word with her?'

'Not yet. I'm biding my time. These things can't be hurried. In dealing with a disgruntled popsy the wise man waits till she has simmered down a bit.'

'How — er — how is she?'

95

'Physically in the pink. Spiritually not so bobbish. She will need careful treatment. You must be patient, telling yourself that her current inclination to dip you in boiling oil will eventually pass. Time the great healer, and all that sort of thing. And as regards tonight you have memorized the drill? Good. Then I will be leaving you. We shall meet at twelve pip emma. Lurk concealed till you hear the hoot of the white owl, and then come running. I think I can manage a white owl all right, but if not I'll do you a brown one.'

7

The clock over the stables was chiming the quarter, with only another quarter to go before twelve p.m., when Gally came out of the portrait gallery carrying the fictitious reclining nude. He was wearing rubber-soled shoes and stepped softly as befitted a man engaged on a perilous mission. Cautiously, for the oak stairs were slippery, he made his way to the hall and the front door that lay beyond it, and shooting back the bolts which Beach had made fast before taking the tray of beverages into the drawing-room at nine-thirty passed through it into the night. He was conscious, as he went, of a momentary pang for the years which the locust had eaten. Just so, he remembered, when his heart was young and every member of the female sex looked like a million dollars to him, had he crept out in the darkness to exchange ideas with a girl named Maud, now a grandmother.

Arriving at his destination, he had no need to imitate the hoot of the white owl, for before he could display his virtuosity in that direction John stepped from the shadows.

'I thought you were never coming,' said John peevishly. He was unused to this sort of thing, and his nerves were on edge. He had reached the sty at eleven-fifteen, and it seemed to him that he had been there, inhaling the Empress's bouquet, since childhood.

With his usual suavity Gally pointed out that he was not late but, if reliance could be placed on the clock over the stables, some ten minutes ahead of time, and John apologized. He said it was the darkness that got him down, and Gally agreed that darkness had its trying side.

'But you can't do these things by daylight. I remember saying that to Bill Bowman, a friend of mine in the old Pelican days. He was in love with a popsy and her parents were holding her incommunicado in the family residence somewhere in Kent. Bill wanted to get a letter to her, telling her to sneak out and run away with him, and his idea was to hide in the grounds till a gardener came along and tip him to give it to her. I told him he was making a great mistake.'

'Do you think we ought to stand here talking?' said John, but Gally proceeded with his tale. It was never easy, indeed it was almost impossible, to stop him when in spate.

' 'Do it by night,' I urged him. 'You know which her room is. Climb up the water pipe to her window, having previously thrown gravel at it — the window, of course, not the water pipe, and get her views face to face. Only so can you hope to bring home the bacon. 'Well, he made some fanciful objection, said climbing water pipes wouldn't do his trousers any good or something frivolous like that, and persisted in his plan. Next morning he went and hid. A gardener came along. He tipped him and gave him the letter. And the gardener, who turned out of course to be the girl's father, immediately got after him with the pitchfork he was carrying. Moreover, he stuck to the tip like glue. Bill has often told me that what really rankled with him was the thought that he had paid a pound just to be chased through a thickset hedge with a gardening fork. He was always a chap who liked to get value for money. So now you see what I meant when I said it's better to do these things at night. By the way, talking of letters, has it ever occurred to you to write one to your popsy?'

John's manner took on a touch of stiffness.

'Must you call her my popsy?'

His tone hurt Gally. He was not conscious of having used a derogatory term.

'Must call her something.'

'You might try Miss Gilpin.'

'Sounds a bit formal. Anyway, you know who I mean. Why not drop her a line?'

John shook his head. A wasted gesture, of course, for a man cloaked in darkness towards another man also cloaked in darkness.

'It wouldn't do any good. I must see her.'

'Yes, on second thoughts you're right. In my younger days I always found that when I wanted to melt the heart of a bookie and persuade him to wait another week for his money, it was essential to confer with him in person, so as to be able to massage his upper arm and pick bits of fluff off him, and no doubt the same principle applies when one is trying to get a girl thinking along the right lines. At any moment you may want to reach out and grab her and shower kisses on her upturned face, and this cannot be done by mail.'

John quivered. Those vivid words had

conjured up a picture which moved him deeply.

'I suppose it really is impossible to get me into the castle?'

The wistful note in his voice, so like that which used to come into his own in the old days when he was having business talks with turf accountants, stirred Gally's sympathetic heart. He would have given much to be able to offer some word of cheer, but he could not encourage false hopes.

'As a friend of mine absolutely impossible. It wouldn't be worth your while to bother to pass the front door. 'Throw this man out', Connie would say to the knaves and scullions on the pay roll, and 'I want to see him bounce twice', she would add. The only way you could remain on the premises for more than ten minutes would be if you put on false whiskers and said you had come to inspect the drains. Which reminds me. A fellow at the Pelican did that once, and — '

But the case history of the fellow at the Pelican who, no doubt from the best motives, had bearded himself like the pard and shown an interest in drainage systems was not to be gone into with the thoroughness customary with Gally when in reminiscent mood. It has been stressed more than once in the course of this chronicle that he was a difficult man to stop, but one of the things that could stop him was the sight at a moment like this of a torch wobbling through the darkness in his direction. He broke off on the word 'and' as if some anecdote-disliking auditor had gripped him by the throat.

John, too, had seen the torch, and a single look

at it was enough to galvanize him into immediate activity. He was gone with the wind, and Gally lost no time in following his astute example. Hilarious though he knew the story of the whiskered fellow at the Pelican to be, he felt no inclination to linger and tell it to the torch-bearer. Better, he decided, to withdraw while the withdrawing was good. He and John had long since exchanged reclining nudes, so there was really nothing to keep him.

Returning by a circuitous route to the house, he was careful to shoot the bolts of the front door, for he had no wish to wound Beach's feelings by leading him to suppose, when he went his rounds in the morning, that he had omitted so important a part of his duties; and, this done, he climbed the stairs to his room.

It was in the same corridor as the portrait gallery, but he did not go there immediately. Hanging the picture was a thing that could be done any time in the next six hours, and the humid night had made him hot and sticky. His first move, obviously, was to take a bath. He gathered up his great sponge and trotted off along the corridor.

II

It was Lord Emsworth who had so abruptly applied the closure to the story of the fellow at the Pelican. As a rule, he was in bed and asleep at this hour, but tonight perturbation of soul had drawn him from between the sheets as if something spiked had come through the mattress. He was consumed with worry about the Empress.

Although, as he had told Vanessa, since the sinister affair of the rejected potato Mr. Banks, the veterinary surgeon, had several times assured him that the noble animal was in midseason form and concern on his part quite unnecessary, he was still as uneasy as ever. Admitted that Mr. Banks was a recognized expert whose skill in his profession had won golden opinions from all sorts of men, he might for once have been mistaken. Alternatively, he might have discerned symptoms of some wasting sickness, and not wanting to cause him anxiety had Kept It From Him.

These speculations made him wakeful, and when at length he did doze off, conditions were in no way improved. Sleep, so widely publicized as knitting up the ravelled sleeve of care, merely brought a nightmare of the most disturbing kind. He dreamed that he had gone to the sty, eagerly anticipating the usual feast for the eyes, and there before him had stood a lean, streamlined Empress, her ribs clearly defined and her whole aspect that of a pig which had been in hard training for weeks, the sort of pig that climbs Matterhorns and wins the annual Stock Exchange walk from London to Brighton.

The shock woke him, but he did not follow his normal practice of blinking once or twice and falling asleep again. He rose, put on dressing gown and slippers and took a torch from the drawer where it nestled among his socks and handkerchiefs. He had to go and reassure himself that the horror he had beheld had been but a dream.

In a less preoccupied mood he might on arriving at the front door have been surprised to find it unbolted, but in his anxious state the phenomenon made no impression on him, and he went on his way unheeding.

It was more as a sort of concession to the lateness of the hour than because he needed its light to guide him that he switched on the torch. When he did so, he instantly became the centre of attraction to a rowdy mob of those gnats, moths and beetles which collect in gangs and stay up late in the rural districts. They appeared to have been waiting for a congenial comrade to come along and give a fillip to their nocturnal revels, and nothing could have been more hearty than the welcome they gave him. He was swallowing his sixth gnat as he reached the sty and paused, filling his lungs with its familiar scent.

The night was very still. From somewhere in the distance came faintly the sound of a belated car as it rounded a corner on the Shrewsbury road, while nearer at hand he could hear a sotto voce something which might have been the hoot of the white or possibly the brown owl. But from the sty not so much as a grunt, and for a moment this deepened his uneasiness. Then reason told him that at such an hour grunts were hardly to be expected. To Galahad, whose formative years had been passed at the Pelican Club, this might be early evening, but it was far too late for a well-adjusted pig like the Empress to be up and about and grunting. She would of course be getting her eight hours in her covered shed.

An imperious urge swept over him to take one look at her, and he made no attempt to resist it. To mount the rail was with him, as the phrase goes, the work of an instant; to slip, overbalance, catch his foot on the rail and fall face downward in the mud the work of another instant. Feeling damp but not discouraged, he rose and came without further misadventure to journey's end, where a fascinating sight rewarded his perseverance. Stretched on her bed of straw and breathing gently through the nose, the Empress was enjoying her usual health-giving slumber, and a glance was enough to tell him how wide of the mark his dream had been. For three years in succession she had been awarded the silver medal in the Fat Pigs class at the annual Shropshire Agricultural Show, and it was plain that had she been entered for the contest again at this moment, the cry 'The winner and still champion' would have been on every judge's lips. Julius Caesar, who liked to have men — and presumably pigs — about him that were fat, would have welcomed her without hesitation to his personal entourage.

It was with a mind darkened by nameless fears that the ninth Earl had embarked on this expedition, but it was in buoyant mood that he returned. That glimpse of the Empress, brief though it had been, had had the most invigorating effect on his morale. All, he felt, was for the best in this best of all possible worlds, and it was only when he reached the house that he was compelled to modify this view in one respect. All would have been for the best in this best of all possible worlds if somebody in his absence had not bolted the front door.

III

It can never be an agreeable experience for a householder to find himself locked out late at night from the house he is holding, and he cannot be censured for allowing it to disconcert him. Of course, if he is a man of determined character, there is a simple and easy way of coping with the situation, always provided that his lungs are in good order. Many years previously Lord Emsworth's father, faced by a similar dilemma on his return in the small hours from the annual dinner of the Loyal Sons of Shropshire, had solved it by shouting at the top of a voice which even in his calmer moments always resembled that of a toastmaster at a public banquet. He also banged on the door with a stout stick, and in almost no time every occupant of the castle, with the exception of those who were having hysterics, had flocked to the spot and admitted him, and with a final brief curse he had thrown the stick at the butler and proceeded bedwards.

His son and heir, now peering dazedly at the door through his pince-nez, had not this resource to fall back on. His father, like so many

Victorian fathers, had had the comfortable knowledge to support him that he was master in his home and that no reproaches were to be expected next morning from a wife who jumped six inches vertically if he spoke to her suddenly. His successor to the earldom was not so fortunately situated.

The thought of what Connie would have to say if roused from her slumbers by shouts in the night paralysed Lord Emsworth. He stood there congealed. The impression prevailing among the gnats, moths and beetles which had accompanied him on the home stretch was that he had been turned into a pillar of salt, and it came as a great surprise to them when at the end of perhaps five minutes he moved and stirred and seemed to feel the rush of life along his keel. It had suddenly occurred to him that on a warm night like this the Duke was sure to have left the french window of the garden suite open. And while Lord Emsworth would have been the last person to claim to be an acrobat and the first person to confess his inability to do anything so agile as climbing water pipes to second storey bedrooms, he did consider himself capable of walking through an open french window. With the feeling that the happy ending was only moments away he rounded the house, and there, just as he had anticipated, was the garden suite with its window as hospitably open as any window could be.

It drew him like a magnet.

It had also, though of this he was not aware, exercised a similar attraction for one of the cats which lived in the stables by day and wandered hither and thither at night. Inquisitive, as is the way with cats, it had been intrigued by the open window and wanted to ascertain what lay beyond it. At the moment when Lord Emsworth tip-toed across the threshold it was investigating one of the Duke's shoes which had been left on the floor and not finding much in it to arrest the attention of a pleasure-seeker.

Lord Emsworth's legs, arriving suddenly beside it, seemed to offer more in the way of entertainment, lending, as it were, the human touch. They had a peculiar scent, but, thought the cat, rather attractive, and being of an affectionate nature it always liked to have a man to rub itself against. Abandoning the shoe, it applied its head to Lord Emsworth's dressing gown with a quick thrusting movement, and Lord Emsworth, filled with much the same emotions as had gripped him in his boyhood when a playful schoolmate, creeping up behind him in the street, had tooted a motor horn in his immediate rear, executed one of those sideways leaps which Nijinsky used to be so good at in his prime. It was followed by the sort of crash an active bull might have produced if let loose in a china shop.

It will be remembered that Lady Constance, having learned from the Duke that he proposed to occupy the garden suite, had hastened thither to make sure that everything in it would be just as he liked it. Among the things she had thought he would like was a piecrust table containing on its surface a clock, a bowl of roses, another bowl

107

holding pot-pourri, a calender, an ashtray and a photograph of James Schoonmaker and herself in their wedding finery. It was with this that Lord Esmworth had collided as he made his entrechat, causing the welkin to ring as described.

It had scarcely ceased to ring, when lights flashed on, revealing the Duke in lemon-coloured pyjamas with a purple stripe.

The Duke of Dunstable, though pop-eyed and far too heavily moustached for most tastes, was no poltroon. Many men, made aware that their privacy had been invaded by nocturnal marauders, would have pulled the sheets over their heads and lain hoping that if they kept quiet the fellows would go away; but he was made of sterner stuff. He prided himself on being a man who stood no nonsense from anyone, and he was certainly not proposing to stand it from a lot of blasted burglars who got up informal games of football outside his bedroom door. Arming himself for want of a better weapon with a bottle which had contained mineral water, he burst upon the scene with the animation of an Assyrian coming down like a wolf on the fold, and there was Lord Emsworth.

His militant spirit was offended by the anti-climax. He had come all keyed up to bean a bevy of burglars with his bottle, and there were no burglars to bean; only his host with a weak smile on his face. He was particularly irked by Lord Emsworth's weak smile. Taken in conjunction with the fact that the latter had wandered into his room at one in the morning, apparently with the object of dancing pas seuls in the dark, it confirmed the impression he had already formed that the man was potty.

Lord Emsworth, though he would have been glad to let the whole thing drop, could not but feel that a word of explanation was called for and that it was for him to open the conversation. It was, he thought, for though vague he had his code, only civil. Smiling another weak smile, he said:

'Er — good evening, Alaric.'

The greeting was unfortunately phrased. Even a colloquial 'Hi' or 'Hullo there' would have had a better chance of mollifying the Duke. It was in no kindly spirit that he replied.

'Good evening? What do you mean good evening? It's the middle of the blasted night. What the devil are you doing here?'

Something had told Lord Emsworth that this interview might prove to be a difficult one, and it was plain to him that that something had known what it was talking about.

'I was just passing through to my room. I'm afraid I disturbed you, Alaric.'

'Of course you disturbed me.'

'I'm sorry. I upset a table. It was quite inadvertent. I was startled by the cat.'

'What cat? I see no cat.'

Lord Emsworth peered about him with the vague stare which had so often exasperated his sisters Constance, Dora, Charlotte, Julia and Hermione. It took him rather longer than the Duke could have wished to discern the catlessness of the room.

'It must have gone.'

'If it was ever there.'

'Oh, it was there.'

'So you say.'

During these exchanges the Duke, with some idea of picking up the table, the clock, the bowl, the other bowl, the ashtray, the calendar and the wedding photograph of Lady Constance and her mate, had approached nearer to his visitor, and as he did so the feeling he had had for some time that it was a little close in here became accentuated. He halted, sniffed, and made an interesting discovery.

'Emsworth,' he said, 'you smell to heaven.'

Lord Emsworth, too, had been conscious of an aroma. Just a suspicion of the scent of new-mown hay, he would have said.

'You've been rolling in something.'

Enlightenment came to Lord Emsworth.

'Ah yes. Yes, yes, yes. Yes, quite. I fell in the sty, Alaric.'

'You did what?'

'I had gone to see the Empress, and I tripped and fell in the sty. It was a little muddy.'

From the very start of this conversation the Duke had been blowing at his moustache at frequent intervals, but never with the vigour which this statement provoked. He sent it shooting up now as if his aim was to loosen it from its foundations. It has not been stated in this chronicle that he had large outstanding ears, rather like the handles of a Greek amphora. We mention them at this juncture because he was feeling that he could not believe them. It was in an almost awed voice that he said:

110

'You went to see that foul pig of yours at this time of night?'

It naturally pained Lord Emsworth to hear the three times silver medallist at the Shropshire Agricultural Show so described, but he was in no position to protest.

'That was how I came to be in your room, Alaric. I was locked out, and your window was open.'

The Duke was still wrestling with the facts placed before him and trying to make some sense of them.

'*Why* did you go and see your foul pig at this time of night?'

Lord Emsworth was able to answer that.

'I had a dream about her. I dreamed she had been slimming.'

An odd guttural sound escaped the Duke. His eyes bulged, and his moustache shot nosewards. He passed a hand over his forehead.

'And that made you . . . at this time of night . . . ' He paused, as if recognizing that it was hopeless to do justice to the occasion with mere words. 'You'd better go to bed,' he said at length.

'Yes, indeed,' said Lord Emsworth. He did not often find himself agreeing with Alaric, but he did this time. 'Good night, Alaric. I hope you are comfortable in here.'

'I am when people don't come barging in and upsetting all the furniture at one in the morning.'

'Quite,' said Lord Emsworth. 'Quite, quite, quite. Yes, of course, exactly.'

He went out and up the stairs, accompanied

111

by a rich smell of pig, but he did not immediately go to his room. Half-way there a thought occurred to him. He would, he realized, have little chance of sleeping unless he soothed his ruffled spirit by reading awhile in some good book with a strong pig interest, and he had left an extremely well-written work on his favourite subject in the portrait gallery that morning, when he had gone to look at the picture of the young woman who reminded him so much of the Empress. It would be pleasant to take another look at her now.

He went there, and switched on the light.

IV

It was about time, Gally reflected as he returned all fresh and rosy from the bathroom, to be putting that picture where it belonged. Then it would be off his mind and he could divert his thoughts in other directions.

As he made his way along the dark corridor he was feeling the agreeable glow which is a good man's reward for doing acts of kindness to his fellows. Admittedly much had still to be done before Johnny's affairs could be said to be in apple pie order, but he had removed — or was on the point of removing — one of the burdens weighing on him. No danger now of ruin overwhelming the Bender Gallery in which the poor young fish had so large a financial interest. As far as that was concerned, there was nothing more to worry about, and a few well-chosen words from one who in his time had made bookies cry would soon adjust the matter of the incandescent popsy.

It was as he meditated with perhaps a touch of smugness on his godson's luck in having a wise elder to whom he could always turn when in difficulties that a sight he had not expected to see brought him to an abrupt halt. Under the door of the portrait gallery a streak of light was shining, indicating that others beside himself were abroad in the night.

He drew back. It was plain that he would have to conduct this mission of his in a less nonchalant spirit than he had anticipated. It would be necessary to be devious and snaky, and with this object in mind he retreated some paces to a spot where darkness would hide him when his fellow prowler emerged.

As to the identity of this prowler and his motives in visiting the portrait gallery at such a time he was completely fogged. The possibility that it might be the Blandings Castle ghost he rejected. Ghosts do, of course, keep late hours, but they do not switch on electric lights. The Blandings Castle ghost, moreover, if he remembered correctly the stories he had heard in childhood, went about with its head under its arm, which would be a handicap to a spectre when looking at pictures.

He had just reached the conclusion that the mystery was insoluble, when the door flew open and Lord Emsworth shot out and started to descend the stairs at an impressive pace. Eyeing him, Gally was reminded of the night when, wishing to take his mind off the troubles on which he had for some days been brooding, he and a fellow altruist had inserted in their friend Plug Basham's bedroom after he had retired to rest a pig covered with phosphorus and had then beaten the gong. Plug, coming down the stairs three at a time, had shown much the same agitation as that now exhibited by Lord Emsworth. He wondered what had occurred to disturb his brother so deeply.

This, however, was not the time for standing speculating on first causes. There was work to be done. The portrait gallery being unoccupied, he hastened there, hung his reclining nude and returned to his base. And he was relaxing there with a cigarette and a novel of suspense, when there came a tapping at the door and the face of Lord Emsworth appeared round it. He still seemed agitated.

'Oh, Galahad,' he said, 'I am so glad you are awake. I was afraid you might be asleep.'

'As early as this? Most unusual if I had been. Take a seat, Clarence. Delighted you dropped in. What's on your mind?'

'I have had a shock, Galahad.'

'Nothing better, they say, for the adrenal glands.'

'And I came to ask your advice.'

'It is at your disposal, as always. What seems to be the trouble?'

'I was wondering if I ought to tell him tonight.'

'Tell who?'

'Alaric.'

'Tell him what?'

'That his picture has been stolen. I was in the portrait gallery just now, and it had gone.'

'Gone? You astound me, Clarence. You mean it wasn't there?'

'Exactly. My first impulse was to go and inform Alaric immediately.'

'Of course.'

'But when I reached his door, I found myself hesitating. You see, most unfortunately I had disturbed his sleep a little earlier, and he had been rather upset about it.'

'How did that happen?'

'I had gone to see the Empress, and while I was in the sty — '

'*In* the sty?'

'Yes, she had gone to bed, and I went in, and I fell in the sty.'

'I thought I noticed something. You might open the window another inch or two. But you were saying?'

'When I got back, I found that someone had bolted the front door.'

'Now who could that have been?'

'And Alaric's french window was open, and all would have been well, if it had not been for the cat.'

'Cat?'

'A cat bumped my leg with its head, and I jumped and upset a table. It made a good deal of noise, and Alaric came out of the bedroom, and he refused to believe that the cat had been there. It was all very unpleasant.'

'Must have been.'

'And I came to ask you if you think it is

115

absolutely necessary to wake him again.'

Gally pondered. It would, of course, be simple for him to set his brother's mind at rest by saying 'First, my dear Clarence, let us go to the portrait gallery and assure ourselves that you are not in error in supposing the picture to have gone. Those optical illusions are not uncommon. It may still be hanging from its hook as snug as a bug in a rug'. But he could not conceal it from himself that a good deal of wholesome fun was to be obtained from waking for a second time an already hotted-up Duke and observing his reactions. And how good it would be for his adrenal glands. Living a placid life down in Wiltshire and seeing nobody but a lot of dull neighbours, his adrenal glands did not get stimulated from one year's end to another. It was only humane to take this opportunity of giving them a prod.

'I think so, Clarence. I feel very strongly that we must tell him at once.'

'We?'

'I shall of course come with you, to lend you moral support.'

'You will?'

'Of course.'

'You are very kind, Galahad.'

'I try to be, Clarence, I try to be. I don't think we ought to leave it all to the Boy Scouts.'

V

It had not taken the Duke long to fall asleep again. He was one of those fortunate men who

116

have no need to count sheep but drop off directly the head touches the pillow. Short though the interval had been since Lord Emsworth's departure, loud snores were proceeding from his bedroom as the two callers entered the garden suite. They ceased abruptly when Gally hammered on the door with the shoe which had made so small an appeal to the recent cat, accompanying the gesture with a cheery 'Bring out your dead'.

The Duke sat up. His first impression was that the house was on fire, but he revised this view when Lord Emsworth put his lips to the keyhole and bleated 'Could you spare a moment, Alaric?' Although nothing could have been more politely phrased than the query, it brought him out of bed with a single leap, full of homicidal thoughts. That Emsworth, of whom he had been confident that he had seen the last, should be playing a return date was in his opinion more than a man could be expected to endure. And when, flinging open the door, he saw that Gally also was present, words — perhaps fortunately — failed him. It was left to Gally to set the conversational ball rolling.

'A very hearty good morning to you, Dunstable,' he said. 'You look astonishingly bright and happy. But I'm afraid those bubbling high spirits of yours are going to sag a bit when you hear what we have come to say. Clarence has an amazing story to relate. Relate your amazing story, Clarence.'

'Er,' said Lord Emsworth.

'That's not all there is of it,' Gally assured the Duke. 'There's a lot more, and the dramatic interest mounts steadily as it goes on.'

'Do you know what time it is?' the Duke demanded, finding speech. 'It's two o'clock in the blasted morning,' and Gally said he had supposed it was something like that. He would, he said, be thinking of bed in another hour or so, for nothing was better for the health than turning in early, ask any well-known Harley Street physician.

'But first the amazing story, and as Clarence shows a tendency to blow up in his lines, perhaps we shall get on quicker if I do the relating. We bring grave news, Dunstable, news which will make your knotted and combined locks to part and each particular hair to stand on end like quills upon the fretful porpentine. You know that picture of yours, the one of the one-girl nudist colony.'

'Two o'clock! Past two! And you come here — '

'It was in the portrait gallery. Note my choice of tense. I use the past deliberately. It was in the portrait gallery, but it isn't. One might put it that Annie doesn't live there any more.'

'What the devil are you talking about?'

'It's quite true, Alaric,' said Lord Emsworth. 'I went to the portrait gallery just now to get a book I had left there, and the picture had disappeared. I was shocked and astounded.'

'To what conclusion, then,' said Gally, 'do we come? If credit is to be given to the testimony of the witness Clarence, somebody with a liking for reclining nudes must have pinched it.'

'What!'

'Well, reason it out for yourself.'

For some moments bewilderment was the only emotion visible on the Duke's face. Then abruptly it changed to righteous wrath. He was not a man whom ideas often struck, but one had just struck him with the force of a bullet, and in the circumstances this was not surprising. It did not require a Sherlock Holmes to solve the riddle. Doctor Watson could have done it easily. Turning as purple as the stripe on his pyjamas, he gulped twice, blew at his moustache, allowed his eyes to protrude in the manner popularized by snails and in a voice of thunder uttered a single word.

'Trout!'

Then, as if fearing that he had not made himself sufficiently clear, he added:

'Trout, curse him! Trout, the larcenous hellhound! Trout, the low-down sneak thief! I might have known it, dammit. I ought to have guessed he would be up to something like this. He doesn't want to pay for the thing like a gentleman, so he steals it. But if he thinks he'll get away with it, he's very much mistaken. I'll confront him. I'll tax him with his crime. I'll make him return my picture if I have to stick lighted matches between his toes.'

Seeing that Lord Emsworth was gaping like the goldfish to which his sister Constance had so often compared him when he failed to grasp the gist, Gally came to his assistance with a brief footnote.

'Dunstable was hoping to sell the picture to Trout, but apparently Trout prefers to get it for nothing, his view being that a penny saved is a penny earned. I've known other men to think along the same lines.'

The Duke continued to sketch out his plans.

'I shall go to him and say 'Trout, you have three seconds to produce that reclining nude,' and if he raises the slightest objection, I shall twist his head off at the roots and make him swallow it,' he said, and Gally agreed that nothing could be fairer than that. Trout, he said, could scarcely fail to applaud such a reasonable attitude.

'I'll go to his room and put it up to him without an instant's delay. Which is his room?'

'I don't know,' said Gally. 'Which is Trout's room, Clarence?'

'I'm afraid I couldn't tell you, Galahad,' said Lord Emsworth, surprised that anyone should suppose that he knew anything. 'There are fifty-two bedrooms in the castle. Many of them are of course unoccupied, as for instance the one where Queen Elizabeth slept and a number of those known as state rooms, but I imagine Mr. Trout would be in one of the others.

Connie is sure to have put him somewhere.'

'Then the thing to do,' said the Duke, who could reason things out as well as the next man, 'is to go and ask Connie.'

It was unfortunate that during this conversation Lord Emsworth should once again have been standing near the table on which the Duke had replaced the two bowls (now empty), the clock, the ash-tray, the calendar and the photograph of James Schoonmaker and Lady

120

Constance on their wedding day, for as these appalling words penetrated to his consciousness he made another of his convulsive leaps and the table and its contents crashed to the floor in the old familiar manner, causing the Duke to exclaim 'Good God, Emsworth!' and Gally to warn 'his brother against getting into a rut.

He was impervious to reproaches.

'But, Alaric!'

'Now what?'

'You can't wake Connie at this time of night!'

'Can't I!'

'I don't know what she will say.'

'Then let's go and find out,' said Gally in his helpful way. 'No need,' he added, for he was a humane man and had no wish to see his brother's adrenal glands stimulated beyond their capacity, 'for you to come, Clarence. Dunstable and I can manage all right, and you ought to be in bed. Good night, sweet prince, and flights of angels sing thee to thy rest.'

VI

To say that Lady Constance was glad to see her visitors when they knocked at her door some minutes later would be an over-statement. She was plainly stirred, and her gaze, resting first on Gally, had in it something of a Medusa quality. Only when she saw the Duke did the flame in her eye diminish in intensity. There was no outrage of which she did not think Galahad capable, but she could not believe that Alaric

121

would come disturbing her slumbers without some good reason.

The Duke was the first to speak. A lesser man would have been taken aback by the spectacle of this majestic woman with a mud pack on her face, but he was not a lesser man.

'Hoy!' he said. 'Where's Trout's room, Connie?'

She answered question with question.

'What in the world are you doing, Alaric, wandering about the house at this time of night?'

The Duke had a short way with this sort of thing. He had not climbed two flights of stairs to take part in a quiz show.

'Never mind what I'm doing wandering about the house. If you really want to know, I'm looking for the reptile Trout.'

'Why on earth do you want Mr. Trout? If you've something to say to him, why can't it wait till you meet him at breakfast?'

'Because it can't, that's why it can't. He'll have made his getaway long before breakfast. I only hope he hasn't made it already.'

So unequal to the intellectual pressure of the conversation was Lady Constance that she actually turned for support to her brother Galahad.

'I don't understand. What does he mean, Galahad?'

Gally was helpful, as always.

'It's quite simple, Connie. He thinks Trout has stolen that picture of his, and he wants to recover it. He feels the thing must be cunningly hidden somewhere by Trout, and his plan, as he outlined it to me, is to stick lighted matches between Trout's toes with a view to persuading him to come clean about its hiding place. Very sensible, it seemed to me. Just the sort of thing to get results.'

Well meant though this explanation was, it left Lady Constance still bewildered.

'But, Alaric, what makes you think Mr. Trout has stolen your picture?'

'Who else could have stolen it?'

'I mean, why are you under the impression that anyone has stolen it?'

'Pictures don't walk away, do they?'

'I don't understand you.'

'If one disappears, somebody must have taken it, and Emsworth was in the portrait gallery just now and says my reclining nude had gone.'

'Clarence!' The mention of her brother's name had had the immediate result of restoring Lady Constance to her normal composure. 'Have you really built up this case against Mr. Trout on the strength of something Clarence told you? You know what he is. You can't rely on anything he says. It's just the same as when he was a child and used to insist that there were Red Indians under his bed.'

The Duke rapped imperiously on the chest of drawers.

'Produce Trout!'

'I will not produce Trout. I am quite convinced that Clarence has made some absurd mistake and that the picture is still there. Let us go to the portrait gallery and see for ourselves.'

It was several minutes before she spoke again.

When she did, it was with the complacency of a woman who is entitled to say 'I told you so'.

'You see,' she said, and the Duke had no reply to make. 'Just as I supposed,' she went on. 'A typical instance of Clarence's muddleheadedness. And now perhaps I may be allowed to go back to bed and, if possible, get some sleep for the remainder of the night.'

She withdrew with a hauteur which none of the portraits of her ancestresses could have exceeded, though many of them had rather specialized in hauteur, and Gally clicked his tongue sympathetically.

'Connie's upset,' he said.

'So am I,' said the Duke.

'Extraordinary that Clarence should have made such a mistake.'

The Duke's pent-up feelings exploded in one of the loudest snorts he had ever achieved.

'Nothing extraordinary about it. Connie may say all she likes about him being muddleheaded, but what he's suffering from isn't muddleheadedness, he's potty to the core, and I can't see the point of trying to pretend he isn't. Goes out in the middle of the night to look at that pig of his because he's had a dream about it. Sneaks into my room and starts upsetting tables, and when asked what the hell he thinks he's up to babbles about non-existent cats. And on top of that can't see a ruddy picture when it's staring him in the face. He ought to be certified.'

Gally stroked his chin thoughtfully. He removed his eyeglass, and gave it a polish.

'I don't think I can go as far as that,' he said,

'but he certainly ought to see a psychiatrist.'

'A what?'

'One of those fellows who ask you questions about your childhood and gradually dig up the reason why you go about shouting 'Fire' in crowded theatres. They find it's because somebody took away your all day sucker when you were six.'

'I know the chaps you mean. They dump you on a couch and charge you some unholy fee per half hour. Only I thought they were called head-shrinkers.'

'That, I believe, is the medical term.'

'I've heard fellows speak of someone called Glossop.'

'Sir Roderick Glossop? Yes, he is generally recognized as at the top of the profession.'

'We'll get hold of him.'

'Unfortunately I read in the paper the other day that he had gone to America.'

'That's too bad.'

'But,' Gally continued, 'by a really extraordinary coincidence I was chatting only this afternoon with his junior partner, a young man named Halliday. I ran into him at the Emsworth Arms. He would be as good for our purpose as Glossop, for they tell me that, though young, he is brilliantly gifted.'

'Think you can get him?'

'I'm sure he would be delighted to come. Connie is the difficulty.'

'Why?'

'Can we get her to invite him to the castle? We want to keep it from her, if possible, that

Clarence is undergoing treatment. You know what women are; they become nervous. Could you pretend he's a friend of yours and persuade her to invite him?'

'Persuade her?' Again a snort like the sound of the Last Trump rang through the portrait gallery. 'I don't have to persuade Connie to invite people. I'll invite him.'

'Splendid,' said Gally. 'It only needs a telephone call. I'll get in touch with him first thing tomorrow.'

8

Lady Constance's boudoir, on the second floor of the castle, looked out on the front drive and the spacious parkland beyond it, and so, two days after the events just recorded, did Lady Constance. She was standing at the window blowing puffs of flame through her shapely nostrils, and every now and then a quiver shook her as if some unseen hand had prodded her with a pin. She was thinking of Alaric, Duke of Dunstable, and a stylist like Gustave Flaubert, with his flair for the mot juste, would have described her as being as mad as a wet hen.

Years ago, in her childhood, a series of governesses had been at pains to implant in her the desirability of self-control. 'Ladies never betray emotion, Connie dear', they had warned her, and she had taken the lesson to heart. But though today she always preserved a patrician calm in public, she considered herself entitled to a certain measure of relaxation when alone in the privacy of her own apartment. And quite rightly, any impartial judge would have said. If, looking out of the window, she frowned and quivered, not even the most censorious of governesses would have held her unjustified in frowning and quivering. She was a proud woman, and this habit of Alaric's of inviting every kind of Tom, Dick and Harry to Blandings Castle without a word to her gashed her haughty spirit like a knife. First Trout, and now this man Halliday, and who knew how many more there would be. She had only one crumb of comfort. Unwelcome though they were, these Trouts and Hallidays might have been worse. They might have been friends of her brother Galahad.

It was as she stood there with her adrenal glands working overtime that the Market Blandings station cab (Jno Robinson, proprietor) drove up to the front door with its usual pants and gaspings, and a young man alighted. This, she presumed, was the Mr. Halliday whom Alaric had inflicted on her, and she followed him into the house with a stare which would have aroused the respectful envy of a basilisk. Not that he had a repulsive or criminal aspect. As far as looks were concerned, he might have been someone she had invited to the castle herself. But it was not at her bidding that he had come, and she was at her iciest when some minutes later he entered the room accompanied by Gally, whom she supposed he had met in the hall and who was bringing him to be introduced to an unwilling hostess. A nervous young man, she noted. He seemed ill at ease.

In this diagnosis she was correct. John was definitely ill at ease. The exhilaration he had felt when informed by Gally that the substitution of the pictures had gone without a hitch and that owing to his, Gally's, superlative generalship he was to come as a guest to the castle had given way to emotions such as a cat might feel which finds itself in a strange alley and muses dubiously on what the future may hold. Gally had spoken of his hostess as a woman whose impulse it would be to attach herself to the scruff of his neck and the seat of his trousers, and start heaving, and looking at her he could well believe her capable of this form of self-expression. The dullest eye could not have failed to detect in her all the qualities which go to make a good chucker-out, and it seemed to him that her fingers were already twitching in anticipation of the task. Recalling what Gally had told him about her being the wife of an American named Schoonmaker, he could not but feel that this Schoonmaker must be a rugged composite of Humphrey Bogart and Edward G. Robinson, who talked out of the side of his mouth and fed on raw meat. Not even when rebuked by the Judge during the case of Onapoulos and Onapoulos versus the Lincolnshire and Eastern Counties Glass Bottling Company had his fortitude so dwindled to the level of that of the common earthworm.

Gally, in sharp contradistinction, was at his perkiest. Connie never had the quelling effect on him that she had on others. When a man has seen a sister spanked with a hairbrush by a disciplinarian Nanny, her spell weakens. Today, moreover, he was loving everybody. If there is one thing more than another which makes a man feel like a benevolent character out of Dickens, it is the thought that he has been instrumental in extracting a fellow human being from the soup which was threatening to engulf him. And nobody could say that he had not performed this kindly office for his godson. Owing to his efforts

John Preferred, which had been down in the cellar with no takers, was now enjoying the most spectacular rise one could wish.

Thinking thus, he bubbled over with cheeriness.

'Hullo there, Connie,' he carolled, more like a lark in Springtime than a disgrace to a proud family. 'This is the Mr. Halliday in anticipation of whose coming you have been counting the minutes. I knew you would want to see him the moment he arrived.'

'Oh?' said Lady Constance. There was no ring of pleasure in her voice. 'How do you do?'

'Great friend of Dunstable's.'

'Oh?'

'And of mine. We have only just met, but already we are like brothers. He calls me Gally, I call him John. Each would lend the other a fiver without a murmur.'

'Oh?'

'It's a great bit of luck getting him here, as he's generally engaged three deep at this time of year. So we must do all we can to make his stay pleasant. What I'm hoping is that he will hit it off with the Gilpin wench. Is she back yet?'

'No.'

'When do you expect her?'

'Some time today, I suppose.'

'Good. Girl called Linda Gilpin who's staying here,' Gally explained to John. 'You'll like her. She went off yesterday in her car to attend some sort of jamboree at her old school. Sports Day or Founder's Day or something. I warned her it would bore her stiff, but she would go. Well, I

130

mustn't stand here talking all the afternoon, I want to show John round the place. So come along, Johnny. You're in luck. If you'd come on Visitors Day, you'd have been soaked half a crown, but now you'll be getting it all for nothing.'

As the door closed behind them, Lady Constance expelled the breath which she had been holding back during these exchanges. In a woman of less breeding it would have come out as an oath, for conversing with Gally had had its usual effect on her, making her feel as if her nerve centres had been scrubbed with sandpaper. It increased her exasperation that she could not in fairness hold him responsible for the intrusion of this man Halliday, the blame resting entirely on Alaric. She looked forward to having a word with Alaric, and a moment later she was given the opportunity of doing so, for the door opened and he came in.

To those familiar with her imperious temperament it will no doubt seem surprising that she should have waited till now to have a word with him, but this is readily explained. The news of John's impending visit had brought on one of those neuralgic attacks to which she was so subject, and she had spent the previous day in bed. The neuralgia having yielded to treatment, she proposed to take up the point at issue and if necessary fight it out, like General Grant, if it took all summer.

It has been stated that Lady Constance had a sisterly affection for the Duke of Dunstable. Of this affection in the gaze she now directed at him there was no trace. She looked more like an aunt than a sister.

'Yes, Alaric?'

'Eh?'

'I said Yes, Alaric.'

'A pretty potty thing to say,' the Duke commented critically. Connie's total lack of sense sometimes made him uneasy, though it was about what you would naturally expect in one of her sex. 'What do you mean, yes? I didn't ask you anything or say it was a fine day or anything.'

Lady Constance, who had stiffened at his entry, stiffened still further. As was his custom when he visited her boudoir, the Duke was pottering about, fiddling with the objects on her desk, picking up a letter, putting it down after giving its contents a cursory glance and looking with offensive curiosity at a photograph of James Schoonmaker on one of the tables. And as always this habit of his made her feel that ants in large numbers were parading up and down her spine. But true to the teaching of the governesses who had told her that ladies never betrayed emotion, she forced herself to be reasonably calm.

'I said 'Yes, Alaric?' because I was anxious to know what your motive was in coming here.'

'Eh?'

Lady Constance's sisterly affection touched a new low. The ranks of the parading ants seemed to have become augmented by new recruits.

'Is there anything I can do for you, Alaric?'

'Yes, I want a stamp. I'm writing to the *Times* about the disgraceful mess the Government has got the country into. Lot of incompetent poops, if you ask me. Do them good if somebody came along and shot them all. Who's Jane?'

'I beg your pardon?'

'This letter is signed Jane. I was wondering who she was.'

'I wish you would not read my letters.'

'No pleasure to me to read them. They're always damned dull. Why has Schoonmaker got that silly grin on his face?'

Several authorities have stated that the thing to do when your self-control seems about to leave you is to draw a deep breath. Lady Constance drew the deepest she could manage.

'I am sorry,' she said, 'that my husband's smile does not meet with your approval, but it is, I believe, customary to smile when you are having your photograph taken. If you wish, I will get James on the transatlantic telephone and acquaint him with your criticism, and no doubt he will arrange his features next time more in accordance with your exacting tastes.'

'Eh?' said the Duke. He spoke absently. He had picked up a letter signed Amy and was finding it better reading than the others. 'What's Fred been doing?'

'I beg your pardon?'

'This woman says she's thinking of divorcing him. Must have been some trouble in the home.'

Lady Constance drew another deep breath.

'Put down that letter, Alaric, and listen to me!'

There was nothing of the sensitive plant about the Duke of Dunstable, but even he could recognize hostility if it was thrust upon him with

133

a heavy enough hand.

'You seem very ratty, Connie. What's biting you?'

'I am extremely annoyed, Alaric. I will not have you inviting people here like this. It seems to be your object to turn Blandings Castle into a residential hotel.'

'Trout, you mean?'

'And this Mr. Halliday.'

Conscious of the excellence of his motives, the Duke was quite willing to explain.

'I had to invite Trout because I want to sell him that picture, and I couldn't do it if he wasn't on the spot.' Even a woman, he told himself, ought to be able to understand anything as simple as that. 'And as for this chap Halliday, I hadn't meant to tell you about him, but as the subject has come up, I may as well.'

'Please do. As a hostess I am naturally interested. Is he, too, one of your customers? Quite a novel idea, turning Blandings Castle into a trading centre. What are you planning to sell him?'

The rule by which Gally lived his life — 'Whenever Connie starts to throw her weight about, sit on her head immediately' — was also the foundation stone of the Duke's domestic policy. There was an authoritative note in his voice as he said:

'No need to get sarcastic, Connie.'

'I disagree with you. There is every need.'

'I'll tell you about Halliday. If I don't, you'll be coming the grande dame over him, and he'll leave us flat. It isn't everybody who can stand

134

that manner of yours. I've often wondered how it goes down with the Yanks. You have a way of curling your upper lip and looking down your nose at people which gives a lot of offence. I've had to speak of it before. Well, here's what happened. After you left us that night — '

'What night?'

'The night Emsworth went off his head and told me my picture had been stolen. By the way, did anybody ever take away his all day sucker when he was six?'

'I haven't the remotest notion what you're talking about.'

'Never mind. We can leave all that to Halliday. Probably the first question he'll ask him. I was saying that after you'd gone off to bed Threepwood and I got talking, and we decided that what Emsworth needs is psychiatric treatment, if you know what that is.'

'Of course I know what it is.'

'Well, that's what we decided he's got to have. It's essential to engage an expert head-shrinker to put a stopper on his pottiness. I recommended this once before, you may remember, when he said he was going to enter his pig for the Derby.'

'Clarence did not say he was going to enter his pig for the Derby.'

'It may have been the Grand National.'

The ants on Lady Constance's spine had now been joined by a good many of their sisters, cousins and uncles and were marching to the tune of The Stars And Stripes Forever. Her voice rose formidably.

'He did not say anything of the sort. I asked

him, and he told me so.'

The Duke remained unmoved.

'Naturally he would deny it. He makes a damaging statement like that in an unguarded moment, realizes how it will sound and tries to hush it up. But the fact remains. I was there when he said it, and I remember telling him that it was very doubtful if the Stewards would accept a pig. However, that is a side issue into which we need not go at the moment. The point is that Threepwood and I were solid on the necessity for bringing in a head-shrinker, and our first choice was Sir Roderick Glossop. He, however, was not available, and we were baffled till Threepwood remembered that he knew Glossop's junior partner, this chap Halliday, so we got in touch with him. He was fortunately at liberty, and we engaged his services. That's how Halliday comes to be at the castle.'

Lady Constance's animosity had waned considerably as this explanation proceeded. She still felt that she should have been consulted before additions were made to the castle's guest list, but on the whole she approved of what had been done. The incidents of that disturbed night had shaken her. She had never been under the illusion that Clarence's was a keen mind, but not till then had he given so substantial a cause for anxiety to his nearest and dearest. Psychiatric treatment was unquestionably called for. Whatever it might do to him, it could scarcely fail to be an improvement. The only doubt that lingered with her was whether this Mr. Halliday was sufficiently mature to undertake the task of penetrating to his subconscious and bringing to the surface the contents of its hidden depths.

'He's very young,' she said dubiously.

The Duke's attention was engaged once more with the photograph of Lady Constance's husband.

'Funny-shaped head Schoonmaker's got. Like a Spanish onion.'

It was a statement which at any other time Lady Constance would have contested hotly, but her mind was on Sir Roderick Glossop's junior partner.

'He's very young,' she repeated.

'I wouldn't call Schoonmaker young. Depends of course what you mean by young.'

'I was speaking of this Mr. Halliday. I was saying he was very young.'

'Of course he's young. Why wouldn't he be? If a man's a junior partner, how can he help being junior?' said the Duke, taking, as so few women were able to, the reasonable view.

Extraordinary, he was thinking, how mingling with those Yanks had sapped Connie's intellect. She didn't seem able nowadays to understand the simplest thing.

II

For perhaps two or possibly three minutes after they had left Lady Constance's boudoir Gally and John preserved an unbroken silence. Gally was plunged again in thoughts of how cleverly he had grappled with the various problems which had confronted him, a feat possible only to one trained in the hard school of the Pelican Club, while John was in the grip of the peculiar numbed sensation, so like that caused by repeated blows on the head from a blunt instrument, which came to all but the strongest who met Lady Constance for the first time when she was feeling frosty. It was as though he had been for an extended period shut up in a frigidaire with the first Queen Elizabeth.

'I think you came through that well, Johnny,' said Gally at length. 'Just the right blend of amiability and reserve. It is not every man who can come through the ordeal of being introduced to Connie with such elan and aplomb. It leads me to hope that when you come up against La Gilpin, she will be less than the dust beneath your chariot wheels. Too bad she's away, but she ought to be with us in an hour or so.'

'By which time I may have started to recover.'

'Yes, I could see that, however little you showed it, you found Connie overpowering. Long association has made me immune, but she does take the stuffing out of most people. Somebody wrote a story years ago entitled The Bird With The Difficult Eye, and I have always thought the author must have had Connie in mind. She takes after my late father, a man who could open an oyster at sixty paces with a single glance. But you mustn't let her sap your nerve, for you'll need all you have for the coming get-together with that popsy of yours.'

'I wish you wouldn't — '

'I am a plain man. I call a popsy a popsy. How

were you thinking of playing the scene of reunion, by the way, always taking into consideration the fact that she, too, will have a difficult eye? Her mood when we were discussing you the other day was not sunny. You will need to pick your words carefully. I would advise the tender reminiscent note, what you might call the Auld Lang Syne touch. Remind her of those long sunlit afternoons when you floated down the river in your punt or canoe, just she and you, the world far away, no sound breaking the summer stillness except the little ripples whispering like fairy bugles among the rushes.'

'We didn't float.'

'Didn't you ever go on the river?'

'No.'

Gally was surprised. He said that in his day you always took a spin with the popsy in a punt or canoe, with a bite to eat afterwards at Skindles. It was the first step towards a fusion of souls.

'Then where did you plan your future?'

'We didn't plan it anywhere. I asked her to marry me and she said she would, and that was that. We hadn't any time to plan futures. It all happened quite suddenly in a taxi.'

'But you must have seen something of her before then?'

'At parties and so on.'

'But not in canoes on long sunlit afternoons?'

'No.'

'Disappointing. When was your first meeting?'

'One morning in her shop.'

'She runs a shop?'

'She used to. It didn't pay.'

139

'What sort of shop?'

'Flower.'

'And you went in to buy long-stemmed roses?'

'No, I went in because I had seen her through the window.'

'Love at first sight?'

'It was at my end.'

'What happened then?'

'We got talking. It turned out that I had been at Oxford with her brother.'

'And then?'

'We met again somewhere.'

'And went on talking about her brother?'

'Among other things.'

'And after that?'

'Some lunches.'

'Many?'

'No. She always seemed to be booked up. She was very popular. Whenever I met her, there was always a gang of Freddies, Algies and Claudes from the Brigade of Guards frisking round her. That's why asking her to marry me seemed such a long shot. I didn't think I had a hope. After all, who am I?'

'You are my godson,' said Gally with dignity, 'and furthermore you have a golf handicap of six. Dash it all, Johnny, Linda Gilpin isn't the Queen of Sheba.'

'Yes, she is.'

'Or Helen of Troy.'

'Yes, she is, and also Cleopatra. You ought to know. You've met her.'

A sidelong glance at his godson told Gally that these words had not been lightly spoken. There

140

was a soul's-awakening look on John's face that emphasized their sincerity. It left no doubt that Linda Gilpin was the girl he wanted and that he was prepared to accept no just-as-good substitute, and it was an attitude Gally understood. He had felt the same himself about Dolly Henderson. Nevertheless, he considered it his duty as a godfather to assume, if only halfheartedly, the role of devil's advocate. He had taken an immediate liking to Linda, but he was not blind to the fact that in making her his wedded wife Johnny would be running up against something hot. She was no Ben Bolt's Alice, who would weep with delight when he gave her a smile and tremble with fear at his frown. She was a girl of spirit, and any husband rash enough to frown at her would very shortly know that he had been in a fight.

This he proceeded to point out to John in well-chosen words.

'I agree,' he said, 'that she is a personable wench and has what it takes, but looks aren't everything. The conversation I had with her when we were going to see the yew alley left me with the conviction that she was anything but meek and insipid. Admittedly the proceedings in the case of Clutterbuck versus Frisby had stirred her up very considerably, but she reminded me of a girl I knew in the old days who once wound up an argument we were having by spiking me in the leg with a hat pin. She recalled to my memory a poem I read in my youth, the protagonist of which was a young costermonger who took his donah to Hampstead Heath on Bank Holiday. The expedition started out well,

141

but when it came on to rain and the ham sand-
wiches got wet, the gentler side of her nature
went into abeyance, and this is how he expresses
himself. 'There is some girls wot cry, says I, while
some don't shed a tear, but just has tempers and
when they has 'em, reaches a point in their
sawcassum wot only a dorg could bear to hear.
Thus unto Nancy by and by, says I'. Linda
Gilpin seemed to me very much the Nancy type.
Are you prepared to face a married life into
which tempers and sawcassum are bound to enter?'

'Yes.'

'You don't feel like calling the whole thing off?'

'No.'

'Taking to the hills while escape is still possible?'

'No.'

'Then,' said Gally, gladly abandoning the
functions of devil's advocate, 'we know how we
stand, and I may say that I agree with you
wholeheartedly. My acquaintance with Linda
Gilpin has not been a long one, but I have seen
enough of her to know that she is what the
doctor ordered. Good Lord, what does an
occasional bit of sawcassum matter? It prevents
married life from becoming stodgy. What we
must do now is think of a good approach for you
to make. The approach is everything. There are
dozens to choose from. There was a chap at the
Pelican who pretended to commit suicide when
the girl turned him down. He swallowed an
aspirin tablet and fell back with a choking cry.
The trouble was that after they had worked on
him with the stomach pump and he went back to

the girl, she simply refused him again, and all that weary work wasted. Still, it was an idea. Something on those lines might be worth trying. It strikes you favourably?'

'No.'

'Then how about having an accident? If she sees you lying on the floor, spouting blood all over the carpet, there'll soon be an end to her sales resistance. I knew a man who won his bride by getting hit over the head with a stone tobacco jar, the sort with the college arms on them which you buy when you're a freshman at the University. Clarence has a stone tobacco jar, and Beach would bean you with it if you slipped him a couple of quid. Indeed, if you played your cards right, he would probably do it for nothing. How about it? No? You're a hard man to help, Johnny. Finnicky is the word that springs to the lips. There seems no way of pleasing you.'

They walked on in silence, John's a thoughtful, Gally's a wounded silence. But it was never the latter's habit to leave a story unfinished.

'There was rather an odd conclusion to that romance I was speaking of,' he said as they came in view of the lake. 'I should have mentioned that the suicide chap's girl was the hat check girl at Oddenino's, and he had left his hat with her before putting on his act. You know how at many restaurants the O.C. in charge of hats sticks a slip of paper with a description of the customer in each lid to assist identification, the idea being that they'll feel complimented at being remembered, which they wouldn't be if they just got a ticket. Mine, for instance, would probably have

143

been something like 'Slim, distinguished, wearing eyeglass'. Well, as I say, this fellow had handed over the headgear, and when they had finished working on him with the stomach pump and he went back to the girl and proposed again and she refused him once more, he thought he might at least save something from the wreck by getting his hat, so he asked for it in a heartbroken sort of way and she gave it to him and he tottered off still heartbroken. His distress was not longlived. He found the girl had forgotten to take out the slip, and it read 'Face that would stop a clock'. He was so indignant that his love died instantaneously and he lived happily ever after.'

John had not given this human drama the attention it deserved. He was staring at the lake with the intensity of Tennyson's bold Sir Bedivere, suddenly conscious of how warm and sticky the sultry summer afternoon had rendered him. He pointed emotionally.

'Could I have a swim before dinner?' he asked, and Gally said he could if he did not take too long over it.

'You'll find trunks, towels and what not in the bath house. My brother Clarence takes a dip every morning, but whether from motives of health or in order to dilute the scent of the pig sty is not known. I shall be in the hammock on the front lawn when you want me.'

He strolled off — slim, distinguished, wearing eyeglass, as the hat check girl at Oddenino's would have said, and a few minutes later John was in the water, revelling in its thereapeutic

144

properties with a gusto which Lord Emsworth could not have surpassed when taking his morning dip, and Linda Gilpin, returning from her visit to the old school and hurrying to the lake for a quick bathe before dressing for dinner, saw him, stood transfixed, and blinked several times as if to assure herself that she had really seen what she thought she had seen. Then, coming to life, she shot off in the direction of the house. It was her intention to find Gally and take up with him the matter of John's arrival, for her woman's intuition told her that if barristers she particularly disliked wormed their way into Blandings Castle, it must be he who had engineered the outrage.

She boiled with justifiable fury, but she was resolved, when she saw Gally, to be very calm and cool and dignified, making it clear to him that though she had been surprised to see John Halliday, his presence at the castle was a thing of supreme indifference to her. To suppose that it mattered to her one way or another was absurd.

Such were her meditations. They were suddenly interrupted. Over lawn and pasture there came stealing a metallic but musical sound, soft in its early stages, then soaring to a majestic crescendo.

Beach was beating the dressing-for-dinner gong.

III

Beach replaced the gong stick with the quiet glow of satisfaction which this part of his duties

145

always gave him. He loved to hear the music swell to the sound of a great Amen and die away in a pianissimo like the last distant murmur of a passing thunderstorm. It had taken him some years to bring his art to its present state of perfection. At the outset of his career he had been a mere crude banger, but today he was prepared to match his virtuosity against any butler in England. Gally, complimenting him once on a masterly performance, had ventured the opinion that it was the large dorsal muscles that did it. Beach himself attributed his success to wrist work and the follow through.

Usually when he had completed his task a restful silence ensued, but this evening the quiet of the hall was broken by a sudden clattering suggestive of coals being delivered down a coal chute. This was caused by Howard Chesney, who, hurrying from upper regions in quest of a mislaid cigarette case, had slipped and made a rapid descent of the last few stairs. He staggered across the floor, clutched at the table on which the papers and magazines were kept, seized it as he was about to fall and stood looking dazed but thankful that he had been spared a worse disaster.

He found Beach at his side. It was Beach's normal practice, when he encountered Howard Chesney, to freeze him with a glance and pass on his way, but Howard's unexpected impersonation of a Gadarene swine rounding into the straight seemed to call for verbal comment. With just the right touch of reserve in his manner, to make it clear that this momentary unbending must not be taken as implying any promise of future camaraderie, he said:

'I trust you have sustained no injury, sir.'

Howard had already assured himself of this by passing his hands rapidly over his person as policemen had sometimes done to him in his native land. Frisking himself, as one might say. Incredible as it would have seemed to him a moment ago, there appeared to be no broken bones.

'No, I'm okay,' he replied bravely. 'I managed to catch hold of the table. Those stairs are slippery.'

'Yes, sir.'

'Why do they keep them that way?'

'I could not say, sir. I was not consulted in the matter,' said Beach austerely. He was willing to sympathize, but not to chat. He made a stately exit, and Howard Chesney after a brief search found his cigarette case. As he did so, Linda came hurrying in from outside. He would gladly have engaged her in conversation, for it was always his policy to talk as much as possible to girls with blue eyes, chestnut hair and graceful figures, but she flitted by and he was obliged to do the next best thing and light a cigarette. He was crushing this out in an ashtray, when Vanessa came down the stairs.

'Hi there, Mr. Chesney,' she said. 'Just the man I wanted to see.'

Vanessa, it will be recalled, had resolved to devote her time to a study in depth of Howard Chesney, with a view to ascertaining whether his moral code was as low as a first glance had told her it was. 'I'm pretty sure he's a crook,' she had said to Wilbur Trout, 'but I'll have to be certain

147

before I start anything.' She had now satisfied herself that it was even lower, and it was with bright confidence that she was now planning to enlist his services.

'Have you seen Wilbur Trout?' she asked, and as she spoke Wilbur appeared from the direction of the billiard room, where he had been practising solitary cannons. 'Oh, there you are,' she said. 'I hoped you would be along. We're going to have a board meeting.'

'A what?'

It was Wilbur who said this. He was staring at her and thinking how particularly attractive she looked. Vanessa liked to dress for dinner in good time, and when she dressed for dinner she always presented a spectacle that took the eye.

'A spot of plotting I should have said, but board meeting sounds better. Come over here where we shan't be heard.'

She led the way to a corner of the hall the only occupant of which was a suit of armour. Thinking it improbable that anyone would be lurking inside this, she resumed.

'It's about that picture, Willie. I've got an idea that looks good. Simple, too. It's always best to keep things simple if you can,' she said, and Wilbur agreed with her. Get too clever, he said, and you were sunk. This had been borne in upon him, he said, when thinking up stories to tell his wives.

'But as Mr. Chesney comes into it,' said Vanessa, 'the first thing to do is to sound him on how he feels about doing a little lawbreaking with no risks attached. Have you any prejudices

148

in that direction, Mr. Chesney?'

Howard Chesney was a cautious man.

'Well, that depends,' he said.

'With no risks attached, I repeat.'

'Well — '

'In that case — '

'Yes, in that case I might sit in. But I'd like to know what the game is.'

'You shall. You've seen that picture that's up in the portrait gallery, the one the Duke brought with him. Willie wants it the worst way, never mind why, and I've contracted to get it for him. Can we count on your assistance?'

'I don't know why not.'

'Bravely spoken.'

'What do I do?'

'Your first move will be to leave.'

'Leave the castle?'

'That's right. You've got your car here, haven't you?'

'Yes.'

'Then off you go.'

'I don't get it.'

'It'll become plainer as I proceed.'

'Why do I have to leave ?'

'So that you won't be a suspect. When the thing's found missing, nobody can say you took it, because you'll have been gone a couple of days.'

'But if I'm not here — '

'How do you do your bit? That's all arranged for. You leave, but you come back and lurk, and you keep on lurking till zero hour, which will be when Willie and I do our stuff. We go to the portrait gallery, you'll be lurking under the window. We lower the picture down to you on a string, and you drive off to London with it. Next morning there'll be a lot of fuss, with everybody running around in circles and yelling Who-dun-it, but where's it going to get them? The Duke'll think it must have been Willie and he'll go through his room with a fine-tooth comb, but there won't be a scrap of evidence and they'll have to settle for burglars. Willie will come out of it without a stain on his character. Then, when the heat's off, he meets you in London, you hand the thing over to him, and there's your happy ending.'

She paused with the air of one waiting for a round of applause. She got it from Wilbur Trout.

'Swell! What a brain!'

'Nice of you to say so.'

'You know, none of my wives had brains.'

'They hadn't?'

'Looks, yes, but not brains. You're a wonder.'

'Thank you, Willie.'

There was a momentary silence, occupied by Wilbur apparently in turning the thing over in his mind.

'The Duke'll be sore.'

'I shouldn't wonder. Still, into each life some rain must fall. And he deserves it for chiselling you out of the picture the way he did. I'll tell you about that some time, Chesney, and you'll agree that he had it coming to him.'

The voice of conscience seemed still to be whispering in Wilbur's ear. A thought occurred to him.

'I'll send him a cheque for what he paid for the thing.'

150

'Thus giving yourself away completely. You might as well mail him a written confession.'

'I'd send it anonymously, of course.'

'An anonymous cheque?'

Wilbur said he had not thought of that.

'It'll have to be cash,' he conceded, and Vanessa shrugged her shoulders.

'I wouldn't if it was me,' she said, 'but if that's the way you want it go ahead.'

The board meeting was over. Wilbur went off to dress. His stay at the castle had been of sufficient duration to give him a pronounced awe of his hostess, and he had no wish to incur her displeasure by being late for dinner. Howard Chesney, who feared only Beach and moreover prided himself on being able to array himself in what he called the soup and fish in ten minutes, remained. An item that should have been on the agenda paper was in his mind, and he was anxious to bring it to the attention of the board's chairwoman.

'About terms,' he said. 'You didn't mention terms.'

Vanessa was surprised. This struck her as rather sordid.

'Terms? I'm doing this to oblige an old friend.'

'Well, I'm not doing it to oblige any old friend. What's there in it for me?'

Vanessa saw his point. The labourer is proverbially worthy of his hire, and it was plain that this labourer intended to get it. And his labour was essential to her scheme. She wasted no time in fruitless argument.

'Yes,' she said. 'I suppose you want your cut.'

He assured her that she was not mistaken.

'Well, Willie's very generous. You won't have anything to complain about with him. He scatters gold with a lavish hand. About how much gold had you in mind?'

'A thousand bucks.'

'You certainly think big.'

'That's my figure.'

'You couldn't shade it?'

'No.'

'All right. I'll take it up with Willie.'

'You do that.'

'Though I still think . . . '

She broke off. Gally and John were coming through the hall. She eyed the latter with interest.

'Hello, who's that? Beach, who would the gentleman be who came through a moment ago with Mr. Threepwood?'

Beach, who had entered and was about to place a tray of cocktail glasses on their table, turned courteously.

'A youngish gentleman, madam?'

'And tallish.'

'That is a Mr. Halliday, madam. He arrived this afternoon.'

Beach completed his task, and withdrew, and Vanessa, turning to Howard Chesney, was surprised to see that he was exhibiting all the indications of having received a shock.

'Something the matter?' she asked, noting his fallen jaw and the glassy stare in his eyes.

Howard Chesney writhed in silence for a moment. When speech came to him, it was bitter. He was patently a man with a grievance.

'If this isn't just my luck! Lawyers crawling all over London, thousands of them, and the one that comes here has to be him. Can you beat it?'

'You know him?'

'Do I know him! Say, listen. The last time I was over on this side a job went wrong and I did a stretch in the coop. And that guy Halliday was the attorney who defended me.'

IV

Vanessa was a girl of cool nerve, but even girls of cool nerve can be shaken.

'What!' she cried.

'That's who he is.'

'Are you sure?'

'Sure I'm sure. And if you're going to say Will he remember me, you bet he'll remember me. It isn't so long ago, and he saw plenty of me. So where do we go from here?'

It was a good question, and Vanessa found herself at a loss to think of an answer. An intelligent girl, she could see that this unfortunate reunion had dealt a mortal blow to the plan of campaign of which she was so proud. The situation was undeniably one that called for thought, and her brain became active.

'Look,' she said. 'This wants talking over, and we can't do it here, because he'll be coming down in a minute. We'll go to the portrait gallery. There won't be anyone there.'

Howard Chesney said that what he was

thinking of doing was sneaking out the back way and getting into his car and driving off without saying goodbye or thanking anyone for a delightful visit, a plan of action rendered additionally attractive because he would not have to tip the butler. Vanessa found it hard to dissuade him from this course, but she managed it at last, and it was to the portrait gallery that they went. And such was the vigour with which she had stimulated her always serviceable brain that by the time they arrived there she was able to announce that she had solved the problem.

'I've got it,' she said. 'What you do is stay in your room and not come down to dinner. I'll tell them you're not feeling well. And tomorrow — '

'Yes, how about tomorrow? I'll meet him then, won't I? And he'll spill the beans, won't he? And the old girl will throw me out on my ear, won't she?'

'If you'll just listen. Tomorrow you leave before breakfast.'

'How do you explain me doing that?'

'You had an early phone call from your lawyer saying it was absolutely vital that you came to London for a conference.'

'You think they'll believe that?'

'Why wouldn't they?'

'Who took the call?'

'I did. I was up early.'

'It sounds thin to me.'

'Well, it's the best we can do.'

'I guess it is, at that. Then what?'

'You go and stay a couple of nights at the Emsworth Arms in Market Blandings.' Howard showed no enthusiasm for the suggestion. He was a man who liked his creature comforts.

'The beds there are the limit. I was talking to a fellow in the bar yesterday, and he said they were stuffed with rocks.'

'Well, go to London if you like, but leave me your phone number, so that I can tell you which night you're to be under that window. We can't get the picture away without you.'

Howard looked at the reclining nude with something of the lack of appreciation shown by Lady Constance on her introduction to it.

'Why does Trout want the thing so bad?'

'She's like his last wife.'

'She looks to me like a pig.'

'So she does to Lord Emsworth. But it doesn't matter if you don't think she's a Miss America. All you have to do is be under the window and earn your thousand dollars. Is it a deal?'

When she put it that way, Howard said it decidedly was.

'Then that's settled,' said Vanessa briskly. 'And you'd best be getting to your room and into bed as quick as you can, because I'm going to tell them to send you up a tray, and it would look funny if you weren't there.'

Howard weighed the advice, and found it good. Soon after she had left he started to follow it. He went to the door, opened it, and immediately closed it again.

The man Halliday was coming along the corridor. He was accompanied by the Duke. Howard got the door shut just in time.

9

John, dressing in the room allotted to him on the second floor, was feeling extraordinarily fit. His swim had invigorated him, and unlike Lord Emsworth, reluctantly donning the soup and fish further along the corridor, he enjoyed dressing for dinner. Physically he could not have been in better shape; nor, he assured himself, was there anything wrong with his mental condition. He would have denied it warmly if anyone had told him he was at all nervous.

Thoughtful, yes. Meditative, certainly. But not nervous. Naturally there was bound to be a certain embarrassment when he and Linda met, but he was confident that the clarity with which he pleaded his case would soon overcome what Gally had called her sales resistance. Linda was a sensible girl. Quite understandably she had been a little annoyed by what had taken place in court when Clutterbuck and Frisby were fighting their legal battle, but now that she had had time to think it over she could hardly fail to see the thing in the right light. He would explain in simple language how he had been placed, love urging him one way, duty another, and she would applaud his integrity, realizing that any girl who got a husband with such high ethical standards was in luck. It would probably end with them having a good laugh together over the whole amusing affair.

It would be ridiculous to describe him as nervous.

Nevertheless, when the door suddenly flew open without warning, he leaped several inches in the direction of the ceiling with a distinct impression that his heart had crashed against his front teeth, nearly dislodging them from their base. Returning to earth, he saw that he had a visitor. A large stout densely moustached man with popping eyes had entered and was scrutinizing him intently, seeming particularly interested in the shirt which he had just pulled over his head. The Duke of Dunstable's inquisitiveness did not confine itself to Lady Constance's correspondence, he could also be intrigued by other people's dress shirts.

'Where you get that?' he enquired.

'I beg your pardon?'

'This,' said the Duke, prodding with a large forefinger, and John replied civilly that he had obtained it at the emporium of Blake and Allsop in the Haymarket; whereupon the Duke, shaking his head reproachfully like one mourning the follies of youth said he ought to have gone to Gooch and Gordon in Regent Street. Better material and cheaper. He, too, he said, had once patronized Blake and Allsop, but had found them too expensive. He advised John to see the error of his ways and go to Gooch and Gordon in future.

'Mention my name.'

He did not give his name. He went on the assumption that everyone knew it instinctively and that the few who did not deserved no consideration. Quick thinking, however, told John that this must be the man who, if all went well at the coming round table conference with Linda, he would shortly be calling Uncle Alaric, and there swept over him the same warm glow of affection which he would have felt for any near relation of the girl he loved. He might have wished her a slimmer uncle and one with a smaller moustache and a more melodious voice, but any uncle of hers was all right with him, and he thanked him for his advice with a respectful sincerity which he hoped would be recognized as coming straight from the heart.

'So you're the head-shrinker.'

On the verge of saying 'I beg your pardon' again, John remembered the junior partnership which entitled him to that description. He said he was, and the Duke said he thought all you fellows had beards.

'You haven't got a beard.'

'No, no beard.'

'That's probably what Connie meant when she was beefing about you being young. You *are* young. How old would you say you were actually?'

'I shall be twenty-seven in September.'

'One of my fatheaded nephews is that, the other a bit younger, but you can't go by age. They would be just as big fools if they were in the fifties. Married against my wishes, both of them. I should imagine you are all right, if you're working with a big pot like Glossop. He's good, isn't he?'

'Very.'

'Right up there at the top?'

'Oh, decidedly. Nobody to touch him.'

'Pity we couldn't have got him. Still, you'll have to do.'

John said he would do his best to do, and the Duke proceeded.

'Did Threepwood explain everything to you? About observing Emsworth and all that?'

'Yes. I understand the situation.'

'You seen him yet?'

'Not yet.'

'You'll be able to run your eye over him at dinner. Threepwood told you he was definitely off his onion, of course?'

'I gathered from what he said that Lord Emsworth was somewhat eccentric.'

The Duke would have none of this evasiveness. Professional caution, no doubt, but it annoyed him.

'Eccentric be blowed. He's potty to the core. Look at the way he talks about that pig of his. Anyone with half an eye can see it's much too fat, and he insists it's supposed to be fat. Says it's been given medals for being fat, from which you will get a rough idea how far the malady has spread. What would a pig do with medals? Threepwood's theory is that he got this way because someone took his all day sucker from him when he was six, but I think it goes deeper than that. I think he was born potty, though he may have been dropped on his head when a baby, which would have helped the thing along. But you'll be able to form your own conclusions when you've observed him for a bit. How do you observe a fellow, by the way?'

It was an awkward question for one so lacking in experience as John, but he did his best.

'Well, I . . . how shall I put it? . . . I, as it were, observe him.'

'Ask him things, you mean?'

'That's right.'

'You can't make him lie on a couch. He'd get suspicious.'

'No, we'll be standing up.'

'It works as well that way, does it?'

'I have always found so.'

'Then I'll leave it to you with every confidence that you'll be able to put your finger on whatever it is that makes him the way he is. Threepwood tells me he will be paying your bill. Is that correct?'

'Yes, that's all arranged.'

'I ask because I'm blowed if I'm going to shell out a lot of money just to be told why Emsworth is potty.'

'Mr. Threepwood will be paying all expenses.'

'Good. I wanted that clearly understood before you start. And a thought occurs to me. While you're about it, why not cock an eye at some of the others here? Do you take on these jobs wholesale, or do you charge so much per person? Not that it affects me, as I'm not paying, but I'm curious.'

'I would make a reduction for quantity. No doubt I could come to some arrangement with Mr. Threepwood. You feel that some of the residents in the castle would be the better for psychiatric treatment?'

'Practically all of them. Blandings Castle at the moment is a hot bed of pottiness. Take that niece of mine . . . What's the matter?'

'Touch of cramp.'

'Thought so when I saw you jump. Used to suffer from cramp myself. My doctor down in Wiltshire cured me. But I was telling you about my niece. The night before I came here she turned up at the hotel humming and giggling, and wouldn't say why. It occurred to me later that she might have been in love, but I enquired of her on her arrival here and she said she wasn't, and she was probably speaking the truth, for I haven't heard her hum and giggle since. I was rather disappointed, for I had been hoping she might be in love with a very fine fellow I know on the Stock Exchange. Very rich. He's been trying to get her to marry him since last November, and he's only got to keep at it. It won't take long, not with one of her branch of the family. Her late father was always falling in love till he married my late sister, when of course it stopped. Yes, I'd like you to keep an eye on her, though, as I say, she hasn't hummed and giggled for some days. One can't be sure it won't break out again. And while you're at it, take a look at a Miss Polk who's staying here. One of Connie's friends. There's something wrong with her. The first day or two after her arrival she was bright and lively: used to talk sixteen to the dozen all the time to Threepwood, though what she found entertaining in him I couldn't tell you: but now she falls into silences when I'm with her. A sort of film comes over her eyes, and she makes some excuse and legs it. That happened only this morning, when she was sitting on a bench in the park and I came along, and we got into conversation. It's a bad sign.'

'Perhaps you touched on a painful subject.'

'No, it couldn't have been that. I was telling her about a speech I made at our local town council. Draw her out and find what the trouble is, and then start observing the others. You needn't bother with Connie, she's more or less all right except for marrying a Yank with a head like a Spanish onion, and you could account for that by the fact that he's got a lot of money, but there's a fellow called Trout who needs attention badly. Keeps on marrying blondes. And of course there's Threepwood.'

'I wouldn't have thought there was anything unbalanced about him.'

'He wears an eyeglass. No, don't you neglect any of them. Watch them all closely. Well, that's that. You've got the idea. Let's go down and have a cocktail. You haven't tied your tie right. Here, let me,' said the Duke, and with skilful hands he converted John's cravat into something that looked like a squashed sock. This done, he led the way to the stairs, speaking as he went of his doctor down in Wiltshire, who, though trustworthy as regarded cramp, went all astray in the matter of ante-dinner aperitifs.

'Says they raise the blood pressure and harden the arteries. Would like me to drink nothing but barley water and lemonade. Potty, of course,' said the Duke, and paused at the head of the stairs to speak further of this misguided physician.

It was at this moment that Howard Chesney, having given them what he thought sufficient time to pass downstairs, opened the portrait gallery door once more a cautious six inches, and peered out. Seeing them still among those present, he was about to dart back into his retreat like a cuckoo in a cuckoo clock, when it was as though his guardian angel had whispered to him that there was a better way. If, said his guardian angel, he were to creep noiselessly up behind John and give him a push, John would infallibly fall down these stairs whose surface had so recently been tested and proved slippery and probably break a leg. A consummation devoutly to be wished, for he would be removed to hospital and there would be no necessity for him, Chesney, to leave the castle in order to avoid a meeting which could not but be fraught with embarrassment.

He stole softly forward like a leopard advancing on its prey.

II

Gally was in the hall when Linda came down from her room. He greeted her with a flashing eyeglass.

'Hullo. You back?'

'I'm back.'

'Have a good time?'

'No.'

'Didn't enjoy yourself?'

'No.'

Gally nodded sagely.

'I feared as much when I saw you drive off. I had an idea you would find the going sticky. I was not educated at a girls' school myself, but I can picture the sort of thing that goes on at these reunions. The tedious playing over of bygone hockey matches, the recapitulation of the rights and wrongs of Angela's big quarrel with Isobel, reminiscences of dormitory feeds and all that Will — you — ever — forget — the — night — when — Flossie — got — so — ill — eating — brown — shoe — polish — spread — on — bread — when — the — potted — meat — gave — out stuff. The discriminating popsy wisely avoids that sort of binge. Well, cheer up, it's over now and you won't be mug enough to go another year, so let's see that beaming smile of yours of which I have heard such good reports. I have a surprise for you.'

The marble of Linda's face was disturbed by a momentary twitch or tremor, but she continued cold and aloof. Gally, eyeing her narrowly, was reminded of a girl he had known in the old days who had played the Snow Queen in a ballet at the Alhambra.

'I know,' she said. 'I went down to the lake.'

'Oh, you've seen him?'

'In the distance.'

'He looks even better close to. Did you shout Yoo-hoo at him?'

She disdained to reply to this question, unless a quick curl of the upper lip could be counted as a reply.

'You really need not have gone to all that

164

trouble, Mr. Threepwood.'

'Call me Gally. What trouble?'

'It must have taken a lot of hard work to get him here.'

'A labour of love.'

'Wasted, because I'm not going to speak to him.'

'No?'

'No.'

'Not even an occasional Good morning?'

'Only if he says it first.'

'You'll hurt his feelings.'

'Good.'

No one could have called her attitude encouraging, but Gally was always difficult to depress. Many of his interviews with bookies in the old days had begun on a similarly unpromising note, and eloquence and persuasiveness had pulled him through in the end. He saw no reason to suppose that a man who had bent to his will tough eggs like Honest Jerry Judson and Tim Simms the Safe Man would be baffled by a mere girl, sore as a sunburned neck though she unquestionably was. He proceeded, unruffled.

'I think you're making a great mistake, my dear child. Surely it's a mug's game to throw away a life's happiness just because Johnny has made you momentarily a bit hot under the collar. You know in your heart that he is Prince Charming and Today's Safety Bet. Do you play golf?'

'Yes. Why?'

'Johnny's handicap is six.'

'I know.'

'What's yours?'

'Eighteen.'

'Well, then. Think how he would improve your game. With him constantly at your side you might get down into single figures. What every girl needs is a husband whose loving task it will be to make her keep her head down and her eye on the ball. And apart from that the mere fact that after only a few meetings you both became convinced that you were twin souls makes it obvious that a merger between you and John Stiffy Halliday is a good thing and should be pushed along.'

In spite of her resolve to keep the scene on a dignified plane and to do nothing that would detract from her cold hauteur, Linda gave a squeak of surprise.

'John *what* Halliday?'

'His father at the christening insisted on the Stiffy. It was his nickname at the Pelican Club, and he wanted it to live after him. His wife objected and the parson wasn't any too pleased, but he won the battle of the font. He was a very determined chap. Johnny's the same.'

'He can be as determined as he likes. I don't want anything more to do with him.'

'That's what you think now.'

'And I shall go on thinking it.'

Gally sighed. He removed his eyeglass and began to polish it. Uphill work, this. A little difficult to know how to proceed. He could understand how those Old Testament snake charmers must have felt who tried to ingratiate themselves with the deaf adder and did not get to first base. He spoke reproachfully.

'You know where you've made your bloomer?'

'Where have I made my bloomer?'

'You've let the sun go down on your wrath, which is the worst possible thing to do. All the nibs are agreed on that.'

Linda was silent for awhile. She seemed to be thinking.

'I suppose I have. Though it isn't wrath exactly.'

'It looks like wrath to me.'

'It was at first, but now it's more like clear vision, if you know what I mean.'

'I don't.'

'It's hard to explain.'

'Have a try.'

'Well, after I'd been thinking about it for a long time it suddenly struck me . . . Have you ever had all your clothes taken off and been tarred and feathered?'

'Not that I remember.'

'Well, that's how I felt when I was in the witness box with him saying 'I suggest' and 'Is it not a fact', and I suddenly realized that if we were married, every time I looked at him I would be thinking of it and a happy marriage would be impossible.'

'What rot.'

'It isn't rot. It's plain sense. The fact is, no girl ought to marry a barrister.'

'Then barristers would become extinct.'

'Which would be fine. The more extinct they become, the better.'

'I disagree with you. Barristers are all right.'

'They're not. They're sadists, never happier than when they're torturing some unfortunate witness.'

'Just doing their duty.'

'Nonsense. It gives them a kick. They love it.'

'Do you think Johnny loved it?'

'Yes, I do.'

'Well, he didn't. He suffered agonies. His soul was twisted into knots. But it was his duty to go all out and win the case for his client. He was taking Clutterbuck's money, and he had to give him a square deal. He couldn't pull his punches just because the other side's star witness happened to be the girl he loved. I admire Johnny intensely. He is an example to all of us. I class him with Lucius Junius Brutus.'

'Who?'

'Haven't you ever heard of Lucius Junius Brutus?'

'No.'

'They don't seem to have taught you much at your school. You ought to have gone to Eton. I suppose you were trying so hard to get into the hockey team that you neglected your studies.'

'I didn't play hockey.'

'Well, lacrosse or ping-pong or whatever it was. Lucius Junius Brutus was a judge of the criminal court in ancient Rome, and one day who should come up before him, charged with some particularly fruity crime, but his only son, the apple of his eye, and as the trial proceeded it became evident that it was an open and shut case and the prosecution had the thing in a bag.

Not even Perry Mason could have got the accused off. But did Lucius Junius Brutus dismiss him with a few fatherly words of caution not to do it again? Did he impose a nominal fine or give him a suspended sentence? No, he saw where his duty lay. He threw the book at the young stinker, and everybody went about saying what a splendid fellow he was. I feel the same about Johnny.'

'I don't.'

'You will. Give yourself time. Don't rush it. The day will come when you'll be proud to marry him.'

'I wouldn't marry him if he were the last man on earth.'

'Well, he isn't, so the question does not arise.'

'I don't think I'll ever marry anyone.'

'Of course you will. You'll marry Johnny.'

'I won't.'

'Want to bet?'

At this moment, when the conversation seemed to have reached a deadlock and stalemate to have set in at the negotiating table, John and the Duke came downstairs, or rather the Duke and John, for they descended in that order. They came not at the leisurely pace customary in good society, but almost as rapidly as if they had slid down the banisters. One moment they were not there, the next they were.

It will be remembered that when last seen these two amateur acrobats were at the head of the stairs and that Howard Chesney was advancing on them like a leopard in quest of its prey, having decided to follow what he could see was the excellent advice of his guardian angel. He reached journey's end just as John was taking his first downward step, he having courteously allowed his elder to precede him. He then, in accordance with his guardian angel's instructions, placed a hand between John's shoulder blades and pushed.

He pushed with the utmost force at his command, and results from his point of view could not have been more satisfactory. The stairs were just as slippery as they had been when he had floated down them, and John, losing his footing, flew through the air like the daring young man on the flying trapeze of whom the poet has sung. He had not proceeded far when he overtook the Duke, and they both flew through the air with, to quote the bard again, the greatest of ease. Arriving in the hall, they separated. The Duke reached the suit of armour in the shadow of which the recent board meeting had been held, while John got only as far as the table where the papers and magazines were kept. Less fortunate than Howard Chesney, he struck it with his head. There was a nasty banging sound and then, as the expression is, he knew no more.

One of the things he did not know was that as he and the table came together Linda had sprung to her feet, uttered a choking cry like Gally's friend who swallowed the aspirin tablet and clutched at her throat in the manner of the heroine of a mystery play when there is a shriek in the night. She then sped across the hall to where the injured man lay, plainly stirred to her depths.

Her display of emotion would have caused Lady Constance's governesses to shake their heads, but Gally, following her at the slower pace fitted to his advanced years, regarded it with an approving eyeglass. It seemed to him that things could not have worked out more satisfactorily. He had recommended his godson to have an accident, and he had had an accident. And getting stunned like this was in his opinion even better than being hit on the head with a stone tobacco jar, and that had been amply sufficient to bring two sundered hearts together. In next to no time, he estimated, the popsy would be flinging herself on that prostrate form and showering kisses on it.

He was right. She did. And John, recovering consciousness and with it the illusion that some practical joker had substituted for his head a large and throbbing pumpkin, looked up dazedly. He had an odd feeling that someone had been kissing him. It hardly seemed possible that it was Linda who had done this, but she was certainly bending over him, and it was worth enquiring into.

'Were you kissing me?' he muttered.

'She was indeed,' said Gally heartily. 'No argument about that, my boy. She was kissing you like a ton of bricks. And I think I speak for her when I say that any little differences you may have had are now all washed up and that the laughing love god has wound his silken fetters about her once more, just as in the good old days when Clutterbuck and Frisby were nothing but a couple of names in the telephone directory. Correct, wench?'

'Quite correct.'

'This poor bit of human wreckage is officially established as the cream in your coffee and the salt in your stew?'

'He is.'

'Then would it be fair to suggest that you take him to the downstairs washroom and bathe his head in cold water. That certainly is a lump you've got, Johnny. I've not seen one as big as that since I used to attend the Saturday night gatherings at the old Pelican. Your father was a great man for getting lumps on his head, generally owing to being hit with bottles. He was always having political disputes with the more quick-tempered members. What the devil's all that noise?' said Gally changing the subject.

III

The noise to which he alluded was proceeding from the Duke. He was lying underneath the suit of armour and giving every indication that, whatever ill effects he might have suffered from his fall, his lungs had remained unimpaired. Gally walked over to where he lay and surveyed him with a sympathetic eye. He was not fond of the Duke, but he had a kind heart and could see that he was in pain.

'Are you all right, Dunstable?' he asked, feeling as he spoke that it was a foolish question, and the injured man told him not to be an ass.

'Of course I'm not all right. I've sprained my ankle.'

172

'Let me have a look. Does that hurt?'

'Ouch!'

'Yes, it's a sprain all right. I can feel the swelling. I'll help you to your room. Oh, Beach,' said Gally, as that interested observer appeared beside them, 'His Grace has sprained his ankle.'

'Indeed, Mr. Galahad?'

'Will you lend a hand. And then you might phone the doctor to come and look him over.'

After a difficult journey the Duke was deposited on the sofa in the garden suite, and Beach withdrew to telephone. Gally, about to follow him, was halted by a sharp 'Hey' from the invalid. He turned, expecting to listen to further observations on the subject of sprained ankles, on which already the other had been far from reticent, but it was on a different topic that the Duke now touched.

'Threepwood!'

'Hullo?'

'Ouch!'

'Agony?'

'Of course it's agony. But it's not that. It's about that niece of mine. What the devil's come over her?'

'How do you mean?'

'You know. You were standing right beside her when she did it. You saw the whole thing. Dammit, man, even if you wear an eyeglass, you aren't blind. She was kissing the headshrinker.'

Gally uttered an exclamation. It was as if his memory had been jogged.

'You're perfectly right. So she was. Yes, it all comes back to me. He was lying on the floor,

173

and she bent over him — '

'What do you mean, bent over him? She flung herself at him like a performing seal going after a bit of fish and kissed him.'

'Yes, I noticed.'

'About fifty times.'

'Yes, that would probably be somewhere near the figure. And you are naturally wondering why. I can explain it in a few words. She's in love with him.'

'Don't be an ass. She's never met him. Not till tonight, I mean. He only arrived this evening. They're perfect strangers.'

Gally saw that the time had come to unseal his lips. He would have preferred to postpone the revelation till he had had his dinner, but this did not appear to be within the sphere of practical politics. It was plain that the invalid would not rest easily on his sofa until presented with a solution of the mystery which was vexing him. He embarked on his narrative with the smooth suavity which had been wont to win all hearts at the Pelican Club.

'I see the time has come to let you in on a little secret, Dunstable, though I wasn't intending to mention it till a more favourable opportunity. In supposing that Johnny Halliday and your niece are perfect strangers you are very wide of the mark. He has known her for quite a time, during which time he never for an instant omitted to press his suit. You know the sort of thing. Flowers, lunches, ardent glances, whispered words and I should imagine, though this is merely a conjecture, bottles of scent. Sometimes

174

he would tell himself that he was making progress, sometimes he would feel that he was getting nowhere and despondency would ensue. He was often to be seen in Hyde Park or Kensington Gardens plucking daisies and murmuring 'She loves me, she loves me not'. And so it went on till some nights ago, stiffening the sinews and summoning up the blood, as the fellow said, he proposed to her in a taxi cab and they became betrothed. That was the night you were so disturbed because she hummed and giggled, giving you the impression that something had gone wrong with the two hemispheres of her brain and the broad band of transversely running fibres known as the corpus callosum and that she was, in your crisp phrase, potty. It was not pottiness, Dunstable, it was the natural exuberance of a young girl who has found love and happiness and is looking forward to the wedding with full choral effects, with the man she adores standing at her side in a morning coat and sponge bag trousers and the bishop and assistant clergy doing their stuff as busily as one-armed paperhangers with the hives. And then the reception and the going-away dress and the sunlit honeymoon and all that applesauce.'

There were several points in this monologue when the Duke would have been glad to interrupt, but the fury with which its subject matter filled him precluded speech, and he could merely splutter. He was still spluttering as Gally proceeded.

'But, as I need hardly tell an old campaigner like you, the course of true love seldom runs

175

smooth. Circumstances arose which led to a rift between the young couple. Johnny unfortunately blotted his copybook and fell back badly in the betting. His only hope of getting things on an even keel again was to come to Blandings Castle and do some heavy pleading. But how to get him there? Ah, that was what wanted thinking out. To tell Connie that he was a friend of mine, in fact actually my godson, would have been fatal, for Connie's attitude towards my circle of intimates has always been austere. Not bothering to make a study of each individual case, she pencils them all in as untouchables. I can see you shuddering at her unreasonableness — at least something seems to be making you shake — but there it is, that's Connie.

'And then I got the idea of bringing him here to psychoanalyse Clarence. I would be killing two birds with one stone, if I may so express myself. He could devote his mornings to pleading with the popsy and attend to Clarence in the afternoon and evening. A perfect set-up it seemed to me. So thanks to you, for you invited him, he came, and most fortunately fell downstairs and bumped his head, with the happy result that your niece, all animosity forgotten, flung herself on him, like as you brilliantly put it a seal going after a bit of fish, started to kiss him and is probably kissing him still. In short, there has been a complete reconciliation, love is working again at the old stand, and you can begin saving up for the wedding present and making notes for your speech at the wedding breakfast.'

Even Gally, practised raconteur though he was, was obliged to stop occasionally and take in breath. He did so now, and the Duke was enabled to convert the monologue into a duet. For the first time he found himself capable of speech.

'I never heard such dashed nonsense in my life,' he said.

Gally was surprised and pained. He had expected a better comment on his eloquence than this. His eyeglass glittered with reproach.

'You amaze me, Dunstable. Don't you approve of young love in Springtime? Not that it is Springtime, but the principle's the same. I would have thought you would have been giving three rousing cheers, only prevented by your groggy ankle from dancing the dance of the seven veils. You seem to me to be on velvet, for though you are losing a niece, you are gaining a nephew.'

'Ouch!'

'Don't say Ouch. Don't you like gaining a nephew?'

'No, I don't. I've got two, and I can't stand them. They both sneaked off and married scums of the earth without a word to me. That isn't going to happen to Linda. I want something better for her than the junior partner of a loony doctor. You can tell your ruddy godson that there isn't a hope of him marrying her. It's no good arguing, I won't consider it,' boomed the Duke, and further discussion was prevented by the arrival of the medicine man, who had his home in the village of Blandings Parva almost in the shadow of the castle walls and so had been able to give prompt service. Gally, relieved by his presence from attendance at the sick bed, returned to the hall, where he found John and Linda, the former looking damp, the latter wearing the contented air of a ministering angel conscious of having done a good job of work. He hastened to acquaint them with the latest developments.

'Well, Johnny, I've just been talking to your future uncle by marriage. Only he says he isn't.'

'Isn't what?'

'Your future uncle by marriage. I explained the position of affairs to him, he being rather at a loss to grasp what was the thought behind all that kissing, and he stoutly denied that you and your little ball of worsted are headed for the altar. He said he wouldn't permit it. What's the matter?'

This to Linda, who had made him jump with a sudden sharp cry, of much the same timbre as the one she had uttered on observing her loved one's head come in contact with the table on which the papers and magazines were kept. The light had died out of her eyes, and those eyes were staring at him in a manner which struck him as extremely odd.

'Did Uncle Alaric say that?' she asked in a hollow voice.

'He did, and it was like his gall. Of all the crust! Where does he get off, trying to dictate to you who you can marry and who you can't? He hasn't any say in the matter at all. It isn't as if he were your father, he's just your uncle and a very inferior uncle at that, the sort of uncle a young

178

bride hushes up and keeps as much as possible in the background. How can he stop you marrying anyone you want to?'

'But he can! He can! Oh, Johnny darling, I couldn't tell you that night in the taxi because there wasn't time, but I'm a ward of court.'

She would probably have gone on to amplify this statement, which had left Gally, for one, completely bewildered, but at this moment Beach began to beat the gong for dinner. And when Beach beat gongs, no human voice could offer competition.

IV

All through the meal Gally continued to ponder on these peculiar words, hoping to read some significance into them, but no gleam of elucidation rewarded him. They seemed to him in a nebulous sort of way to convey a suggestion of the legal and if so had no doubt had a meaning for John, but with Connie present he could not apply to John for enlightenment. Nor could he go to the fountain head and ask Linda. He did enquire of Vanessa, who was seated next to him, if she knew what a ward of court was, but as she said she had an idea it was something to do with tennis, he made no real advance.

Dinner at the castle under Lady Constance's regime was a formal affair with no mass exit of the two sexes at the end of it. The gentlemen were left to their port precisely as the gentlemen of her father's day had been left to theirs. It was consequently only after the ladies had withdrawn and Lord Emsworth had gone to his room to take his collar off and get into bedroom slippers that Gally was able to put the question uppermost in his mind. With an abruptness excusable in the circumstances he interrupted Wilbur Trout, who had begun to tell a story about a travelling salesman, and said:

'Do either of you know what a ward of court is?'

Wilbur, abandoning his anecdote with his usual amiability, said he thought it was the fellow who did the fetching and carrying when the District Attorney asked the Judge if the murder weapon or the bloodstained handkerchief or whatever it might be could be placed in evidence as Exhibit A. Gally thanked him.

'No, it's a girl of some sort,' he said. 'I was talking to a girl not long ago, and she told me she was a ward of court, and I've been wondering what she meant.'

John through the greater part of dinner had been sitting in silence, and Gally had supposed that this was because his head was hurting him. The heads of the younger generation, he told himself, were not like the heads he had known at the old Pelican, where it had been unusual for members to take much notice even when struck with a side of beef. He now spoke, the first time he had done so since the fish course.

'I know what a ward of court is.'

'Ah! I thought it was something legal.'

'It's the same as a ward in Chancery,' said John, and Gally uttered a brief 'Oh, my God'.

Whether from his reading or because he had heard somebody say something on the subject, he had a rudimentary acquaintance with the status of wards in Chancery. He began to grasp the seriousness of the situation.

John continued to explain in a toneless voice like that of one speaking from the tomb. He was wearing the same wan look which had caused remark in the garden of the Emsworth Arms and distressed the personnel of Paddington.

'A girl who is a ward of court comes under the ruling of the Guardianship Of Infants Act. She cannot marry or accept proposals of marriage without the consent of the court. When the consent of the court is not given, an injunction of restraint is made against the other intended party.'

Having mentally translated this into English, Gally removed and began to polish his eyeglass, a thing which, as has been shown, he seldom did except in moments of profound emotion. When he spoke, it was as though another voice was joining in the conversation from another tomb.

'You mean they put a stopper on the marriage?'

'Exactly.'

'Still they might not.'

'They would if some near relative of the ward of court — her uncle, for instance — objected to it.'

Gally burnished his eyeglass feverishly. He seemed to be praying for strength.

'Are you telling me that if a ward of court wants to marry a fellow who is one of the best and her uncle, a notorious louse, doesn't approve, the court would tell her she mustn't?'

'Yes, if he stood to her in loco parentis.'

'Monstrous!'

'It's the law.'

'Who made that law?'

'I couldn't tell you offhand.'

'Well, it's a damned outrage.'

Wilbur Trout, who had been listening with great interest, put the question which would naturally occur to the lay mind.

'What happens if the other intended party tells the court to go fry an egg and marries the girl anyway?'

'He gets sent to prison.'

'You're kidding.'

'No, that's the law. It's a very serious offence.'

'So the way it works out is that you just can't marry a ward of court?'

'Not with near relatives objecting.'

'Well, I wish some of my wives had been wards of court with near relatives objecting,' said Wilbur. 'I'd have saved money.'

V

Shortly after uttering these wistful words Wilbur, having like the stag at eve drunk his fill, left the table, saying that he thought he would go and do a bit more practising in the billiard room, and Gally was at liberty to speak freely.

'Well, this is a nice piece of box fruit, Johnny.'

'Yes.'

'You couldn't have got your facts wrong?'

'No.'

'Then things don't look so good.'

'I've known them better.'

'Why do you suppose Dunstable made her a ward of court?'

John's reply to this was a little brusque. He was not feeling his usual amiable self.

'Considering that it was only about an hour ago that I found out she was one and that I've had no opportunity of asking her since, I can't tell you.'

'It must have been his experience with her brothers that put the idea into his head. He was telling me about them. They both married girls he disapproved of, and no doubt he said to himself that he was not going to have that happen to Linda.'

'Probably.'

'Just the sort of low trick that would have occurred to him.'

'Yes.'

'Is it really true that you would be slapped in the jug if you married her?'

'Yes.'

'You couldn't reason with them and drive it into their fat heads that yours was a special case?'

'No.'

Gally heaved a sigh. He was a doughty warrior and never gave in readily when in receipt of the slings and arrows of outrageous fortune, but reviewing the position of affairs he was compelled to recognize that the outlook could not be called promising. Any knowledgeable turf accountant like Honest Jerry Judson, he felt, would hesitate for a long time before giving odds shorter than a hundred to one against the triumph of young love. And everything till now had seemed to be working out so smoothly.

'It's very bitter,' he said, heaving another sigh, 'that after negotiating with such success all the Becher's Brooks and Canal Turns in love's Grand National we seem to be pipped on the post. Though I ought not to say that. We mustn't be defeatist. Always keep your chin up, is my motto. There must be any number of ways of dealing with the situation.'

'Name three.'

'It will want thought, of course.'

'Quite a good deal.'

'The great thing is that you are solidly established at the castle, cheek by jowl, as you might say, with Dunstable, and so are in an excellent position to ingratiate yourself with him and get him to look on you as a son. He must learn to love you. You must see to it that your nature expands before him like some beautiful flower. You want to get him saying to himself 'By golly, I was all wrong about this chap. Now that I've come to know him better I can see he's the salt of the ruddy earth, and it will be a pleasure and privilege to dance at his wedding.' Have you been to see him yet with sympathetic enquiries?'

'What about?'

'His ankle. He sprained it and is lying prone on a bed of pain. This is your moment. Go and cheer him up.'

'Must I?'

'It might just turn the scale. Do it now.'

'Or tomorrow perhaps? Or the day after?'

'No, now. Why the hesitation?'

'He's rather a formidable character.'

'Nonsense. Mild as a lamb.'

'H'm.'

'Don't say 'H'm'. No one ever got anywhere by sitting on his trouser seat and saying 'H'm'. You want to marry the popsy, don't you? Well, obviously the first step is to give Dunstable the old oil. So off you go. Cluster round him like a porous plaster. Dance before him. Ask him riddles. Tell him bedtime stories. Sing him lullabies. Amuse him with simple card tricks.'

'Well, if you say so,' said John, dubiously.

His acquaintance with the Duke of Dunstable had been brief, but he was conscious of no eagerness to extend it.

10

Lord Emsworth went to bed that night in something of a twitter. To a sensitive man the spectacle of a cascade of people falling downstairs is always disturbing, and his reaction to the events that had preceded the evening meal had been a heightening of the blood pressure similar to that which his doctor down in Wiltshire had warned the Duke against. His nerve centres were still vibrating when he reached his room, and it is not surprising that it was a long time before he was able to get to sleep.

And even when slumber at last came to him it was short-lived, for at about three in the morning there occurred one of those annoying interruptions to repose which are not uncommon in the rural districts. A bat, flitting in the darkness outside, took the wrong turning as it made its nightly rounds and came in through the window which had been left healthfully open. It then proceeded to circle the room in the aimless fat-headed fashion habitual with bats, who are notoriously among the less intellectually gifted of God's creatures. Show me a bat, says the old proverb, and I will show you something that ought to be in some kind of a home.

It was not immediately that Lord Emsworth became aware that he had a room-mate, for when asleep he was difficult to rouse. But after

186

the creature had whizzed past his face once or twice he began to have the feeling, so often experienced by people in ghost stories, that he was not alone. He sat up in bed, blinked several times, and was eventually able to verify this supposition.

Though of a dreamy temperament and inclined in most crises to sit still and let his lower jaw droop, he could on occasion be the man of action. He took up a pillow and by flapping at the intruder with it succeeded at length in persuading it to go outside where it would be appreciated, but by now he was so wide awake that he knew that sleep would be impossible until he had soothed himself by reading a pig book for awhile. He had at his bedside a new one which had arrived by the morning post and he had so far merely dipped into it. He took it up, and was soon engrossed.

It turned out to be one of those startling ultra-modern pig books, the work no doubt of some clever young fellow just down from his agricultural college, and it shocked him a good deal by its avant-garde views on such subjects as swill and bran mash, views which would never have done for orthodox thinkers like Whiffle and Wolff-Lehman. It was, however, undeniably interesting. It gripped. He had to read on to see how it all came out in the end, and, so doing, he arrived at Chapter Five and the passage about the newly-discovered vitamin pill for stimulating the porcine appetite.

'All nonsense', Whiffle would have said, 'Poppycock', Wolff-Lehman would have called it, but on his credulous mind it made a profound impression. It left him feeling like some watcher of the skies when a new planet swims into his ken or like stout Cortez when with eagle eyes he stared at the Pacific. Something on these lines was precisely what he had hoped to find ever since the Empress had declined that potato. Banks, the Market Blandings veterinary surgeon, and Cuthbert Price, his pig man, had tried to lull him into a false security by insisting that no significance was to be attached to what they maintained was a mere passing whim on the noble animal's part, but they had not really set his mind at ease. He remained convinced that an artificial stimulant was needed, and here in Chapter Five of *Pigs At A Glance* was what looked like the very thing. To be administered twice a day in a little skim milk, the author recommended, and while he did not actually say in so many words that if this policy were pursued the patient would leap with wiggling tail on everything on the menu, one could see that he was confident that that was what the outcome would be, for he promised specifically that at least an inch would be added to the waist line in a matter of days.

There was probably some good stuff awaiting him in Chapter Six, but Lord Emsworth was too impatient to lie there and read on. He sprang from his bed, his pince-nez quivering on his nose. J. G. Banks had to be informed of this sensational discovery without an instant's delay. He could hardly wait to get him on the telephone.

He did, however, after finding his bedroom slippers, one of which had hidden itself under the bed, wait for quite an appreciable time, for he had just remembered that the only telephone available was the one in the library, and to reach the library it would be necessary to pass by the room in which his sister Constance slept. And as the picture rose before his eyes of Connie darting out and catching him, he experienced much the same sensation as comes to those who have lived in the East when they get a recurrence of their old malaria.

It was but a passing weakness. He thought of his Crusading ancestors, particularly Sir Pharamond, the one who did so well at the Battle of Joppa. Would Sir Pharamond with all his mentions in dispatches have allowed a sister to intimidate him? Of course it was possible that Sir Pharamond had not had a sister like Connie, but even so . . .

Two minutes later, nerved to his perilous venture, he had started on his way.

II

It is not too much to say that at this point in his progress Lord Emsworth was feeling calm, confident and carefree; but a wise friend, one who had read his Thomas Hardy and learned from that pessimistic author's works how often and how easily human enterprises are ruined by some unforeseen Act of God, would have warned him against any premature complacency. One

189

never knew, he would have pointed out, around what corner Fate might not be waiting with the stocking full of sand. 'Watch your step, Emsworth,' he would have said.

This, however, owing to the darkness which prevailed, Lord Emsworth was unable to do, and there was nothing to tell him that a considerable Act of God was lurking outside Lady Constance's door, all ready for his coming. His first intimation that it was there occurred when he put a foot on it and the world seemed to come to an end not with a whimper but with a bang.

It is to be doubted whether even Sir Pharamond in such circumstances would have been able to preserve his equanimity intact, tough guy though he was admitted to be by his fellow Crusaders. The shock paralysed his descendant. Lord Emsworth stood gulping, gripped by the unpleasant feeling that his spine had come out through the top of his head. He was not a particularly superstitious man, but he had begun to think that night prowling was unlucky for him.

Mingled with his dismay was bewilderment. He recalled how his brother Galahad had urged him not to allow the upsetting of tables in the small hours to become a habit, but this thing with which he had collided was not a table. It was too dark for him to make a definite pronouncement, but it seemed to be a tray containing glass and china, and he could think of no reason why the corridor should be paved with trays.

The explanation was one of those absurdly

simple explanations. Lady Constance sometimes found a difficulty in dropping off to sleep, and her doctor in New York had recommended as an assistance to the sand man a plate of fruit and a glass of warm milk, to be taken last thing at night before retiring to rest. These consumed, it was her practice to put the tray outside her door, ready for the housemaid to remove in the morning and ready also, as has been shown, for her brother Clarence to step into with a forceful bedroom slipper. Thomas Hardy would have seen in the whole affair one more of life's little ironies and on having it drawn to his attention would have got twenty thousand words of a novel out of it.

Conditions being as described, a quicker thinker than Lord Emsworth would have extracted his feet from the debris and faded into the night with a minimum of delay. He, however, continued to stand transfixed, and was still doing so when, just as had happened on his last night out, the door opened and light flashed on the scene. It was accompanied by Lady Constance in a rose-coloured dressing gown, looking like something out of an Elizabethan tragedy. Laying a good deal of emphasis on the first syllable, she said:

'CLARence!'

It is possible that something of the spirit of his ancestors lingered in Lord Emsworth, or it may have been that a shock is always apt to stiffen the sinews of the mildest man. Whatever the motivating cause, he presented a splendidly dauntless front and was swift with the telling riposte. It ran as follows:

'What's that tray doing there?'

It was a testing question, but Lady Constance was not easily worsted in verbal give-and-take. As a girl she had been on the debating team at Roedean. Her reply, and it was a good one, came without hesitation.

'Never mind what *it's* doing. What are *you* doing?'

'Trays all over the floor!'

'Do you know what time it is?'

'I might have injured myself severely.'

'You might also have gone to bed.'

'I've been to bed.'

'Then why didn't you stay there?'

'I couldn't sleep.'

'You could have read a book.'

'I did read a book. It was that new pig book that came this morning. Extraordinarily interesting.'

'Then why aren't you reading it now, instead of wandering about the house at four o'clock?'

She had a point there. Lord Emsworth was a reasonable man, and he could see that. Moreover, the spirit of his ancestors had begun to die out in him, to be replaced by a mood that was apologetic rather than Crusading. He felt that he owed Connie an explanation, and fortunately he had an excellent one to hand.

'I was going to phone Banks.'

'You were *what?*'

'I was going to get Banks on the telephone.'

Lady Constance was obliged to swallow twice before finding further articulation possible.

When she spoke, it was almost in a whisper. Strong woman though she was, he had shaken her.

'Are you under the impression that your bank will be open at four in the morning?'

This illustration of woman's tendency always to get things muddled up amused Lord Emsworth. He smiled indulgently.

'Not my bank. Banks, the vet. I want to tell him about this wonderful vitamin pill for pigs that has just been discovered. It was in the book I was reading.'

Lady Constance swallowed again. She was feeling oddly weak. Lord Emsworth, though not usually observant, noted her agitation, and an idea struck him.

'It's rather late, of course.'

'A little.'

'He may have gone to bed.'

'It is possible.'

'Do you think I ought to wait till after breakfast?'

'I do.'

It was a thought. Lord Emsworth weighed it gravely.

'Yes, you are quite right, Connie,' he said at length. 'Banks might have been annoyed. He wouldn't like having his sleep broken. I see that now. Sensible of you to suggest putting it off. After breakfast will do perfectly well. Then I'll say good night. You'll be getting back to bed, of course?'

'I shall be thankful to.'

'Capital, capital, capital.'

III

The thoughts of youth, said Henry Wadsworth Longfellow (1805-1882), are long long thoughts, and so, when the conditions are right, are those of middle-age. Lady Constance's prevented her going to sleep for quite some time after she was between the sheets again. Her mind was wrestling feverishly with the problem presented by the apparently borderline case with whom she had recently been conversing.

Coming fresh to Lord Emsworth, as it were, after a longish sojourn in New York, where she had met only the most rational of men, dull some of them and inclined to restrict their conversation to the vagaries of the Stock Market, but nevertheless all perfectly rational, she had found him, even more than when last encountered, a fitting object for anxiety.

No sister could view him now without concern. There was an expression she had heard her husband James Schoonmaker use to describe an acquaintance of whose mentality his opinion was low, which seemed to her to fit the ninth Earl of Emsworth like the paper on the wall. It was the expression 'He has not got all his marbles'. What had occurred in the past few days, and particularly what had occurred tonight, had left her with the conviction that, whatever the ninth Earl's merits, he offered an open target for her James's criticism. He was amiable, he was clean, sober and obedient, but the marbles in his possession were virtually non-existent.

Sift the evidence. He wandered to and fro at night, not just one night but practically every night. He tripped over cats that were not there. He asserted that pictures had disappeared which were in full view, staring him in the face. And but for her restraining influence he would have rung up a hardworking veterinary surgeon on the telephone at four in the morning to tell him about vitamin pills for pigs. It was an impressive list of qualifications for admission to some good nursing home where he would get sympathetic treatment and bright cheerful society.

Of course, it might be that the ministrations of this Mr. Halliday would effect an improvement, bringing his stock of marbles up to a passable level, but she was unable to share the confidence which Alaric and her brother Galahad appeared to have in Mr. Halliday. Happening to meet him on her way to her room, she had questioned him as to his methods, and his answers had seemed to her vague and confused. This might no doubt have been due to the inability of an expert to make himself clear to the lay mind, but it had left her uneasy.

And he was so young. That perhaps was where the trouble lay. She had no objection to some men being young — waiters, for instance, or policemen or representatives of the country in the Olympic Games — but in a man whose walk in life was to delve into people's subconscious and make notes of what came up one expected something more elderly.

It was with this thought in her mind, vexing

her like an aching tooth, that Lady Constance fell asleep.

When she woke, it was still there, and her misgivings grew with breakfast, when she had ample opportunity of observing him and weighing him in the balance. She rose from the table more convinced than ever that in the matter of correcting her brother Clarence's deviations from the normal he was far too juvenile a reed on which to lean.

After breakfast she went to the garden suite to see the Duke and give him womanly sympathy, hoping that his injuries would not have had the worst effect on his always uncertain temper. Far less provocation in the past than a sprained ankle had often left him in one of those testy moods when a sympathetic woman closeted with him got the illusion that she was in the presence of something out of the Book of Revelations.

To her relief he appeared reasonably placid. He was sitting up in bed smoking a cigar and reading the local paper, the *Bridgnorth, Shifnal and Albrighton Argus*, with which is incorporated the *Wheat Grower's Intelligencer and Stock Breeder's Gazette*.

'Oh, it's you,' he said.

She would have preferred a more effusive welcome, but she reflected philosophically that it was better than some of the welcomes she might have received. She summoned up a bright smile.

'Well, Alaric, how are you this morning?'

'Rotten.'

'Does your ankle hurt?'

'Like hell.'

196

'Still, it could have been worse.'

'How?'

'You might have broken your neck.'

'Not that blasted head-shrinker's fault I didn't.'

'I wanted to talk to you about Mr. Halliday. I've been thinking about him.'

'So have I. Bullocking into people and boosting them downstairs.'

'He's very young.'

'That's no excuse. When I was his age, I didn't go about boosting people downstairs.'

'I mean I really do not feel he is old enough to be of any help to Clarence. I can't think why you engaged him.'

'Had to engage someone, hadn't we? Emsworth needs the promptest treatment.'

'Yes, that is true. I quite agree with you about that. Do you know, Alaric, he was wandering around the house at three o'clock in the morning. He said he was going to telephone the veterinary surgeon about some vitamin pill for pigs he had found in a book he had been reading.'

'At three o'clock?'

'It was nearer four. He woke me up.'

'So that's why you've got that horrible pasty look,' said the Duke, glad to have solved a mystery. 'You look like something the cat brought in. Always that way if you don't get your proper sleep. Well, there you are, then. His pottiness is spreading, and Halliday's presence is essential. He must get to work immediately, not a moment must be wasted. Today Emsworth phones people at four in the morning, tomorrow he'll probably be saying he's a poached egg. It's a pity in a way that you've got to go back to America. Not that you'd be much use if you hadn't, but the more persons keeping an eye on him the better, and you can't expect me to stay here for ever. As soon as my ankle's all right I must be down in Wiltshire, seeing to it that they're getting on with the repairs to my house. You've got to watch those fellows like a hawk.'

'But, Alaric — '

'They don't do a stroke of work unless you're there to keep after them all the time. I'm not paying them good money just to stand around like statues, nothing moving except their lips as they tell each other dirty stories, and the sooner they understand that, the better.'

'But, Alaric, I am not going to America.'

'Yes, you are.'

'I'm staying here for the rest of the summer.'

'No, you aren't.'

'And James is joining me when he has finished this deal he is working on.'

'No, he isn't. It's going to take him longer than he had expected, and he wants you to come back right away. It's all in his letter. Oh, I forgot to tell you. He's written you a long letter, and it got mixed up with mine.'

A sharp gasp escaped Lady Constance.

'You *read* it?'

'Most of it. I skipped some of the dull bits.'

'Well, really, Alaric!'

'How was I to know it wasn't for me?'

'From the name on the envelope, I should have thought.'

'Didn't notice it.'

'And the opening words.'

'It began 'My darling'. No mention of you at all. What does it matter, anyway? I've given you the gist. No need for you to read it.'

'I want my letter!'

'Then you'll have to crawl under the bed, because that's where it's fallen,' said the Duke with the smugness of a member of Parliament making a debating point. 'The breeze through the window caught it. You'll get pretty dusty, because it's somewhere right at the back.'

Lady Constance bit her lip. It hurt her a little, but it was better than biting Alaric, Duke of Dunstable.

'I will ring for Beach.'

'What's the good of that? Beach can't crawl under beds.'

'He will send the boy who cleans the knives and boots.'

'All right, let the child come. But I'm not going to tip him,' said the Duke, and on this sordid note the conversation ended.

Lady Constance left the sick room in a state of considerable agitation. It always irked her to have to alter her plans, and now it was particularly upsetting. She had been looking forward so eagerly to having her James with her at the castle, not merely because she loved him and felt that a holiday in these peaceful surroundings would do him so much good, but because his calm sensible companionship would be so beneficial to Clarence. The thought of leaving the latter in the care of a mere boy like this immature Halliday, she far away and unable to superintend his course of treatment, chilled her. Who could say what blunders the stripling might not commit? And who, an inner voice reminded her in case she had overlooked it, could say what Clarence might not be up to in her absence? Probably taking all his meals in the library and sneaking off all day and never allowing Halliday to get near him.

She reached her boudoir, rang for Beach, told him to instruct the boy who cleaned the knives and boots to proceed to the garden suite and start crawling: then for several minutes she stood looking out of the window, deep in thought, and was rewarded with an idea.

At the time when his services had been desired Sir Roderick Glossop had not been available, away no doubt on some case to which he had been pledged. But it was possible that he would now be free to spend a few days at the castle, and even a few days of such an expert might be enough. It was at any rate worth trying.

She took up the telephone, and a secretarial voice answered her.

'Sir Roderick Glossop's office.'

'Could I speak to Sir Roderick?'

'Ay am sorry, he is in America. We are turning all our cases over to Sir Abercrombie Fitch. Shall I give you his numbah?'

'No, I think not, thank you. I suppose you mean all the cases not handled by his partner?'

'Pardon?'

'His junior partner.'

'Sir Roderick has no junior partner.'

Lady Constance remained calm, at least as far as her diction was concerned. Ladies never betray emotion, Connie dear, even on the telephone.

'There seems to be some confusion. I am Lady Constance Schoonmaker, speaking from Blandings Castle in Shropshire. There is a young man at the castle named Halliday who according to my brother is Sir Roderick Glossop's junior partner. You know nothing of him? He could not be Sir Abercrombie Fitch's partner?'

'Sir Abercrombie has no partner.'

'You are sure?'

There came a sharp intake of breath at the other end of the wire. The question had given offence. You cannot go about asking secretaries if they are sure. Ice crept into this one's reply.

'Ay am quate sure.'

'Thank you,' said Lady Constance, but her tone as she offered these thanks was not warm. She replaced the receiver, breathed heavily once or twice, and went off on winged feet to see the Duke. The situation, to her mind, called for clarification, and he was the man to clarify it.

The doctor was with him when she burst into the bedroom, and she was obliged to wait fuming while he went about his bathing and bandaging, accompanying his activities with amiable observations on the weather and other subjects. At long last he said Well, we seem to be getting on quite nicely, and took his departure, and the Duke relit the cigar which he had temporarily laid aside.

'Seems a pretty competent chap, that chap,' he

said. 'What would he make a year, do you think? Can't be much money in being a country doctor, though my fellow down in Wiltshire does fairly well. But then he has a number of good steady alcoholics, which always helps.'

Lady Constance was in no mood to speculate on the incomes of rural physicians. She plunged without delay into what lawyers call the *res*.

'Alaric, I want to know all about this man Halliday.'

The Duke puffed at his cigar for some moments as if turning this demand over in his mind.

'How do you mean all about him? I don't know anything about him except that he's Glossop's junior partner and has the ruddy audacity to want to marry my niece. But I've put a stopper on that all right. She's a ward of court and can't get spliced without my consent, and he's got about as much chance of getting that as he has of flying to the moon. If he thinks he can spend all his time bullocking people downstairs like a charging rhinoceros and expect to marry their nieces, he's very much mistaken. He was in here last night trying to suck up to me, but I sent him off with a flea in his ear.'

Lady Constance had come to the room with the intention of confining the discussion of John to his claim to be a figure in the psychiatric world, but this extraordinary statement led her to broaden the scope of her enquiries.

'What did you say?' she gasped. 'He wants to marry your niece?'

'That's what he says. In love with her, apparently.'

'But he only got here last night. How can he be in love with her if he's only known her a few hours?'

'See that?' said the Duke. 'I've blown a ring.'

Lady Constance's interest in smoke rings was on a par with that which she felt for the finances of members of the medical profession practising in the country. She repeated her question, and the Duke said Yes, that had puzzled him, too.

'But Threepwood tells me the fellow's known her for a long time. Been giving her ardent glances and bottles of scent for months, blast his impudence. Threepwood was saying something about their having quarrelled about something and the fellow jumped at the opportunity of coming here because he hoped that if he was on the spot he could square himself. He's Threepwood's godson, by the way. Just the sort of young hound who would be. Why are you looking like a dying duck?'

Lady Constance was looking like a dying duck because a sudden bright light had flashed upon her. The mists had cleared, and she saw what is generally described as all. She was in possession of the facts, and they could have only one interpretation. Like a serpent, though perhaps not altogether like a serpent, for serpents do draw the line somewhere, her brother Galahad had introduced another impostor into the castle.

Blandings Castle in recent years had been particularly rich in impostors. One or two of them had had other sponsors, but as a rule it was Gally who sneaked them in, and the realization that he had done it again filled her, as she had so

203

often been filled before, with a passionate desire to skin him with a blunt knife.

Once, when they were children, Galahad had fallen into the deep pond in the kitchen garden, and just as he was about to sink for the third time one of the gardeners had come along and pulled him out. She was brooding now on the thoughtless folly of that misguided gardener. Half the trouble in the world, she was thinking, was caused by people not letting well alone.

She strode purposefully to the bell, and pressed it, a gesture that puzzled the Duke.

'What,' he asked, 'do you think you're doing?'

'I am ringing for Beach.'

'I don't want Beach.'

'I do,' said Lady Constance grimly. 'I am going to send him to tell Mr. Halliday that I would like a word with him.'

11

It was Gally's practice, when he favoured Blandings Castle with a visit, to repair after breakfast to the hammock on the front lawn and there to ponder in comfort on whatever seemed to him worth pondering on. It might be the Cosmos or the situation in the Far East, it might be merely the problem of whether or not to risk a couple of quid on some horse running in the 2.30 at Catterick Bridge. This morning, as was natural in a conscientious godfather, his thoughts were concentrated on the sad case of his stricken godson, and when, after he had been giving it the cream of his intellect for some ten minutes, he opened his eyes and became aware that John was standing beside him, he broached the subject without preamble.

'Hullo, Johnny, I was just thinking about you. How did you get on with Dunstable last night? Was he chummy?'

John's voice as he replied was sombre, as was his whole appearance. He looked like a young man who had had even less sleep than that notorious night bird the ninth Earl of Emsworth.

'Not very,' he said briefly.

The words and the tone in which they were uttered were damping, but Gally refused to be damped.

'Don't let that worry you.'

'No?'

'Certainly not. You couldn't expect him to be brimming over with the milk of human kindness right away. One of the lessons life teaches us is never to look for instant bonhomie from someone we have rammed in the small of the back and bumped down two flights of stairs. That sort of thing does something to a man. I noticed when I was talking to him that the iron seemed to have entered into his soul quite a bit.'

'I got that impression, too. Apparently he thinks I did it on purpose.'

'Very unjust. Better men than you have slipped on those stairs, myself for one. Still, you might have been more careful. No doubt you wanted your cocktail, but you needn't have come rushing to get it.'

'I wasn't rushing. Do you know, Gally, I had a feeling that somebody had pushed me.'

'Absurd. People don't go pushing people downstairs even at Blandings Castle.'

'No, I suppose it was just my imagination.'

'Must have been. But never mind that. The important thing is did you soothe him?'

'No.'

'You asked after his ankle?'

'Yes.'

'And when he had stopped talking about that?'

'I said I believed he had known my father at one time.'

'Oh, my God!'

'Was that a mistake?'

'The gravest of errors. He couldn't stand your father. He once hit him with a cold turkey.'

'He hit my father?'

'No, your father hit him. It was one night when we were all having supper at Romano's, and they had disagreed about the apostolic claims of the church of Abyssinia, which was odd because it was generally about politics that Stiffy disagreed with people. The supper had been a festive one, to celebrate the victory of a horse on whom as the result of a tip from the stable we had all had our bit, and I suppose they were both somewhat flushed with wine, for this argument started. Dunstable maintained that those claims were perfectly justified, and your father said the church of Abyssinia was talking through its hat, and things got more and more heated, and finally Dunstable took up a bowl of fruit salad and was about to strike your father with it, when your father grabbed this turkey, which was on a side table with the other cold viands, and with one blow laid him out as flat as a crepe suzette. The unfortunate thing was that it was all over so rapidly that one had no opportunity of placing a wager on the outcome. Otherwise, I would have cleaned up by putting my little all on Stiffy, whom I knew as a man never to be more feared than when with cold turkey in hand. I had once seen him stun a fellow named Percy Pound with the same blunt instrument. So Dunstable has not forgotten and forgiven after thirty years. At least I gather from your manner that the episode still rankles.'

'He certainly went up in the air when I said whose son I was.'

'It just shows what a beautiful cold turkey your father used to swing in his prime. I have always thought it a pity that there was no event of that kind in the Olympic Games. But do you know what I find the strangest aspect of the whole affair? That either of them should ever have heard of the church of Abyssinia. You wouldn't have thought they would have recognized the church of Abyssinia if it had been served up to them on a plate with watercress round it. Yes, Beach?'

Unobserved by them, Beach had approached the hammock, panting a little, for he had been instructed to make haste and he was not the slim footman he had been eighteen years ago.

'Her ladyship would be glad if she could have a word with Mr. Halliday, Mr. Galahad.'

Gally had removed his eyeglass and had been polishing it. He replaced it, but with the feeling that he might soon have to polish it again. Long experience had taught him to expect trouble when Connie wanted words with people.

'Any idea what about?'

'No, Mr. Galahad. Her ladyship did not confide in me.'

'Well, better give her five minutes, Johnny.'

Left alone, Gally returned to his meditations. It was a lovely morning of blue skies and summer scents. Birds twittered, bees buzzed, insects droned, and from the stable yard came the soft sound of chauffeur Voules playing his harmonica. The cat which helped Lord Emsworth upset tables sauntered along and jumped on Gally's stomach. He tickled it behind the ear with his customary courtesy, but he tickled with a heavy heart. He was musing on John, and he was uneasy. He had said that they must not be defeatist, but it was extremely difficult to avoid being so. With Connie wanting words with John, he could not regard the position of affairs as good.

As he lay there, frowning thoughtfully, he was made aware that he had another visitor. Linda was standing by the hammock. She was wearing the unmistakeable air of a ward of court who has recently learned that an injunction of restraint is about to be made against the other intending party, and he saw that she would need a good deal of cheering up if the roses were to be brought back to her cheeks. As buoyantly as he could he said:

'Hullo, my dear. I was just chatting with this cat. Have you seen Johnny?'

'No.'

'He was here a moment ago. He went in to talk to my sister Connie. I don't know how long she'll keep him, but after they're through he ought to look in on your foul uncle again.'

'Has he seen Uncle Alaric?'

'Last night. In the flesh.'

'What happened?'

'Nothing very good to report so far, but it was a start. The thing for him to do now is to keep popping in on the old bounder and omitting no word or act which may help to conciliate him. If he plays his cards right, I don't see why a beautiful friendship should not result.'

'Very unlikely.'

Gally adjusted the cat on his stomach, and frowned disapprovingly.

'You mustn't talk like that.'

'Well, I do.'

'It's not the right spirit. You ought to be saying to yourself 'Who can resist Johnny?''

'And the answer would be 'Uncle Alaric can'.'

There was a silence, except of course for the birds, the bees, the insects and Voules the chauffeur's harmonica. Linda broke it with a question. It was one that had been constantly in her thoughts.

'Do you think you really do go to prison if you marry a ward of court when they've told you not to?'

Gally would have given much to be able to reply in the negative, instancing the cases of fellows at the Pelican who had done it dozens of times with impunity, but facts had to be faced.

'I'm afraid so. Johnny says you do, and he ought to know.'

'Suppose I told them he's the only man in the world I can be happy with and I'll just pine away to a shadow if I can't get him. Mightn't they skip the red tape?'

'I doubt it. These chaps who make the laws of England are pretty hardboiled blokes. No sentiment.'

'Johnny says he's quite willing to take a chance.'

'Don't let him. Don't dream of letting him.'

'Of course I won't. Do you think I'm going to have that precious lamb sewing mail bags in an underground dungeon where he'll be gnawed to the bone by rats? It's so unfair,' cried Linda passionately. 'Just because I'm female, I mean. Both my brothers married girls Uncle Alaric couldn't stand at any price, but he couldn't make them wards of his beastly court because they were men. He huffed and puffed, but there wasn't a thing he could do about it. But just because I'm a — '

She broke off abruptly. Jno Robinson's station taxi had drawn up at the front door, and from the front door Beach emerged bearing a suitcase. He was followed by John. He placed the suitcase in the cab, and John climbed in after it. Jno Robinson set his Arab steed in motion and with a clang and a clatter it vanished down the drive, just as Linda with another passionate cry made for the house.

There was a pensive look on Gally's face as he removed the cat and extricated himself from the hammock. He did not need to be told what lay behind these peculiar happenings. How it had come about he could not say, but plainly his best-laid plans had gone agley, just as the poet Burns had warned him they might. He reached automatically for his eyeglass and was polishing it meditatively when Linda returned.

'He's gone!' she said in a hollow voice.

'Yes, I saw.'

'Lady Constance has thrown him out.'

'I gathered that.'

'I don't understand,' said Linda, who seemed dazed. 'Beach says it's because she has found out he's not a psychoanalyst. Why should he be a psychoanalyst? Lots of people aren't. It doesn't make sense.'

Gally shook his head sadly. To him it made sense.

'I think I can explain,' he said, 'but later, when

we have more leisure. It's a long story. How does Beach know all this?'

'His shoelace had come untied outside Lady Constance's door, and he stooped to tie it.'

'And happened to overhear what was passing within?'

'Yes.'

Her story rang true to Gally, though he found it hard to believe that a man of Beach's build could have stooped.

'This,' he said, 'undeniably complicates things. I had been relying on Johnny making an extended stay at the castle with plenty of time to work on your ghastly uncle and gradually get him into a more reasonable frame of mind. We are now in something of a dilemma. But don't despair. There must be a way out, there's always a way out of everything, and I'm sure to spot it sooner or later. Hullo, here's Beach again, and five will get you ten that he's come to tell me her ladyship would like a word with me. Yes, Beach?'

'Her ladyship would like a word with you, Mr. Galahad.'

'Then what a pity,' said Gally, 'that she isn't going to get it.'

'Sir?'

'You hunted high and low, you turned stones and explored avenues, but you couldn't find me. You think I must have gone to Market Blandings to buy tobacco. That is your story, Beach, and be careful to tell it without any of the hesitations and stammerings which are so apt to arouse suspicion in the auditor. Above all, remember not to stand on one leg. What you will be aiming at in her ladyship is that willing suspension of disbelief dramatic critics are always talking about. Tell your tale so that it can be swallowed. In this way much unpleasantness will be avoided,' said Gally.

He was an intrepid man and was not afraid of his sister Constance. He merely thought it wiser not to confer with her until the hot blood had had time to cool. He had pursued the same policy in the past with Honest Jerry Judson and Tim Simms the Safe Man.

II

Beach made the telling of his tale as succinct as possible, and after Lady Constance had clicked her tongue, as she did on receipt of the news, he did not linger to offer her silent sympathy for her disappointment, but passed from the presence as quickly as was within the scope of a man of his portliness. He was anxious to get back to his pantry and resume the perusal of a letter which had come for him by the morning post.

The letter was from a Mrs. Gerald Vail, formerly Miss Penelope Donaldson, younger daughter of the Mr. Donaldson of Donaldson's Dog Joy whose elder daughter had married Lord Emsworth's son Freddie. During her recent visit to the castle a warm friendship had sprung up between her and Beach, and since her marriage to the health cure establishment in which her husband was a partner they had been in regular correspondence. She would give him the latest hot news from the health cure establishment, and he would reciprocate with an up-to-date account of doings at Blandings Castle.

Her letters were always fraught with interest, for the health cure establishment as seen through her eyes appeared to be peopled by eccentrics of the first water, and he chafed at any interruption which delayed the reading of them. It was consequently with annoyance that as he crossed the hall he found his progress arrested by Vanessa Polk. He liked and admired Vanessa Polk, but he wanted to get to his pantry.

'Oh, Beach,' said Vanessa, 'I'm looking for Mr. Trout. You haven't seen him, have you?'

'No, miss.'

'Very difficult finding people in a place this size. What Blandings Castle needs is a troupe of bloodhounds. I'd see that a few were laid on, if I were you. You never know when they won't come in handy. Well, if you see him, tell him I'm up on the roof.'

She passed on, and he was able to continue heading for the pantry.

The letter was on the table where he had left it when rung for by Lady Constance, and he resumed his reading of it with the enjoyment Penny Vail's letters always gave him. He had just reached the postscript, when the door opened and Gally came in. Thinking it over, Gally said, he had come to the conclusion that Beach's pantry was the one spot in the castle where a man with whom Lady Constance would like to have a word could feel safe from having that word said to him.

214

'The chance of her ladyship dropping in on you for a glass of port and a gossip is, I take it, slim. And it's nice to get away from the women now and then. I have read in novels that there is nothing more delightful than a tête-à-tête with a cultured member of the other sex, and perhaps there isn't, but the time for it should be carefully chosen. It's not a thing to rush into with your eyes shut. Having stooped to tie your shoelace outside her door while she was in conference with Mr. Halliday, you are aware that the lady up top is for the moment better avoided. Later on, possibly . . .'

Gally paused. His auditor, he saw, was not giving him his attention. Beach, usually so imperturbable except when visitors put water in their claret, was showing unmistakeable signs of agitation.

'Something the matter, Beach?'

'Yes, indeed, Mr. Galahad.'

'Tell me all.'

'I fear this will come as a shock.'

'What does one more shock matter nowadays? Explode your bomb.'

'I have received a letter from Mrs. Vail.'

'Who? Oh, Penny. Nothing sensational about that, is there? You told me you corresponded regularly.'

'Yes, Mr. Galahad. But in this letter she . . . I must mention that in my last communication I informed Mrs. Vail that we had the daughter of the well-known American financier Mr. J. B. Polk staying with us. I thought it might interest her.'

'I don't know why it should, but go on.'

'And in her reply . . . this is what gave me such a shock, Mr. Galahad . . . she states that Mr. Polk has no daughter.'

'What!'

'Precisely that, Mr. Galahad.'

'Well, I'll be dashed.'

'And Mrs. Vail cannot be mistaken. She says in her letter that her father Mr. Donaldson is an intimate friend of Mr. Polk.'

'So she would know if he had a daughter.'

'Exactly, Mr. Galahad. One is reluctantly forced to the conclusion that the lady calling herself Miss Polk is an impostor.'

'And presumably up to something. I wonder what.'

A respectful shrug of his ample shoulders indicated that this was a mystery that Beach was unable to solve. Gally stood frowning.

'Well,' he said, 'the obvious thing is to go and ask her. Any idea where she is?'

'Yes, Mr. Galahad. She informed me that she was about to visit the roof.'

'When was that?'

'Only a short time ago.'

'Then she's probably still up there. I'll go and see.'

Gally spoke without enthusiasm. It would be necessary, he realized, when he met Vanessa, to be stern and austere, and sternness and austerity did not come easily to him. He was by nature a tolerant man, always inclined to let everyone do what he or she liked. It was a frame of mind habitual with members of the Pelican Club. 'Nothing to do with me', the Pelicans would say if they saw someone up to something, and Gally always said the same.

But this was a special case. Here he was in a sense representing the family, and whatever this girl was contemplating it was presumably something opposed to the family interests. He must not allow an easygoing Pelican-Club-bred turn of mind or his liking for her, which was considerable, to put him in the position of an indulgent spectator.

All that was clear enough. Nevertheless he was not happy as he started on his mission. He was about to have a tete-a-tete with a cultured member of the other sex, but he was not looking forward to it.

III

Though not much frequented by residents and visitors, the roof was a feature of Blandings Castle that well repaid inspection, for from it it was possible to see a fascinating panorama of Shropshire and its adjoining counties. To reach it the explorer went past the great gatehouse, where a channel of gravel separated the west wing from the centre block, and came on a small door leading to mysterious stone steps. Mounting these, he found himself on a vast flat surface bordered by battlements, on its edge the flagstaff from which flew the gay flag announcing, in case the information was of any interest to anyone, that Clarence, ninth Earl of Emsworth, was on the premises. As a boy, when it had so often been imperative to find a quiet hideaway when his father was looking for him, Gally had spent many a happy hour there.

Vanessa was standing gazing over the battlements. He hailed her, and she turned with a start.

'Oh hi,' she said.

'Hi to you,' said Gally. No sense in being stern and austere till one had to. 'Taking a look at the countryside?'

'It's a wonderful view. What's that hill over there?'

'The Wrekin.'

'Where's this Bredon that A. E. Housman writes about?'

'Good heavens, do you read Housman?'

'Why not?'

The discomfort Gally had been feeling became intensified. She seemed so wholesome, so like the sort of girl you brought home to meet mother. To denounce her was not going to be easy, and for an instant he toyed with the idea of abandoning the whole project. Curiosity was probably what decided him to continue. Sleep at night would be impossible until he had informed himself of her motives in undertaking the perilous task of starting funny business with so hard-boiled an egg as Connie.

'You're a very remarkable girl,' he said.

'Because I read poetry?'

'I was thinking more of what you do when you aren't reading poetry. Only a very remarkable girl would have been capable of doing what you did.'

'What was that?'

'Kidding my sister Constance into believing that you are the daughter of J. B. Polk. I learn from a reliable source close to him that he hasn't one.'

Gally paused, inviting comment. When it came, it was not the comment he had expected. He had been prepared for the guilty start, the sudden pallor and possibly the flood of tears, but he had not anticipated that she would be amused. She laughed, a jolly ringing laugh, the laugh of a girl with a sense of humour who can join in the merriment though the joke is on her.

'I was afraid this might happen,' she said. 'I read it in the tea leaves.'

'It's surprising that it didn't happen sooner. I'd have thought you would have come a purler at the first fence. Connie's married to a big pot in the world of finance. Polk is also a big pot in that world. The betting would have been that she was bound to have met him. Why didn't she?'

'Mr. Polk doesn't meet anyone. He's a recluse. The only person he sees outside business hours is a Mr. Donaldson who sells dog biscuits.'

'And Donaldson has a daughter who is a great friend of Beach. She was the reliable source I mentioned. Beach has just had a letter from her in which she states that J. B. Polk has neither chick nor child.'

'He would hate having either. He lives alone with four dogs and seven cats, and loves it.'

'You seem to know a lot about him.'

'Oh, one gets around. As a matter of fact, I'm his secretary.'

'I see. And as a good secretary should, you look on him as a father. So when you told Connie you were his daughter, you were just speaking figuratively.'

'I like that way of putting it.'

'It is rather tactful. Connie would say in her blunt way that you had wormed yourself in under a false name.'

'Who's wormed herself in under a false name? Not me. I may have gone a little astray in describing myself as J. B's daughter, but I'm Miss Polk all right. My father was P. P. Polk, formerly from Norfolk, later an American citizen. Polk's a good Norfolk name.'

'Is it?'

'So they tell me.'

'Don't two Polks in the office cause confusion? If I walked in and shouted 'Polk!', which of you would bound forward?'

'Neither of us. You wouldn't have a hope of seeing him or me without an appointment. But if what you're trying to say is Did the coincidence of our having the same name distress J. B. Polk, the answer is No. He was amused. In fact, I think that's why he made me his confidential secretary.'

'Confidential, eh?'

'Very confidential. J. B. has no secrets from me.'

'Must be a well-paid job.'

'Very.'

'Then,' said Gally, frankly bewildered, 'I don't get it. What's your game?'

'I beg your pardon?'

'What are you after? Are you working for some museum that wants to get hold of Clarence's bedroom slippers? The Smithsonian would probably pay a large sum for them. Are you connected with a secret society which is plotting to kidnap Beach? Dash it, my good wench, you must have had *some* reason for coming here under false pretences.'

'It's quite simple. I wanted to see Blandings Castle.'

'Just that?'

'Just that.'

Something of the sternness which had so far been absent from it crept into Gally's manner. He spoke severely.

'I resent having my leg pulled.'

'I'm not pulling your leg. I wanted to see it, and when I say see it, I mean *see* it. Live in it, soak myself in it, not just come on Visitors Day and be one of a mob shown around by the butler.'

Gally could make nothing of this.

'This is most extraordinary. Gratifying, of course, to one of the family to hear such a plug for the old dosshouse, but where did you get all this enthusiasm? I wouldn't have thought that living in New York you would ever have heard of Blandings Castle. We aren't Buckingham Palace or the Tower of London.'

'That was my mother.'

'What do you mean, that was your mother? What *was* your mother?'

'She used to talk about Blandings all the time when I was a child — or chick, if you prefer it.

The park, the lake, the yew alley, the amber drawing-room, everything. It fascinated me. I could never have enough of it, and I made up my mind that some day I'd get there.'

'And you've got.'

'Temporarily, shall we say.'

'But how did your mother become such an authority on the place? Used she to stay here?'

'In a sense. She was one of the parlourmaids.'

'What!'

'That surprises you?'

'It does indeed. You're not pulling my leg again?'

'Why again? I've never pulled your leg.'

'I suggest, as my godson would say, that you are. How on earth would a Blandings parlourmaid get to New York?'

'It can be done, given the right sequence of events. My father was valet to an American millionaire. They came to the castle on a visit. My father was naturally thrown into my mother's society. They fell in love and got married, and then they all three went back to America, where they lived happily till after several years the millionaire died of a heart attack. All straight so far?'

'Quite.'

'As for my becoming J. B. Polk's girl Friday and the friend of Lady Constance, that perhaps requires a lengthier explanation. Would you care to hear the story of my life?'

'I'd love it. Not omitting your reasons for settling in as J. B. Polk's daughter.'

'No, I'll be coming to that. But first, I think, a

cigarette, if you've got one.'

Gally produced his case. Vanessa stood looking over the battlements, a rather rapt expression on her face.

'I suppose your ancestors used to pour boiling lead on people from up here?' she said.

'All the time. Made them jump.'

'That's just the sort of thing I find so romantic about the place.'

'I can see how you might. Very attractive, those old English customs. But don't go wandering off on the subject of my ancestors. Let's have the story.'

'Ready?'

'And waiting.'

'Then away we go. Where did the last instalment end?'

'Death of millionaire.'

'Oh, yes. Well, he left my father a bit of money, enough to buy a little restaurant. It prospered, and I was able to go to a good school and after that to college. I had always wanted to be a secretary, so I boned up on shorthand and efficiency and all that, and I got a job, then a better job, till climbing the ladder rung by rung I got taken on by Polk Enterprises, finally, as told in an earlier chapter, becoming J. B. Polk's confidential secretary. Am I boring you?'

'Not at all.'

'It sounds pretty dull to me. But keep on listening, for the plot now thickens. One day about three weeks ago I came into the office and found my employer tearing what remained of his hair. It seemed that he had a colossal law suit on, with millions at stake, and he had just learned on the grapevine that the opposition were going to subpoena me as a witness. And if I gave evidence about a certain letter he had dictated to me, he would be in a spot. The letter apparently had been lost, but I could testify to its contents, and bang would go all hope of his winning the case. See where I'm heading?'

'I think so.'

'I'm sure you do. He told me I must get out of the country quick. England, he said, would be the best place to lie hid, which suited me, because though I had heard so much about England I had never been there. He gave me liberal expense money and booked me a passage on the boat. That's how I came to meet Lady Constance. And now you will be wanting to know how she came to mistake me for J. B's daughter.'

'Just what I was going to ask.'

'It came about quite naturally. After we had got friendly she used to talk a lot about Blandings Castle, but though I made it clear enough that I was perfectly willing to join her there she did not issue an invitation. It was as if she was wary about getting too friendly with strangers she met on ocean liners. And then one day the ship's paper had a bit in it about J. B. Polk, something about his dogs and cats, and she asked me if I was any relation, and feeling that it might just turn the scale and bring about the happy ending I said I was his daughter. It did turn the scale. I got my invitation instantly. That is how our heroine comes to be at Blandings

Castle. And now,' said Vanessa, 'I suppose I had better be going and starting my packing.'

Gally stared at her, amazed.

'You aren't thinking of leaving?'

'I certainly am. I don't propose to be among those present when you pass my story along to Lady Constance. You don't catch me waiting to be looked at through a lorgnette as if I were a deceitful cockroach. Never outstay your welcome is the motto of this branch of the Polks.'

It was very rarely that Gally, who prided himself on his ability to preserve an unmoved front on all occasions, was heard to emit a gasp of horrified incredulity, but he did so now. It sounded like the bursting of a paper bag.

'You don't think I'm going to squeal to Connie?'

'Aren't you?'

'Of course I'm not.'

'But I'm an impostor.'

'And why shouldn't you be? Practically everyone else who comes here is. Man and boy I have seen more impostors at Blandings Castle than you could shake a stick at in a month of Sundays. It would have surprised me greatly if you *hadn't* been an impostor. You've gone to endless trouble to get here. Do you think I'm going to dash the cup from your lips? Secrecy and silence, my wench, secrecy and silence.'

Vanessa was visibly moved.

'I call that pretty good of you.'

'Not at all.'

'I don't know what to say.'

'Say nothing. And I'll impress it upon Beach

that he must do the same. His lips must be sealed. I'll go and seal them now,' said Gally.

He had scarcely trotted off, all zeal and willingness to oblige, when Wilbur Trout appeared on the roof.

Wilbur was looking pale and anxious. He had just come from the portrait gallery, where he had been scrutinizing the reclining nude with a good deal less enthusiasm than he usually accorded it.

At the time when she had outlined it, Wilbur, it may be remembered, had expressed whole-hearted approval of Vanessa's scheme for the picture's removal, but with the passing of the hours doubts had set in. Except in the matter of marrying blondes he was not an adventurous man, and contemplation of the shape of things to come, as sketched out by Vanessa, had had the worst effect on his nervous system.

When, therefore, her opening words as he joined her on the roof were 'Willie, we'll have to get that picture tonight', it was with panic rather than joy that his heart leaped up. His emotions were not unlike those which he had experienced in mid-air as he dived into the Plaza fountain — regret that he had undertaken something which had seemed a good idea at the time, and the disturbing realization that it was too late to go back now.

Having gulped twice, he said:

'Why the hurry?'

'Essential, I'm afraid. If Lady Constance finds out — '

'Finds out what?'

'Something about me.'

226

'What about you?'

'Something Gally Threepwood has discovered. If she hears of it, I shall be thrown out of the place on my ear not more than sixty seconds later. He says he won't breathe a word, but you can't be sure. It's such a good story that he may not be able to resist telling it. No, we can't take a chance. Chesney will have got to London by now. I'll phone him this afternoon and tell him to be waiting under the window at two in the morning. You can go to sleep till then. I'll knock on your door and wake you. What's the matter? You don't seem pleased.'

'Oh, I am.'

'You ought to be. Think of having that picture for your very own. You ought to be strewing roses from your hat. Though Genevieve would say 'woses', wouldn't she?'

'She always did.'

'No wonder you miss her,' said Vanessa.

12

The alarm clock beside Vanessa's bed tinkled softly, announcing that the hour was two in the morning, and she sat up and brushed the last vestiges of sleep from her attractive eyes. She had retired early in order to approach the tasks of the night with a clear mind, and it was with a clear mind that she now examined the programme in detail and found it satisfactory. She had the torch and the stout cord which is so essential when pictures of stout nudes in stout frames have to be lowered from second storey windows, and in addition to these she had remembered to equip herself with a large flask in case her colleague's morale should require building up. It was a possibility that unquestionably had to be budgetted for. At their last meeting she had noticed that he seemed to be suffering from an attack of nerves, but nothing, she felt, that a good flask could not cure.

Strange, she was thinking, that a big strong man who had once won fame on the football field should be so timorous in a situation which she, a poor weak woman, was regarding merely as a pleasant and stimulating deviation from the dull round of everyday life, but timorous apparently he was. Where she looked forward with bright anticipation to what lay before them, he, unless her senses deceived her, was what Lady Macbeth would have called infirm of purpose. A flask, accordingly, would seem to be indispensable.

As she slipped a becoming peignoir over her pyjamas, she mused on Wilbur and was surprised at the warmth and tenderness with which she found herself thinking of him.

At the time of their brief engagement he had aroused in her only a mild liking, but in these last days at Blandings Castle liking had become something more.

No question that for her he was an easy man to get along with — pleasant, amiable and speaking her own language. Not too many brains, either, which was an added attraction, for she mistrusted clever men. Too bad, she thought, that he was such an answer to the gold-digger's prayer. What he needed was someone to look after him, to protect him, to check that disastrous tendency of his to make a fool of himself at the slightest opportunity, and unfortunately there was no chance that she would be able to take on the assignment, for once in possession of the picture he would be off with it to New York, and the next thing she would hear would be that he had married another repulsive female and more work for the divorce lawyers. It saddened her.

However, brooding on the matrimonial future of Wilbur Trout was not business. Briskly she collected cord, torch and flask and started to grope her way along the dark corridor.

Wilbur's room was the one in which, according to legend, an Emsworth of the fifteenth century had dismembered his wife with a battle axe, as husbands in those days were so apt to do when the strain of married life became too much for them. The unfortunate woman must have experienced a good deal of apprehension when she heard him at the door, but not much more than did Wilbur when Vanessa's knock sounded in the silent night. Not even Lord Emsworth at the top of his table-upsetting form could have produced a deeper impression. After lying awake for several hours he had at last fallen into a doze, and the knock had coincided with the point in his nightmare when a bomb had exploded under his feet.

What was causing Wilbur's lack of enthusiasms for tonight's operation was principally the fact that it was at Blandings Castle that it was to be carried out. He feared interruption by the castle's chatelaine. What the Duke had described as Lady Constance's habit of coming the *grande dame* over people had daunted him from their first meeting, when she had been in a mood much the same as that in which she had greeted John. In his wide experience he had never encountered anything like her before, and what was chilling him as he answered Vanessa's knock was the thought that she might join them just as they were getting down to the work of the night. His imagination pictured her striding into the portrait gallery with a 'What the hell goes on here?', or whatever it is that British aristocrats said when they found their guests looting the premises at two in the morning. Contemplating his chances of getting through till daybreak without a nervous breakdown, he thought very little of them.

It was consequently with profound relief that

he saw the flask, and not for the first time since their reunion he was conscious of a surge of admiration for this super-efficient girl who thought of everything.

'Gimme,' he said, for at times like this he was a man of few words, and she gave it to him. What seemed a torchlight procession wandering through his interior had the effect of banishing temporarily the terror beneath which he had cringed, and it was with quite a gay insouciance that he said:

'You look like a million dollars in that bath robe.'

It was a stately compliment, and Vanessa accepted it gratefully.

'It happens to be a peignoir, Willie, but thanks for the kind words.'

'Genevieve has one rather like that.'

Vanessa's lips tightened, but she controlled herself. There was nothing in her voice to show that he had touched on a distasteful subject.

'Has she now? That's very interesting. Tell me more about Genevieve.'

The request seemed to find Wilbur at a loss. He fingered his chin dubiously.

'There isn't much to tell.'

'Search the memory.'

'She was a great looker.'

'I'll bet.'

'Blonde.'

'I was betting on that, too.'

'She hadn't much to say.'

'One of those strong, silent girls.'

'Except when she got mad at me.'

'That made her chatty?'

'Generally. Though sometimes she would just throw things at me.'

'What sort of things?'

'Oh, anything that came to hand.'

'Woses, perhaps?'

'And she used to lock me out a good deal. I remember one time we got arguing about something at a night club, and she beat it back to the apartment, and when I got there she had smashed every stick of the furniture with a poker, all the pictures and everything. 'Hi, honey', she said. 'I've been cleaning house.' Then she chased me out with the poker.'

'And then she got a divorce?'

'Soon after that.'

'On what grounds?'

'Inhuman cruelty.'

'Poor soul, how she must have suffered.'

'But of course the real reason was that she had got this crush on this trumpeter.'

'Oh yes, I was forgetting the trumpeter. Not in a name band, I think you told me.'

'No, that's what puzzled me. I always thought she was kind of choosy about who she mixed with.'

'Very much the lady?'

'Oh, quite.'

'Well, it ought to be some consolation to you to think that she's chasing him with a poker now. Finished that flask?'

'There's still a little left.'

'Save it for a celebration later. Come on,' said Vanessa. 'Let's go.'

It had been her intention to confine the illumination of the proceedings to the torch, but it's thin gleam made the portrait gallery seem so sinister and ghostly that in deference to Wilbur's tremors she switched on the light. She could hardly have done anything more encouraging to those tremors. The sudden brilliance threatened to undo all the stiffening of the backbone he had derived from the flask's liquid fire. It revealed rows of Emsworth ancestors staring out of their frames with a silent rebuke which had the worst effect on his nervous system. He had not been present when the Duke in an inspired flight had compared them to the occupants of the Chamber of Horrors at Madame Tussaud's, but had he been he would have endorsed the critique with the utmost fervour. The Earls, in his opinion, were bad enough, but their Countesses eclipsed them. To his fevered eye they all looked like Lady Constance's twin sisters.

'Gimme that flask again,' he muttered.

Vanessa performed the humane act as requested, but she did it absently like one whose thoughts were elsewhere. Though not oppressed as was Wilbur by the Earls and Countesses, she had lost the gay exuberance with which she had started out on this expedition. A feeling that something was wrong was beginning to creep over her.

Two o'clock sharp, she had told Howard Chesney on the telephone that afternoon, and he had said 'Okay, two o'clock sharp. Right', but though it was now long past the hour a glance from the window showed that he was not at his post. In the world outside there were rabbits, weasels, moths, bats and even the white owl of which Gally had spoken to John, but no Howard Chesney. Beach would have felt that this was just what the grounds of Blandings Castle needed to bring them to perfection. Vanessa was unable to share such a sentiment. She had no deep affection for Howard Chesney, but his presence was essential to her plan of campaign, and his absence bred the suspicion that all was not well.

Gradually the suspicion grew, and at last the clock over the stables crushed any faint hope that might have lingered by chiming the half hour. With the dull weight of failure on her which all good organizers dislike so much, she turned to break the news to Wilbur.

She was a good loser. She saw eye to eye with the philosopher, whoever he was, who first deplored the futility of crying over spilt milk. This, she told herself, was just one of those things, and nothing to be done about it. Where Howard Chesney was concerned, she had no hard feelings. She knew that only some misadventure on a major scale could have prevented him coming to collect a thousand dollars. All she felt was sympathy for Wilbur's disappointment.

'I'm afraid, Willie,' she began, but got no further, for she saw that for the time being explanations and commiserations would be wasted. Sunk in a chair, his long legs stretched out and his head on one side, Wilbur Trout was catching up with his sleep.

She stood watching him, and was surprised at

the wave of maternal tenderness that surged over her. His best friends would not have claimed that Wilbur, asleep in a chair with his head lolling to one side, was a feast for the eye, but for her the spectacle had an appeal that grew stronger with every minute that passed. She felt that she could have stayed drinking it in for ever.

This, however, in the circumstances was scarcely advisable. No invasion of their privacy had occurred as yet, but there was no saying how long this happy state of things would last. Reluctantly she became her practical self again. Attaching herself to his ginger hair, she gave it a pull.

'Bedtime, Willie.'

He came slowly to life with a grunt and a gurgle.

'Eh?'

'Time for bye-bye.'

'What?'

'Oh, wake up. The party's over.'

Wilbur sat up, blinking.

'Was I asleep?'

'Fast asleep.'

'Odd thing, that. It isn't as if I wasn't used to late nights.' His eye fell on the reclining nude. He registered surprise. 'Hullo! It's still there. What's the time?'

'It must be nearly three.'

'And Chesney hasn't got here yet? Something must have happened to him.'

Wilbur's surmise was right. Headed in his car for Shropshire and his thousand dollars, Howard Chesney had won through only as far as

Worcestershire. He was lying with a broken leg in the cottage hospital of the village of Wibley-in-the-Vale in that county, a salutary object lesson to the inhabitants of the hamlet not to go to sleep at the wheel of a car when on the wrong side of the road with a truck laden with mineral water bottles coming the other way.

'Yes, something must have happened to him,' Vanessa agreed, 'and we can't do anything without him, so, as I said before, the party's over. I'm sorry.'

Wilbur did not speak. He had gone to the picture and was staring at it, deep in thought. Slowly he became aware that he had been spoken to, and he turned.

'What was that?'

'Nothing.'

'You said something.'

'Only that I was sorry.'

'Why?'

'Well, aren't you?'

'You mean about this?'

'I know how much you wanted it.'

'Listen,' said Wilbur. 'Let me tell you something. I don't want the damned thing.'

'What!'

'And it beats me how I ever got the idea that I did. I wouldn't have it as a gift. It makes me sick to look at it. You know what I do want?'

'What?'

'You.'

'Me?'

'Yes, you. I realize now what a sap I was letting you go and wasting my time marrying a bunch of

236

blondes who didn't amount to a row of beans. I ought to have known they were a lot of false alarms and that you were the only one for me. I could kick myself. It just shows what a fool a guy can make of himself when he tries. I ought to have my head examined. Well, how about it?'

Vanessa was conscious of a thrill of happiness which had the effect of making even the Earls and Countesses appear beautiful. Their painted eyes seemed to gaze benevolently from their frames as if this romance pleased them. Even the third Earl, who could have walked into any gathering of Chicago gangsters and been welcomed by all present as one of the mob, had taken on the aspect of a kindly uncle. She drew a long breath.

'Willie! Is this a proposal of marriage?'

'Sure it's a proposal of marriage. What did you think it was?'

'Well, one never knows. Of course I'll marry you, Willie.'

'That's the way to talk,' said Wilbur.

He crossed to where she stood and folded her in his arms with the practised dexterity of a man who had been folding girls in his arms since he was a slip of a boy, and would have been content to let this state of things continue indefinitely, but she released herself and stepped back.

'Yes, I'll marry you, Willie, but I think it's only fair that you should know what you're letting yourself in for.'

'What do you mean?'

'Just this, that if I marry, it'll be for keeps. When I take you for my wedded husband, you'll stay taken. You're going to have me around for an awful long time, Willie.'

'Suits me.'

'You're sure?'

'Sure I'm sure.'

'Then I see no objection to you folding me in your arms again. It felt kind of good the first time. And now,' said Vanessa, 'we might be going off and seeing if we can get some sleep. And tomorrow we'll say goodbye to Blandings Castle and drive to London and hunt up a registrar. You don't get married by Justices of the Peace over here, you go to a registry office.'

13

The following morning found Gally in his hammock as usual, but without his eyeglass. He had removed it and closed his eyes in order to assist thought, for he had much intensive thinking to do. Once more the cat from the stables, who knew a kindred soul when she met one, jumped on his stomach and purred invitingly, but this time he was too preoccupied to tickle it behind the ear. He was friendly, but aloof.

The Pelican Club trains its sons well, teaching them, no matter what their troubles and anxieties, always to preserve outwardly the poker-faced nonchalance of a red Indian at the stake. Nobody seeing him as he lay there could have guessed at the pangs he was suffering as he mused on the tangled matrimonial affairs of a loved godson. To Vanessa, coming to the hammock's side, he seemed his customary unruffled self.

'Hullo there,' she said. 'You look very comfortable. Don't get up. The etiquette books say that a gentleman should always rise in the presence of a lady, but that doesn't apply when the gentleman is reclining in a hammock with a cat on top of him. I've only come to say goodbye.'

It meant adjusting the cat, but Gally was obliged to sit up. He replaced his eyeglass and gazed at her with incredulity not unmixed with reproach.

'You're leaving?'

'In a minute or two.'

'You said you weren't going to.'

'I've altered my plans. Don't look so reproachful. It isn't that I don't trust you not to give me away. I know the word of the Threepwoods is their bond. But something's happened since our chat on the roof. Can I speak freely before the cat? I ask because it's a secret for the moment and I wouldn't want it to be noised abroad. I'm going to be married.'

'What!'

'Yessir, it's all fixed.'

A horrible suspicion caused a shudder to pass through Gally's dapper frame. His voice shook.

'Not Dunstable?'

'Good heavens, no. What made you pick on him?'

'A girl as rich as he thinks you are is always bound to exert a spell on a man as fond of money as he is. He's been courting you for days. Ask Connie if you don't believe me.'

'So that's what he's been doing! It puzzled me.'

'That's what. But if it isn't Dunstable — '

' — it must be Wilbur Trout. It is. Now say it.'

'Say what?'

'H'm.'

'I wasn't dreaming of saying H'm.'

'I thought you would. Disapprovingly.'

'I don't disapprove. Why shouldn't you marry Trout? Everybody else does.'

'I nearly did some years ago. We were engaged.'

'All I was asking myself was Is he good enough for you? Any girl who can make a fool of Connie as you've done deserves the best of husbands.

And while Trout is admittedly the most frequent of husbands, is he the best?'

'He's going to be. I have all sorts of plans for Willie. I'm going to make him get a job and cut down on cocktails and generally realize that life is stern and life is earnest. He'll be fine.'

'And you feel that you can correct that tendency of his to become over-cordial when he meets a blonde?'

'Sure. It's just a nervous habit.'

'Then accept my congratulations.'

'Thank you.'

'You won't mind if while giving you them I heave a sigh?'

'Go right ahead, if you want to. But why?'

'I'm thinking of my godson Johnny Halliday.'

'What's wrong with him?'

'Everything. It's a tragedy. He loves the Gilpin wench, and she loves him, but they can't get married because Dunstable won't give his consent.'

'For heaven's sake. I thought that consent stuff went out with Queen Victoria.'

'It did as a general rule, but Linda Gilpin's a ward of court, and that means that the court won't allow her to marry what they call the intending party unless her guardian gives them the green light. Her guardian is Dunstable.'

'So that's why you were asking me at dinner about wards of court. And the Duke won't give the green light?'

'Not unless I can find some way of making him. And so far I've not been able to think of one. What I want is to get some hold over him. You don't know of any guilty secrets he might have?'

241

'I'm afraid I don't.'

'Nor do I. I see now that it was a shortsighted policy turning him down when he came up for election at the Pelican Club. If he had been let in, one would have been able to keep a constant eye on him and assemble any amount of material for blackmail, but as it is, I'm helpless.'

'It's difficult.'

'Very difficult.'

'It's the sort of situation where you want the United States Marines to arrive. Oh, that's Willie,' said Vanessa, alluding to the rhythmic tooting of a horn that was proceeding from an ornate car outside the front door. 'I must rush. Will you be in London soon?'

'I shouldn't wonder. Not much use staying on and reasoning with Dunstable unless I have definite information as to where the body's buried.'

'Give me a ring. I'll be at Barribault's. Goodbye. And keep an eye skinned for those United States Marines. I'm sure they'll be along.'

She ran off, leaving Gally sufficiently restored to be able to tickle the cat behind the ear. He could not share her optimism, but she had cheered him up a little.

II

The car rolled off down the drive, and Lady Constance, as she turned from speeding it on its way, erased from her lips the bright smile they had worn while she was making her farewells. She was conscious of a growing uneasiness.

Wilbur's attitude while settling himself at the steering wheel had disturbed her.

Having seen in her time so many romances run their course at Blandings Castle, she had become expert at recognizing the symptoms, and she was oppressed by the conviction that she had been present at the early stages of another. She was telling herself that if what she had detected in the eyes of Wilbur Trout had not been the love light, she did not know a love light when she saw one.

And the solicitous way he had fussed over the girl in the seat beside him. Did she want a rug? Was she sure she didn't want a rug? Wouldn't she be cold without a rug? Well, all right if she was really sure she didn't want a rug, but would it be okay if he lit a cigarette? The smoke might blow in her eyes. Would she mind the smoke blowing in her eyes? Oh, she would have a cigarette, too? Fine. Swell. Capital. Splendid. And she needn't worry about him driving too fast. No risks for him, no, *sir*.

The whole of his dialogue could have been written into *Romeo And Juliet* without changing a word. Taken in conjunction with the love light in his eyes, to which reference has already been made, it sent her hurrying to the garden suite to warn the Duke that he had a rival to his wooing and that he would do well to accelerate that wooing in no uncertain manner. It would, she would tell him, though not in those words, be necessary for him to pull up his socks and get a move on.

She found him in the frame of mind which

causes strong men to pace to and fro with knitted brows. His injured ankle, of course, prohibited anything in the nature of pacing to and fro, but his brow was definitely knitted. A recently received piece of information had stirred him to his depths.

'Hoy!' he boomed as she entered. 'What's all this Beach tells me about Trout leaving?'

'Yes, he has just gone.'

'Where?'

'London.'

'And not coming back?'

'No.'

The Duke could put two and two together. He scorched her with a burning eye.

'You've been coming the *grande dame* over him!'

'I have not.'

'But he's gone?'

'Yes.'

'And no chance now of selling him that picture. It required constant personal super-vision. Another week and I'd have got him where I wanted him. Are you sure you've not been looking down your nose at him?'

Lady Constance lowered herself into a chair. A woman of lesser breeding and self-control would have slumped into it like a sack of coals.

'Quite sure. And I am not worrying about the picture, Alaric. It is much more serious than that.'

'How do you mean it's more serious? How can anything be more serious? Now I'll have to sell it at Sotheby's or somewhere for about half what

244

I'd have got from Trout. What makes you say it's more serious? What's more serious?'

'Vanessa went with him.'

'What! She's left, too?'

'Yes.'

'Why?'

'Trout must have persuaded her to go with him. He's in love with her.'

'Don't be an ass.'

'I tell you he is. I could see by looking at him.'

'Well, she can't be in love with him. He's got ginger hair and a broken nose.'

'I don't suppose she is. But that is not to say that she won't marry him if he is persistent. You must act at once, Alaric.'

'Act? Act how?'

'Write to her immediately. She will be at Barribault's.'

'I've lunched there. They charge you the earth.'

'And ask her to be your wife. Say you will get a special licence. It will show how eager you are. You get it from the Archbishop of Canterbury.'

'I know you do, and he soaks you worse than Barribault's.'

'What does that matter?'

'It matters to me. You're like all women, you seem to think a man is made of money.'

'Good heavens, Alaric, is this a time to economize? Have you forgotten that Vanessa will be one of the richest women in America? She's J. B. Polk's daughter, J. B. Polk's *daughter*. She'll inherit millions.'

She had found the talking point. The Duke's

eyes gleamed with a new light. It differed in quality from the love light which Wilbur Trout had recently been spraying over Vanessa, but it was fully as noticeable. His voice rang out like a clarion.

'I'll write that letter!'

'It's the only thing to do. And Beach can take it to Market Blandings and have it registered.'

'But I don't know what to say.'

'I'll tell you what to say. You could begin by telling her that the reason you hesitated to speak before was that you felt you might be a little old for her.'

'Old?' The Duke started. He was — by about thirty years — past his first youth, but like all men so situated he regarded himself as just approaching the prime of life. 'What do you mean, old?'

'And then . . . No, you'll never be able to write the sort of letter this has to be. It wants the most careful phrasing. I'll do it, and you can copy it out.'

As Lady Constance seated herself at the desk and took pen in hand, the Duke's emotions were mixed. A proud man, he resented having his love letters written for him, but on the other hand he could not but feel that in the present crisis a ghost writer would come in uncommonly handy, for he had to admit that, left to his own devices, he would not even know how to start the thing, let alone fill the four sheets which could be looked on as the irreducible minimum. He was a great writer of letters to the *Times*, the Government could not move a step without hearing from him, but this one called for gifts of which he knew himself to be deficient. It was, accordingly, with approval that he watched his collaborator's pen racing over the paper, and when she had finished, he took the manuscript from her with pleasurable anticipation of a treat in store.

It was a pity, therefore, that perusal of it should have brought out all the destructive critic in him. He scanned the document with dismay, and delivered his verdict with asperity. He might have been one of those Scotch reviewers Byron disliked so much.

'This,' he said, his eyes popping as they had rarely popped before, 'is the most god-awful slush I ever read!'

If Lady Constance was piqued, she did not show it. She may have raised an eyebrow, but scarcely so that it could be noticed. Like all authors, she knew her output was above criticism.

'Indeed?' she said. 'Perhaps you will tell me what jars on your sensitive taste.'

'Well, this for a start — 'I can't go on living without you'.'

'You think it should be changed to 'without your money'?'

'It's too damned grovelling. Puts her above herself right from the start. But that's not so bad as this poppycock about the church steeple. 'I love you as the church steeple loves the cloud that settles above it'. Is that a way to talk? She'll think I'm potty.'

'Not at all. A charming thought. Do you

247

remember Bertie Weaver? No, you wouldn't, he was only at the castle for a short time. He was my father's secretary, and he said those very words to me one evening when we were walking by the lake. I've often wondered where he got them, because he was not the poetic type, he had been a Rugby football Blue at Cambridge. From some play he had seen, I suppose. It's the kind of thing they say in plays. It impressed me enormously, and I'm sure it will impress Vanessa. Any more complaints?'

'I don't like any of it.'

'Well, it's all you're going to get. I take it that even though you have a sprained ankle you can manage to go to the desk. Do so, and copy out what I have written word for word, for I certainly do not intend to compose a revised version.'

And with this ultimatum Lady Constance withdrew haughtily, leaving the Duke, as so many men have been left by women in their time, with the loser's end of the debate.

For some minutes after she had gone he huffed and puffed, as his niece Linda would have said, but not surprisingly it got him nowhere. No matter how often he blew at his moustache and muttered 'Women!' he could not evade the inevitable.

Half an hour later, when his task was done and he had sealed and directed the envelope, there was a deprecating knock on the door and Lord Emsworth came in.

It was not sheer goodness of heart that had brought the latter to the sick chamber. Any etiquette book would have told him that a visit of enquiry was due from a host to a guest who has sprained his ankle by falling down his, the host's, personal stairs, but he would certainly have ignored this ruling had it not been for the conviction that, if he did, he would have a painful interview with Connie. 'Have you been to see Alaric?' he could hear her saying, and an 'Eh? What? Alaric? Oh, you mean Alaric. Well, no, as a matter of fact, not yet' would have the worst results.

He could only hope to be able to make his stay a short one, and, as it happened, the Duke proposed to make it even shorter. Talking to Lord Emsworth was one of the many things that exasperated him.

'Oh, it's you,' he said. 'You can do something for me, Emsworth. This letter. Most important. Has to go immediately. Give it to Beach and tell him to take it to Market Blandings post office and register it. At once.'

The elation Lord Emsworth felt at this early conclusion to a visit that might have dragged on interminably was mixed with less agreeable feelings. Wonderful to be in a position to say to Connie when she questioned him, 'Been to see Alaric? Of course I've been to see Alaric. We had a long and interesting talk', but he did not like this reference to Beach and Market Blandings.

'Ask Beach to walk to Market Blandings? In this weather?'

'Do him good.'

'I don't know what he'll say.'

'If he utters a word of protest, kick his spine up through his hat.'

249

'Very well, Alaric.'

'And don't just stand there. Get moving.'

'Yes, Alaric.'

'That letter must go without delay.'

'Yes, Alaric.'

'Oh, and one other thing,' said the Duke. 'I almost forgot to tell you. I'm suing you for heavy damages for this ankle of mine. We won't discuss it now, you will hear from my solicitors in due course.'

III

Gally, in his hammock, had closed his eyes again and was thinking once more of John and Linda and the United States Marines. He was roused from his reverie by a voice bleating his name, and opening his eyes was annoyed to find his brother Clarence drooping over him. The interruption had derailed his train of thought, and though that train had shown no signs of going anywhere, he resented this.

Annoyance changed quickly to concern as he observed his visitor's agitation. Unlike the members of the Pelican Club, Lord Emsworth, when on the receiving end of the slings and arrows of outrageous fortune, always allowed his doubts and fears to be visible to the naked eye.

'Something wrong, Clarence?'

'Yes, indeed, Galahad.'

'Connie, I suppose? Don't let her worry you. Get tough. Talk back at her out of the side of your mouth.'

'It is not Connie, it's Alaric.'

'Pursue the same policy.'

'But he says he is going to bring an action against me because he sprained his ankle on those stairs.'

Gally uttered a defiant laugh.

'Let him. He hasn't a hope.'

'You really think so?'

'Brief a good counsel for the defence and watch him tear the man to pieces. He'll go through him like a dose of salts. 'Is it not a fact that you were galloping down those stairs at sixty miles an hour in order to get at the cocktails?' 'Would it be fair to say that you had been mopping up the stuff like a vacuum cleaner all the afternoon?' 'I suggest that you were as tight as an owl.' He'll have him tied up in knots in the first two minutes, and the jury will stop the case.'

Lord Emsworth seemed to expand like a balloon. Galahad, he was thinking, could always be relied on to appreciate one's difficulties and make valuable suggestions for dealing with them.

'Well, you have relieved me greatly, Galahad. I wish you could be equally comforting about this letter. Alaric has given me a letter to give to Beach to take to Market Blandings.'

'And what's your problem?'

'I can't ask Beach to make that long walk on a hot morning like this.'

'Why not put it on the hall table with the rest of the letters?'

'Alaric made such a point of it that it should go at once. It has to be registered.'

'I see.'

'I don't suppose Beach will actually give notice if I tell him to go to Market Blandings, but he won't like it at all. I shall have to take it myself, and I have an appointment to meet Banks at the sty.'

Gally's was a feeling heart, and as he had said to his brother on a previous occasion he did not think it right to leave acts of kindness entirely to the Boy Scouts. He extricated himself from the hammock.

'I'll take it, if you like.'

'Oh, Galahad! Will you really?'

'I shall enjoy the stroll.'

'Here is the letter.'

'Right.'

'Thank you so much, Galahad.'

'Not at all. Always glad to oblige. Hullo, this is odd. It's addressed to Vanessa Polk.'

'Banks and I are going to discuss a new vitamin pill for pigs which I have been reading about. To be taken in a little skim milk.'

'What would he be writing to her for?'

'Supposed to be wonderful. Thank you again, Galahad. It really is extremely good of you.'

Gally slipped the letter into his pocket, a thoughtful frown on his face. He could imagine no reason for this sudden urge on the Duke's part to become a Vanessa Polk pen pal. And he was still as far as ever from a solution of the mystery and was half inclined to go to the length of applying for one to the Duke, when his meditations were again interrupted by a voice, and he saw that he had been joined by his sister Constance.

'Oh, there you are, Galahad,' she said.

There was no trace in her manner of the pique she had felt a short while before when leaving the garden suite. Two things had combined to restore her equanimity. The first was the comforting reflection that her recent critic was a dull clod temperamentally incapable of recognizing good writing when it was put before him; the second that she was about to make Galahad feel extremely foolish, a pleasure she was able only rarely to enjoy.

'I was looking for you,' she said. 'I wonder if you remember a conversation we had not long ago.'

'I recollect having a word or two with you about my godson Johnny Halliday.'

'I was not referring to that. I mean about Alaric.'

'Alaric? Did we have a conversation about him? Ah yes, it's beginning to come back to me. You said you were hoping he would marry Vanessa Polk — '

' — And you said he was too self-centred and too fond of his comforts ever to think of marrying again. Well, it may interest you to know that he has written a letter to Vanessa, asking her to be his wife, and Beach is taking it to the post office in Market Blandings.'

'Good Lord! You're not pulling my leg?'

'No.'

'He's really written to the popsy proposing?'

'Yes.'

'How do you know?'

'He showed me the letter. She's bound to

accept him. Any girl would want to become a Duchess. And it will be an excellent marriage for Alaric.'

'She being the daughter of J. B. Polk, the loaded tycoon.'

'Exactly. Well, Galahad, it would seem that you were not such a good judge of character as you thought you were.'

'That would seem, wouldn't it?'

'You have always been much too sure you were right and everybody else was wrong.'

'Don't rub it in. Would it be premature if I went and congratulated Dunstable?'

'Considering how improbable it is that Vanessa will refuse him, I see no objection.'

'I'll go at once. Hark! Can you hear something?'

'No.'

'I can. The tramp-tramp-tramp of marching feet and a thousand manly voices singing 'from the halls of Montezuma'. How right the Polk popsy was. The United States Marines have arrived.'

IV

Lying on his sofa, watching the shadows flit across the lawn outside, the Duke was in what practically amounted to a sunny mood. Serene is perhaps the word one is groping for. He was feeling serene.

But when some human substance appeared in the french windows and he saw that it was Gally,

254

his benevolence noticeably waned. He had never been fond of this companion of his early days, and his stare was the cold stare of a man anxious to know to what he is indebted for the honour of this visit.

'I thought I'd look in,' said Gally.

'Oh?'

'To ask after your ankle.'

'Oh?'

'How is it?'

'Bad.'

'Good. I mean, I'm sorry. What does the doctor say? Any signs of gangrene? That's what you want to watch out for, gangrene. Do you remember a fellow in the old days called Postlethwaite? He was bitten in the leg by a Siamese cat, got gangrene and as near as a toucher passed beyond the veil. You will probably argue that you have not been bitten in the leg by a Siamese cat, and that's of course a good point, but even so you can't feel safe. Have you a funny burning sensation? High temperature? Floating spots before the eyes? But, good heavens,' said Gally, 'I ought not to be talking to you like this. The great thing when visiting the afflicted is to present a cheerful front, to be all hearty and jolly and make them forget their troubles. I should be cheering you up with something funny. But what? Ha! Of course, yes, the Polk wench. That'll amuse you. It turns out that she's an impostor. It's an odd thing about Blandings Castle, it seems to attract impostors as catnip does cats. They make a bee line for the place. When two or three impostors are gathered together, it's only a question of time before they're saying 'Let's all go round to Blandings', and along they come. It shakes one. I've sometimes asked myself if Connie is really Connie. How can we be certain that she's not an international spy cunningly made up as Connie? The only one of the local fauna I feel really sure about is Beach. He seems to be genuine. Returning to the case of the Polk wench — '

All through this long harangue the Duke had been struggling to speak, but had failed to do so, partly because he lacked the special gifts which a man had to have if he hoped to interrupt Gally, but principally owing to a restriction of his vocal cords, which seemed to have seized up, preventing speech. He now contrived to utter. His words came out in a hoarse whisper, but they emerged.

'What's that?' he said. 'What's that? Are you telling me Vanessa Polk is not Vanessa Polk?'

'Well, yes and no.'

'What the devil do you mean, Yes and no?'

'It's a bit intricate, but I think I can explain. She's Vanessa Polk all right, but not, as she gave us to understand, the daughter of the plutocratic J. B. Polk. She is the offspring or issue of P. P. Polk, one of the Norfolk Polks. Polk is a good Norfolk name, so they tell me. He was a valet.'

'What!'

'Or gentleman's personal gentleman, if you prefer it. Her mother used to be a parlourmaid here. The popsy herself is a secretary. Makes you laugh, doesn't it, to think of Connie of all people being taken in. It'll be a lesson to her not to be so fussy about impostors sponsored by others.'

The Duke was not laughing. The sound that had escaped him had been more like a death rattle. His jaw had dropped, and his eyes were threatening to part from their sockets.

'Threepwood!'

'Yes?'

'I . . . I . . . '

'Yes?'

'Threepwood, I have written that woman a letter, proposing marriage!'

'So Connie told me, and I was thrilled. It's a real Cinderella story — the humble little secretary marrying the great Duke,' said Gally. He had been about to say 'the popeyed Duke', but thought it more tactful to substitute the other adjective. 'You'll never regret it, Dunstable. You will be getting a prize. One of the nicest girls I ever met. You couldn't have a better prop for your declining years.'

The Duke snorted emotionally.

'You don't think I'm going to marry her now, do you?'

'Aren't you?'

'Of course I'm not.'

'How about her suing you for breach of promise?'

'She mustn't get that letter! Ring for Beach.'

'Why?'

'He may not have started yet.'

'With the letter?'

'Yes.'

'But Beach hasn't got it. I have. Clarence was concerned about asking Beach to go hiking with the sun's ultra-violet rays so sultry, so I said I would take it. I have it here.'

The Duke expelled a deep breath. His lower jaw resumed its place, and his eyes returned to their sockets.

'Thank heaven! You might have told me before,' he added with a venomous glance. 'I was half out of my mind.'

'I know. But it was great fun, wasn't it?'

'Give it to me!'

'Certainly, my dear fellow. It was what I came here to do. But before the handing-over ceremony I shall have to make one or two simple conditions. Clarence tells me you are planning to bring an action against him for having such slippery stairs. That must be dropped.'

'Of course, of course, of course. To hell with Emsworth and his stairs. Give me that letter.'

'Just one more article of agreement, if that's the right expression. You must also jettison these fanciful objections you have to my godson marrying your niece.'

'What!'

Gally was all sympathy and understanding. His voice was very gentle.

'I know just how you feel. Every time your ankle gives you a twinge you think harsh thoughts of him, and I'm not surprised. But there it is. Nothing to be done about it. You must bite the bullet. Because, if you don't, this letter goes to La Polk, registered.'

A silence of the kind usually described as pregnant fell on the garden suite. It might have been broken by the Duke calling Gally a low

258

blackmailer and he had every inclination to do so, but even as his lips started to frame the words, prudence told him that they were better left unsaid. The thought of that breach of promise case restrained him.

He knew all about breach of promise cases. He had had one himself in his youth. They read your letters out in court, and everybody there laughed his or her fat head off. And it all came out in the papers next morning. To yield was bitter, but rather that than to have to sit and listen while a blasted barrister intoned that bit about the church steeple and the cloud. He swallowed several times, and eventually was able to speak. When he did so, it was in a peevish vein.

'What the devil does he want to marry her for?'

'Love, Dunstable, love.'

'She hasn't got a penny.'

'That doesn't weigh with these vintage Lochinvars.'

'Has he any money?'

'Quite enough.'

'I mean, they won't expect me to support them?'

'Good Lord, no. He's doing well at the bar, and he has an interest in that gallery where you bought the picture. It's a very prosperous concern. Mugs coming in all the time with their cheque books and fountain pens. You need have no anxiety about Johnny's finances. So is it a deal?'

'I suppose so.'

If a criticism could be made of the Duke's

vocal delivery as he said these three words, it would be that it lacked geniality and enthusiasm. It fell somewhat short of the snarl of a timber wolf which has hurt its shinbone on a passing rock, but it was not enthusiastic and genial. Gally, however, found no fault in it.

'Good,' he said. 'Excellent. Capital. Then all that remains is to complete the formalities by putting it in writing. Can you hop to that desk?'

'I suppose so.'

'Then hop,' said Gally.

14

Another summer day was drawing to a close, and dusk had fallen once more on Blandings Castle. The Empress had turned in. Chauffeur Voules was playing his harmonica. The stable cat was having a quick wash and brush up before starting on its night out. And in the kitchen Mrs. Willoughby, the cook, was putting the final touches on the well-jammed roly-poly pudding which Beach would soon be taking to the library, where Gally and Lord Emsworth were enjoying their dinner of good plain English fare. Now that they were alone, Lord Emsworth had said, it was cosier there than in the vast *salon* where the meal had been served during the reign of Lady Constance, who was now on the ocean with only a few hours to go before her reunion with James Schoonmaker.

Through the open window the scent of stocks and tobacco plant floated in, competing with the aroma of the leg of lamb, the boiled potatoes and the spinach with which dinner had begun. Beach brought in the roly-poly pudding and withdrew, and Lord Emsworth heaved a contented sigh. In Lady Constance's time it would have made his stiff shirt front go pop, but now it merely stirred the bosom of his shooting coat with the holes in the elbows. His toes wriggled sensuously inside his bedroom slippers.

'This is very pleasant, Galahad,' he said, and

Gally endorsed the sentiment.

'I was thinking the same thing, Clarence. No Connie, no Dunstable. Peace, perfect peace with loved ones far away, as one might say. I'm sorry I'm leaving.'

'You must, I suppose?'

'I doubt if the marriage would be legal without me.'

'Someone you know is being married?'

'My godson.'

'I've never met him, have I?'

'Certainly you have. The chap who falls downstairs.'

'Ah yes. Who is he marrying?'

'Linda Gilpin.'

'Who is Linda Gilpin?'

'The girl who kisses him after he's fallen downstairs. I am to be Johnny's best man.'

'Who — '

'Yes, I see I'm confusing you, Clarence. Johnny and my godson are one and the same. All straight now?'

'Perfectly, perfectly. Your godson Johnny is marrying Linda Gilpin.'

'You put it in a nutshell. And I have to be there when the firing squad assembles. Furthermore, Trout and Vanessa Polk insist on me dining with them before they go off on their honeymoon.'

'Who is Trout?'

'The chap who has married Vanessa Polk.'

'Who is Vanessa Polk?'

'The girl who has married Trout. They've both married each other, and they're going for the honeymoon to Nassau.'

'That's where the Falls are, isn't it? People go over them in barrels, which is a thing I don't suppose many young couples would care to do. But no doubt Mr. and Mrs. Trout will find some other way of passing the time. Vanessa Polk, did you say? Wasn't she staying here?'

'That's right, and so was Trout.'

'I thought the names were familiar. Nice girl. Very sound on pigs. I hope she will be very happy.'

'I'm sure she will.'

'And I hope your godson will be very happy.'

'Have no uneasiness about that. He loves his popsy.'

'I thought you said her name was Linda.'

'Popsy is the generic term. By the way, did Connie confide in you much while she was here?'

'Not very much.'

'Then you probably don't know that serious obstacles had to be surmounted before the Johnny-Linda Gilpin merger could be put through. It was touch and go for quite a time. Snags arose. Tricky corners had to be rounded. It was only at long last that they were given the green light. But all that's over now. It makes me feel as if I were sitting in at the end of a play, one of those charming delicate things the French do so well. You know the sort of thing I mean — lightly sentimental, the smile following the tear. I am having my dinner. The storm is over, there is sunlight in my heart. I have a glass of wine and sit thinking of what has passed. And now we want something to bring down the curtain. A toast is indicated. Let us drink to the Pelican Club, under whose gentle tuition I learned to keep cool, stiffen the upper lip and always think a shade quicker than the next man. To the Pelican Club,' said Gally, raising his glass.

'To the Pelican Club,' said Lord Emsworth, raising his. 'What is the Pelican Club, Galahad?'

'God bless you, Clarence,' said Gally. 'Have some more roly-poly pudding.'

www.raintreepublishers.co.uk
Visit our website to find out
more information about
Raintree books.

To order:
☎ Phone 0845 6044371
🖨 Fax +44 (0) 1865 312263
✉ Email myorders@raintreepublishers.co.uk

Customers from outside the UK please telephone +44 1865 312262

Raintree is an imprint of Capstone Global Library Limited,
a company incorporated in England and Wales having its
registered office at 7 Pilgrim Street, London, EC4V 6LB
– Registered company number: 6695582

First published by Stone Arch Books in 2011
First published in the United Kingdom
in hardback and paperback in 2012
The moral rights of the proprietor have been asserted.

Art Director: Bob Lentz
Designer: Hilary Wacholz
Production Specialist: Michelle Biedrischied
Editor: Vaarunika Dharmapala
Originated by Capstone Global Library Ltd
Printed and bound in China by Leo Paper Products Ltd

ISBN 978 1 406 22719 2 (hardback)
15 14 13 12 11
10 9 8 7 6 5 4 3 2 1

ISBN 978 1 406 22726 0 (paperback)
15 14 13 12 11
10 9 8 7 6 5 4 3 2 1

British Library Cataloguing in Publication Data
A full catalogue record for this book is available
from the British Library.

CONTENTS

CHAPTER 1

HOLIDAY'S OVER!

Green Lantern Hal Jordan leaned back and smiled. Today was the first time since joining the Green Lantern Corps that he could take a day off. With no missions to save the universe on his schedule, Hal flew to a beach on the beautiful planet Orios. With his ring, the super hero constructed a big green hammock. He lay looking out at the ocean, watching many alien animals he had never seen before.

WHOOOOSH! A giant, scaly creature jumped out of the water.

At first, Hal thought it was a dolphin, but as he looked closer, the strange orange fish appeared more like a horse. At that same moment, three purple birds flew overhead. **CRUNCH! CRUNCH!** The strange creature opened its jaws, swallowed up the birds, and splashed back down in the water.

Hal was not surprised. Ever since he had become a Green Lantern and travelled around the universe, the super hero had seen all sorts of animals. Most of them looked very different from those on Earth.

After watching the creatures for a moment, Hal lay back in his hammock. He closed his eyes and decided to take a much needed nap.

BEEP! Suddenly, Hal's Green Lantern ring demanded his attention.

A green hologram of an alien with four arms popped out of it. Hal's hammock disappeared. He fell down on to the sand.

THUD!

It's Salaak, Hal thought. *Must be time for a new mission.*

"Hal Jordan, your rest is over," the image of Salaak said.

"I had a feeling," Hal said, smiling, "but I didn't even get to catch up on my sleep."

"You need to report to the planet Nokyo One," the alien continued. "I've received reports of Manhunter robots attacking a human city there, and you are the closest Green Lantern. I have sent the directions to the planet to your ring. Travel to Nokyo One and protect the city. Good luck, Hal." The hologram of Salaak disappeared.

Manhunters? thought Hal. Manhunters were a race of androids the Guardians of the Universe had created before they formed the Green Lantern Corps. The androids were built to maintain peace, but had become corrupted and very dangerous.

"Time to save the universe again," he said to himself. With that, he raised his fist into the sky and took off through space.

*   *   *

When Hal arrived on Nokyo One, he immediately saw the Manhunter robots as he flew towards the city. *That's strange,* Hal thought. *There aren't enough robots to take over a planet. What are they doing here?*

As he reached the surface of the planet, Hal willed his ring to construct two boxing gloves.

Hal placed the superpowered gloves on each hand and flew directly at a group of the Manhunters.

"In this corner, a broken robot!" Hal shouted. **Ka-Prannng!** He punched a Manhunter as hard as he could. A thousand tiny pieces flew through the air.

Hal did not have time to celebrate. Another Manhunter robot was flying straight at him. "Come on, then!" he yelled, transforming his boxing gloves into a green cricket bat.

KRAK! He swung the bat at the charging Manhunter and destroyed it. The people who had gathered on the streets to watch the Green Lantern save their city began to cheer. Suddenly, Hal heard a woman scream. "Help!" the woman cried. "That building is burning! Save us!"

Hal looked around. Out of the corner of his eye, he spotted a large block of flats. It had caught fire during his battle with the Manhunters. He thought quickly, deciding the best way to put out the blaze. Then the super hero spotted a large river a few hundred metres away.

With his ring, the super hero made a fire hose and pointed it at the river. It quickly filled with water. Then Hal pointed the hose at the building and unleashed the water.

Splash! Within seconds, the building had stopped burning.

The people trapped inside came running out on to the street, relieved and grateful.

"Thank you!" a woman said to Hal.

"No problem," Hal replied. "Just doing my job –"

"Look out behind you!" another person interrupted.

Hal turned around just in time to see ten more Manhunter robots flying at him.

"That's enough!" Hal said. He pointed his ring at the robots and created a giant bubble around them. They were trapped. Hal flung the bubble into space, sending the robots far away, where he hoped they would never cause trouble again.

"Another planet saved!" Hal said.

Then suddenly, Hal's ring cried out, "WARNING! Incoming enemies!"

Hal looked up at the sky. Hundreds more robots were heading straight towards the city! "Perhaps I spoke too soon," the super hero said.

CHAPTER 2

ATTACK OF THE MANHUNTERS

I've never fought this many enemies at once! Hal thought as he flew towards the incoming robots. The Green Lantern needed a weapon to fight with. Using his ring, Hal created a giant green sword. As soon as he was close to the attackers, he swung the sword as hard as he could at the robots.

CLANK! The first five Manhunters exploded on impact.

"Power levels at 50 per cent," said Hal's green ring.

Through the smoke of the destroyed robots, Hal could see hundreds more coming towards him. He gulped. *I need to do better than that!* he thought.

Hal focused hard, attempting to create another giant sword with his ring. But the weapon did not appear.

"Power levels at 10 per cent," said his ring.

Hal weakened as well. *I've got to keep fighting!* he thought.

The Green Lantern flew towards the nearest robot and fired a beam of energy from his ring. The robot dodged it and blasted Hal with its own laser beam.

"Power levels at 1 per cent," said Hal's ring. The super hero's eyes began to close, and he was about to pass out.

Suddenly, Hal felt power growing within.

"Power levels at 30 per cent," exclaimed Hal's ring.

What? the Green Lantern thought.

"Power levels at 100 per cent," said the ring.

What's going on? Hal felt all of his strength flowing back and prepared to attack the robots again.

"Power levels at 200 per cent," Hal's ring said.

"Two-hundred per cent?" Hal shouted.

"Do not worry, Green Lantern Hal Jordan," said a calm voice. "All is well."

Hal did not have time to look for the source of the voice. The Manhunter robots were about to reach the planet's surface.

Hal focused again. This time, he felt a massive amount of energy flow through him. He channelled the energy into a giant green blast and shot it at the Manhunters.

KA-BOOM! The blast was larger than any Hal had ever created. It destroyed nearly every robot. Only a handful had escaped. They quickly retreated into space.

"Got them!" exclaimed Hal.

The calm voice spoke again. "Excellent work, Hal Jordan."

Hal spun around. Floating behind him was an alien with white skin, no nose, and a long tentacle at the back of his head. The alien wore a uniform like Hal's – except it was blue. "It is I, Saint Walker," said the alien, "and this is Brother Sepdifer." He pointed to a figure beside him.

Hal had encountered Saint Walker in previous adventures, but he had never met Brother Sepdifer. "Thanks for the help, Walker," Hal said. He pointed at Brother Sepdifer. "Is he a Blue Lantern, too?"

"Correct, Hal Jordan," said Saint Walker. "We are both Blue Lanterns."

"Were you the ones who super-charged my ring?" asked Hal.

"Yes. We are fuelled by the power of hope," explained Saint Walker. "We channelled all the hope from the citizens of Nokyo One into your ring. The power of hope became your strength."

"Thank you for the help," said Hal.

"You are welcome, Hal Jordan," said Saint Walker. Brother Sepdifer stood silently, nodding his head with approval.

"Why doesn't he talk?" asked Hal.

"Brother Sepdifer has pledged a vow of silence. He is currently spending one year without speaking to show his dedication to the Blue Lantern Corps and to the power of hope," replied Saint Walker.

Hal grinned. "You lot are crazy," said the super hero with a smile.

"We are not crazy, Hal Jordan," said Saint Walker, "but we must ask you to come with us."

"Come with you where?" asked Hal.

"You must travel with us to the Blue Lantern home planet of Odym," said Saint Walker. "You will train to become a Blue Lantern and join our quest to spread hope throughout the universe."

Hal began to laugh. "You really are crazy! I'm not coming with you anywhere! I'm a Green Lantern. I'm powered by my will!" shouted Hal. "And right now, my will is to go after the rest of those Manhunters!"

"I am sorry, Hal Jordan," said Saint Walker, "but your mission must wait. It is most important that you come with us to Odym *now*. There is no time to waste."

"Look, I appreciate your help earlier," said Hal. "But I have to follow those robots and make sure they never return. *That* is what's most important." To show off his power, Hal created a green fighter jet.

"You must learn about the power of hope!" shouted Saint Walker. Even though he had raised his voice, it was still very calm and peaceful. He spoke to Hal as if he were already his close friend.

"I'm sorry, but hope alone isn't enough to save the universe," said Hal. "The only way I can make a difference is by using my will power to get things done. Thanks again for your offer, but I'm going to stop the Manhunters now."

Hal jumped into the cockpit of the jet and blasted off for space. He left the Blue Lanterns behind.

Saint Walker turned to Brother Sepdifer. "Hal Jordan is not yet aware of the bond between hope and will power," he said to his silent comrade.

Brother Sepdifer shook his head. The two Blue Lanterns watched as Hal's jet flew towards the stars.

CHAPTER 3

VOYAGE TO KIRDON

As he left Nokyo One's atmosphere, Hal spoke to his ring. "Can you trace the fuel trails that the fleeing robots left behind?" asked Hal.

"One moment," chimed the ring.

A few seconds later, Hal's ring had the answer. "Locked on to Manhunter robot fuel trails. They lead to the planet Kirdon, which is approximately 7.63 million kilometres from our present location."

"We'd better hurry up then," said Hal.

"Affirmative. Focusing all power on acceleration," replied his ring. The green jet sped up, and Hal was flying faster than he ever had before.

*　　*　　*

After several hours, Hal could see the planet Kirdon from the cockpit of his green jet. The planet was a bright orange orb. It looked like a giant fireball.

"Ring, are you sure this isn't a star?" asked Hal.

"Correct. This is not a star. It is the planet Kirdon," answered the ring.

If you say so, thought Hal. *It doesn't look like any planet I've ever seen, though.*

As Hal flew closer to the planet, his ring alerted him again.

BEEP! BEEP! BEEP! BEEP!

"WARNING!" said the ring. "Kirdon's temperatures are incredibly high! Keep your shield up at all times while on the surface."

"Good to know," Hal said.

He streaked towards the planet. Nearing the surface, the Green Lantern noticed that Kirdon did not just *look* like it was on fire – it was covered with flames! Smoke and molten lava blanketed the planet's entire landscape.

How could a Manhunter base be here? Hal wondered. *Nothing could survive in this environment.*

Hal continued to fly over the fires. He looked for a place to land. After a few minutes, he spotted a large rock sticking up out of the sea of lava. He landed his jet on the rock and jumped out.

"Shields at 100 per cent," said his ring.

"Thanks," said Hal. "Can you find the actual location of the Manhunter base?"

"The base is thirty kilometres north of our present location," replied the ring.

"Let's go!" said Hal. He jumped in the air and began flying north towards the robots' headquarters. His ring kept a shield around him to protect him from the heat.

After flying north for a few moments, Hal dodged a giant pillar of fire that shot up into the air. *WHOOOOSH!* It nearly knocked Hal out of the sky.

"WARNING! Shields at 80 per cent!" exclaimed Hal's ring.

I need to be more careful, thought Hal, tumbling towards the sea of lava beneath him. He quickly recovered in mid-air.

"Approaching Manhunter base," warned Hal's ring. "Proceed with extreme caution."

"What are you talking about?" asked Hal. "I don't see anything that looks like a base. All I see is fire!"

Hal stopped flying and floated above the fires. He looked in every direction for signs of the Manhunter headquarters.

"Aha!" Hal finally exclaimed. Out of the corner of his eye, Hal spotted a small mountain peak sticking out of the flames. It looked like a volcano that had sunk into the sea of lava.

An underground base, Hal realized. *That's got to be it.* He flew over to the mountain peak and hovered high above it.

"Multiple Manhunter signals detected below," said his ring.

The Green Lantern flew down to the mountain. On the peak, a huge crater seemed to lead inside the base.

"We're going in!" yelled Hal with a grin.

THWOOOOMMMMM! The Green Lantern dived down into the giant hole, flying at full speed. The crater led to a long dark tunnel within the mountain. He sped through the tunnel, the bright green light of his ring guiding the way.

Hal began to think that his ring had made a mistake and that this was not the Manhunters' base after all. He was about to turn around when his ring finally spoke.

"Approaching a large chamber," said the ring. "Use caution."

Finally! thought Hal. *This has got to be their headquarters.*

Suddenly, Hal could see a light at the end of the tunnel. He flew towards it and into a massive stone room. The super hero realized he had reached the centre of the mountain. Glancing around, he quickly realized that this was not just a hollowed-out mountain. Hundreds of high-tech machines filled the room. Some were repairing broken robots. Others looked like they were creating new ones. Hundreds of Manhunters hung on the walls, plugged in and charging like oversized computers.

This is definitely their base, thought Hal. *Now I just need to work out how to destroy it!*

Hal did not have time to think. **THUD!** Something smacked the back of his head, knocking him to the ground.

"Welcome, human," said a booming, robotic voice. "Prepare for elimination!"

CHAPTER 4

ENTER THE GRANDMASTER

Hal looked up from his position on the ground. Towering over him was a robot unlike any that he had ever seen before. It was more than thirty metres tall and fifteen metres wide. The giant machine resembled a Manhunter, but something about it was different. Hal looked closer at his attacker. Not only did it resemble a Manhunter, it was made up of thousands of Manhunters!

Hal realized that he might be in trouble.

"Shields at 70 per cent," his ring warned.

Hal climbed to his feet and faced his opponent. "You must be the one behind the attacks on Nokyo One!" he shouted.

"Correct, human," answered the colossal robot. "I am the Grandmaster. The Manhunter army is under my command."

"You attacked innocent people! Why?" asked Hal.

"Our planet is dying," Grandmaster said. "The core is erupting, and the entire surface is covered in flames. It will not be long before Kirdon explodes."

"But why attack Nokyo One?" asked Hal. The super hero was growing impatient.

"Nokyo One is the closest suitable planet for our needs. We plan to eliminate the human population there and colonize the planet," said the Grandmaster.

"Sorry," said Hal, raising his ring out in front of him, "but I can't let you do that."

Hal created a giant green lasso and spun it around in the air. *WHOOOOSH!*

He tossed it at the Grandmaster, catching the massive robot around its left leg. Hal tugged on the lasso, attempting to pull the Grandmaster to the ground.

The Grandmaster did not move an inch. Instead, it ripped the green lasso off its leg. "Eliminate him!" it screamed.

Hearing their master's command, hundreds of smaller Manhunters detached themselves from the walls and flew directly at Hal. "NO MAN ESCAPES THE MANHUNTERS!" they all yelled in menacing robotic voices.

Stay sharp, Hal told himself.

Hal created a huge pair of green shears with his ring. He used it to chop two of the closest robots in half. Then he changed the shears into a hammer, and swung it at the next closest robots. **THUD!** Hal destroyed five more Manhunters. Then, Hal realized that these basic tools would not be enough to defeat the entire army.

I need some back-up, he thought.

Hal thought of his fellow Green Lanterns back on the planet Oa. He focused all his will power into his ring and tried to make the strongest constructs he could. Out of his ring emerged several green holographic versions of his Green Lantern friends, including Kilowog, Arisia, and Salaak.

The constructs of the Corps members flew at the attacking Manhunter robots, firing energy beams at them.

They were able to destroy almost fifty robots, but Hal was only strong enough to maintain the constructs for a few seconds before they disappeared.

"WARNING!" chimed his ring. "Power levels at 15 per cent."

"I only have one more chance," Hal said. "I need to focus all my will."

Another swarm of Manhunters zoomed towards Hal. "Time for some target practice!" shouted Hal.

He shot a dozen green energy beams at the attacking robots. Most of the energy beams hit the Manhunters in the middle of their helmets, causing them to explode. Other energy beams were so powerful that they were able to destroy two robots at once. **KA-POW!**

More Manhunters quickly approached Hal from the side, and he fired another series of energy beams at them. One energy beam tore straight through a Manhunter, hitting the wall of the mountain and creating a giant hole.

WHOOOOSH! Lava suddenly rushed into the chamber through the hole in the side of the mountain.

"WARNING! WARNING!" said Hal's ring. "Temperatures in this chamber will soon reach critical levels. Evacuation is highly recommended."

"I've worked out how I'm going to destroy the base!" Hal shouted with a grin.

ZZRRRRTT! From out of nowhere, the Grandmaster knocked Hal to the ground with a laser blast.

"Power levels at 4 per cent," warned Hal's ring.

A Manhunter landed on the ground next to Hal, and placed its foot on Hal's neck. "NO MAN ESCAPES THE MANHUNTERS!" the robot yelled.

I'm doomed, Hal thought.

ZZZAPPPPPPP! Then suddenly, a blue energy beam blasted through the Manhunter's chest and destroyed it.

Hal was saved!

From behind Hal, Saint Walker, the Blue Lantern, stepped out of the shadows. Brother Sepdifer was again floating beside him. "As I told you before, Hal Jordan," Saint Walker said, "you must never give up hope!"

CHAPTER 5

RETURN OF THE BLUE LANTERNS

Hal could already feel the power flowing back into him, which he now knew was a result of the Blue Lanterns' presence.

"I didn't realize that you could fire energy beams or make constructs," Hal said to the Blue Lanterns. "I thought you were just living, breathing power-chargers."

"Our rings possess many of the same abilities as yours," answered Saint Walker, "but with an important restriction."

"What's that?" asked Hal.

"Our rings work only when in the presence of a Green Lantern. Hope is useless without the will power to act upon it, Hal Jordan," explained Saint Walker.

"Well, then it's a good thing I'm here to rescue you!" Hal joked. "Now, let's get rid of this Grandmaster – *and* his army!"

Hal, Saint Walker, and Brother Sepdifer fired energy beams in every direction.

Within seconds, they had destroyed nearly every Manhunter in the chamber. The remaining robots flew over to the Grandmaster and attached themselves to his casing.

The massive machine was now even larger and more powerful than before.

"Lanterns!" the machine bellowed. "I will extinguish your light forever!"

"Not going to happen!" yelled Hal.

Hal nodded at the Blue Lanterns. All three created constructs of giant superpowered chains. Hal wrapped his chains around the Grandmaster's legs, while the Blue Lanterns chained together the Grandmaster's arms.

"Take him down!" shouted Hal.

On his command, each Lantern pulled hard on their chains. The Grandmaster began to wobble. Hal tensed his muscles and pulled as hard as he could. The Grandmaster fell to the ground of the chamber – and into the molten lava!

The lava immediately started melting the Grandmaster's armour.

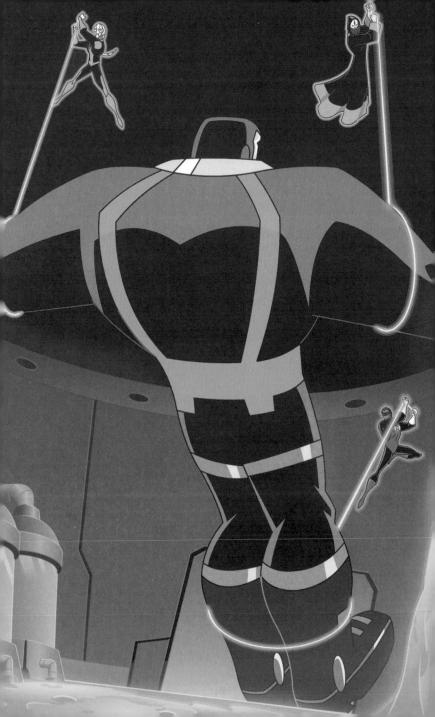

Hal's ring sounded an alert. "WARNING! The Grandmaster is about to explode, which will destroy this entire mountain. Evacuate immediately!"

"You heard the ring!" yelled Hal to the Blue Lanterns. "Let's get out of here!"

The three Lanterns rocketed through the tunnel opening, racing towards the surface. **KA-BOOM!** The Lanterns heard a loud explosion beneath them. "That must have been the Grandmaster," said Saint Walker. "Good riddance."

Suddenly, fire shot up through the tunnel. **FWOOOSHHHHHH!** The three Lanterns flew at super-speed, barely escaping the tunnel before it was fully consumed in fire. As they reached the surface, the entire mountain crumbled into the sea of lava.

Hal and the Blue Lanterns watched in awe as the planet collapsed in on itself.

Saint Walker turned to face the Green Lantern. "Hal Jordan, we followed you to this planet in order to bring you back to Odym with us," said Walker. "But we see now that we cannot simply have you join our ranks as a Blue Lantern."

Walker smiled at Hal. "The fusion of hope and will is the most powerful force in existence," he said. "If the universe is to be protected, it must include both Green *and* Blue Lanterns."

"I couldn't have said it better myself," replied Hal.

"I am glad that you agree," said Saint Walker. Despite the danger they had just faced, his voice was completely calm.

"So … can your rings do any other tricks?" asked Hal.

"We know no tricks," said Saint Walker. "But our rings do possess another ability in addition to those of your ring."

"Oh? What's that?" asked Hal, curious.

"We can create a construct of a person's most hopeful future," revealed Saint Walker.

"Can you show me mine?" said Hal.

Saint Walker closed his eyes. He placed one hand on Hal's shoulder and put his other hand out in front of him.

All of a sudden, a blue construct of a man appeared before them. He resembled Hal, but appeared slightly older. He was wearing a Green Lantern uniform similar to Hal's.

The hologram looked very regal, almost as if he were a king.

"Who ... who is this?" asked Hal.

"This is you, Hal Jordan," answered Saint Walker. "This is who the universe hopes you will become – the greatest Green Lantern of all."

BLUE LANTERN CORPS

BASE: Odym

OFFICIAL NAME: Blue Lantern Corps

LEADERS: Ganthet and Sayd

ENEMIES: Orange Lantern Corps, Red Lantern Corps, Sinestro Corps

POWERS/ABILITIES: Unmatched hope for the future; ability to aid other corps by enhancing the Power Rings of their comrades.

BIOGRAPHY

Although exiled for their individuality, former Guardians of the Universe, Ganthet and Sayd, had great hope for the future. With this emotion, they created Blue Power Rings and founded the Blue Lantern Corps. Members of this group, including Saint Walker and Brother Sepdifer, use their rings to aid other Lantern Corps. Although extremely powerful, Blue power rings must be near a Green Lantern ring to function properly.